Untamable

A Romantic Comedy

JAMIE SCHLOSSER

Here, kitty kitty ...

Sarah~

Emery will tame your

Jamie

Untamable
A Romantic Comedy
By Jamie Schlosser

Cover Design: Jay Aheer at Simply Defined Art
Formatting: Jill Sava, Love Affair With Fiction
Editing: Emily Lawrence at Lawrence Editing

Dedication

To Dad—the best storyteller I know.

Prologue

Two Years Ago

Emery

"Emery! We need you in exam three."

I lifted my head out of the cage I was cleaning and glanced at Christine.

Ignoring her panicked whisper, I asked, "Who put the regular cat litter in Fritzy's box? The note specifically says he likes the newspaper shreds."

Wide-eyed, she anxiously tugged at the hem of her zoo-themed scrub top. "I'm serious. Doctor Carson is about to blow a gasket."

"See, the problem is," I continued, wiping down the stainless-steel cage, "he won't go to the bathroom in there. So he pees outside of the box, then sits in it. Now he needs a bath."

"We can get to that later." Swiping the frizzy hair away from her face, the middle-aged woman huffed. "We've got bigger problems right now."

I let out a sigh. "All right. What's going on?"

"It's Arnold Miller."

Ah. That explained the terror-stricken look on Christine's face. She'd been a vet tech for decades. She knew all the ins and outs of this business, but no one put the fear of God in her like Arnold Miller.

The cat was hostile. Vicious. A pain in everyone's ass.

Arnold was a cat whose full name was actually Twinkle Star Snowy Nose Tickle Toes. I had no idea where the hell that name came from, or why his owner called him Arnold. But his unfortunate title had nothing to do with the fact that he was an asshole.

Honestly, he was just misunderstood. I wouldn't want to get shoved into a crate and brought to the doctor against my will either. Being aggressive was a natural fear-based response.

A low howl escalated to a high screech, and Christine shuddered as it echoed through the building. I sighed before quickly placing some fresh newspaper down for Fritzy, then I moved toward the awful sound coming from the exam room.

Christine didn't follow.

When I got inside, there was a man I didn't recognize in the far corner. Dressed in a sleek black suit, he looked extremely out of place among the linoleum floors and the cute kitten posters tacked to the wall. A hairball lingered near his shiny shoes. He glanced up from his cell phone with a bored expression, then went back to typing over the keys.

Next, my eyes went to Marty Miller, Arnold's fearless owner. With his long gray beard, shaved head, and leather biker jacket, some people found him intimidating. But in the four years I'd worked at Remington Animal Medical Center, I'd gotten to know him pretty well.

Marty was a big softie who loved his asshole cat.

"Hey, Emery." He gave a tight smile as he struggled with the angry animal on the metal exam table. "This tough guy got into a fight with the neighbor's cat the other day. He's got an infected bite on his hind leg."

"Is he limping?" I asked.

"No. But he won't stop licking at it and it's oozing now. Probably got an abscess. You know how it goes."

I nodded. This wasn't the first time Arnold had been in here for this, and it wouldn't be his last.

Doctor Carson cleared his throat. He was a few feet away, armed with the protective gloves. That was a mistake on his part.

"You won't get anywhere near Arnold with those things on," I told him. "He hates the gloves."

He gave me an annoyed look. "I can't risk getting injured."

Going over to the cabinet, I pulled out an old towel and slid it across the table to Marty. Knowing the drill, he unfolded it and began wrapping it around the black furball in his arms.

I faced Doctor Carson to give him the rundown.

"He's gonna swaddle Arnold like a baby, nice and snug. You've got about sixty seconds to get what needs done before he loses it." The more I talked, the wider his eyes grew, his face getting paler with every word. Telling Dr. Clueless what to do was overstepping, and I knew it. But fuck if anyone was going to stop me. "Here's what we can do. We can sedate him or we can go straight to an antibiotic shot. Either way, we'll need to get close enough to give him an injection, so my vote goes for the meds."

Nodding, he got rid of the gloves and fumbled with a syringe.

The doc was fresh out of vet med school. He'd started working here a few months ago, and I'd hoped to see him become more confident in his new position.

Unfortunately, I was beginning to think this profession just wasn't his thing.

A sheen of sweat broke out on Doctor Carson's forehead, right below his perfectly coiffed hair. Nervously shifting toward Arnold, he took a deep breath. Trembled. Hesitated. He was taking too long.

As if the cat read my mind, he let out an impatient growl, and Doctor Carson jumped back.

Oh, for fuck's sake.

I grabbed the syringe from his hand and quickly administered the antibiotic shot to Arnold's rump, dodging his hind legs as they kicked with claws ready for scratching. It was over before anyone could object to my interference.

I'd given injections before, but technically I wasn't certified to do that. Was it unethical? Yeah, sort of.

Was I going to get into trouble? Judging by the grateful expressions on the faces around me, I highly doubted it.

I handed the empty syringe back to Dr. Carson.

"Right, then. Thank you, Emery." Standing tall, like he didn't just nearly piss his pants, he turned to Marty. "Let us know if he shows signs of not feeling well…"

His voice faded away as I quietly slipped out of the exam room to go back to my previous task. I'd just finished bathing Fritzy when the mysterious spiffy-suit dude approached me.

"You're pretty good with cats," he stated.

"Yeah, you could say that." I closed the metal cage with a clank.

He handed me a business card. "We're looking for someone like you. I don't know how you feel about being on a documentary…" He trailed off, his face screwing up with distaste as he eyed my dirty scrubs. "But it's a better opportunity than working here."

"A documentary about cats?"

He waved his hand. "Reality show, documentary… Same thing."

"Reality show?" I shook my head. "I don't know."

"Well, I think you'd look great on camera. We'd need to get some meat on your bones, but the man bun thing is really popular these days." He gestured toward me. "It gives you a certain ruggedness we're going for."

My hand went to the mass of light brown hair tied at the back of my head. I didn't wear my hair like this because it was trendy; I just didn't have the time or money for regular haircuts.

"Consider it," he insisted. "You've got nothing to lose. Call that number if you want to set up an audition." With a final nod, he left.

I glanced down at the card.

Steve Feldman. Talent Scout/Producer.

As my eyes traveled around the room, I thought about all the work I still had to do before my day was finished. Litter boxes needed to be changed. The kennels disinfected. The old mop bucket waited for me in the corner, filled with bleach water and soap.

I thought about the measly paycheck that wouldn't

even come close to covering all the expenses I had. It was plain pasta and hot dogs on the menu for dinner again tonight. Yeah, it was nasty shit, especially when I'd eaten that the past three nights in a row, but I only had twenty dollars left to last me the rest of the week.

Then I thought about Dr. Carson, too incompetent and fearful to perform a job I would do just about anything for. Being a veterinarian had been my dream since I was five years old, but college wasn't in the cards for me. Instead, I settled for being a peon at a vet clinic. I'd clean up crap all day if it meant I got to work with animals.

Spiffy Dude was right about one thing—I didn't have anything to lose. When you're at the bottom of the barrel, you've got nowhere else to go but up.

Taking a deep breath, I whipped out my cell phone and made a call that would change my life.

Chapter 1

Present Day

Emery

"I'M EMERY MATHESON, and I will tame your pussy." I shot my signature grin into the dark lens, the large green screen glowing behind me.

Steve poked his head around the camera man and squinted his eyes.

"Can I get a little more feeling behind that?" he asked seriously. "I really need to *believe* that you're going to tame my pussy."

My lips twitched as I fought a smile. I had no idea how he could say that with a straight face. Adjusting the fluffy Himalayan in my arms, I squared my shoulders and repeated the line, this time with *a little more feeling*.

Steve seemed satisfied. "That's a wrap, guys. I'll see you all at the location on Monday morning."

Everyone started to disperse as I gently placed Princess back in her kennel. Her blue eyes peered back at

7

me and I felt a niggling of guilt knowing she'd be going back to the animal shelter. She'd spent the past two days on the set, being passed from person to person without one complaint.

The local shelter had allowed us to use her for our latest promotional shoot in exchange for a donation. Honestly, I would've given them the money either way. I had a soft spot for all the animals that sat there for months waiting to be adopted.

But Princess wouldn't have any trouble finding a home. She was beautiful, docile, and sweet.

"Bye," I whispered, giving her one last scratch under the chin.

We were gearing up for the first shoot of season three. The cable channel we worked for—Night Time Television—was only a few years old and instantly popular. And The Pussy Tamer was the network's most popular show.

The idea was genius—a late-night reality show that targeted a predominantly female audience by combining cute, flawed animals and an attractive man who dedicated his life to fixing them. Filled with humor, heart, and sexual innuendo, it was the perfect recipe for success.

A panicked-looking guy scurried by as he yammered into his headset about technical issues with his sound equipment. Several caterers refreshed the sandwich spread on a nearby table. The amount of manpower that went into production behind the scenes never ceased to amaze me. There were assistant producers, stylists, lighting specialists, caterers, the camera crew.

And I was the center of it all.

People constantly buzzed around me, asking if I

needed anything. Powdered my face when it got shiny. Made sure my hair wasn't out of place. If it was too hot, someone found a fan. Too cold, and they turned up the heat.

The only person who didn't seem overly concerned about my well-being was Steve.

"Hey, you got a sec?" I called to my producer as he walked by. He didn't look up from his phone but motioned at me like he was listening. "I want to do some kind of promotion for the shelter. I was thinking we could feature some of the animals at the end of every episode. Maybe gain some interest—"

"Yeah, that sounds great," he cut me off, obviously distracted. "I'll get someone on that."

God, he was such a dick. A dick I owed everything to, but still a dick.

I'd come a long way from the lanky, broke-as-a-joke guy Steve found cleaning kennels two years ago. In my time as The Pussy Tamer, I'd traveled all around the country, made more money than I ever thought possible, and most importantly, I had made a difference in people's lives.

Nothing felt better than getting letters and pictures from the families I helped.

Well, almost nothing.

A few months ago, I'd acquired my vet tech certification—paid for by the show. I wasn't a doctor— yet—but I was one step closer to my goal.

The producers had said they wanted me to have adequate medical training, and I couldn't agree fast enough. It eliminated the need for them to hire a tech, and now I was able to do basic exams and administer certain medications when needed.

"You ready for this next one?" Rhonda, my favorite assistant producer, handed me the information packet on the next client. "It's a lot different than anything we've done before. Steve says it'll be the most dramatic season yet."

"I'm always ready," I replied, shooting her a cocky grin. "And doesn't he say that every time?"

"Just wait till you check out the specs on this project." Wrapping both hands around my bicep, she let out an impressed whistle. "Look at these arms."

"Thanks. The personal trainers have been kicking my ass for the last two months. I'm ready for a cheeseburger."

Lifting my T-shirt, she lightly slapped my stomach. "I'd say you deserve one. That's a nice eight-pack you've got there."

Although she admired my body, her interest wasn't the least bit sexual.

Rhonda was in her mid-forties and she used to do semi-professional body building in her younger days. Although she claimed she was too old for it now, fitness was still a big part of her life. She had a short, no-nonsense hairstyle and an intimidating personality to match. Sometimes she was a bit of a drill sergeant, other times she was a mother hen.

It was what made her so good at her job. Everyone knew one thing: You don't fuck with Rhonda.

Adjusting the stack of folders in her arm, she took a giant gulp from her Starbucks coffee cup. The team had a long night ahead. I almost felt bad about the fact that I got to go home while everyone else had to prepare for the shoot.

"Are you sure there's nothing I can help with around here?"

That earned a stern glare. "Go home, Emery. Get some rest. You'll need it."

"All right. Don't work too hard."

"You know I always do," she replied before chasing down one of the camera men.

Holding onto the Manila folder, I headed for the exit. The heavy door swung open, and I took a deep inhale of the cool fall air as I left the studio.

Sunsets were hard to see in Chicago, but an orange glow emitted from behind the skyscrapers, matching the vibrant colors of the autumn leaves at the park in the distance. The city skyline was beautiful—there was nothing like it—but it was a lot different from where I spent my first twenty-two years.

For a second, old memories seeped in. The sound of crashing waves, the smell of the sea, and the gritty sand between my toes as I watched the bright orb sink below the horizon.

Living just an hour away from the beach had been my favorite part about growing up in South Carolina. The roots I often longed for were still planted there, an invisible tie that would always pull me back.

As I strode across the parking lot, that longing grew until it felt like an anvil in my chest.

I pushed it down.

Raking a hand through my hair, I shook myself from the reverie of the life I left behind as the gravel crunched under my boots. Being homesick seemed to be a regular occurrence these days, but it wasn't on my agenda tonight.

Instead, I focused on the new haircut I'd gotten yesterday.

The stylists had finally decided to do away with the man bun. At first, I was excited. I missed having short hair. But they left it longer on top, then put a shit-ton of product in it to make it look 'wild and effortlessly sexy.' Judging by the thirty-five minutes it took to get it *just right*, it was anything but effortless.

Some of the light-brown locks fell in front of my eyes and I growled. I shoved them back, but the persistent chunks blocked my vision again.

Fuck this. Maybe I'd see if they would let me buzz it off.

Just as I reached my Range Rover, my phone started ringing, and I let out an annoyed groan when 'unknown caller' flashed across the screen. Normally I wouldn't answer, but I felt like I could use the entertainment today.

"Hello?"

"Can you tame me, big boy?" A deep purr came through the speaker.

A dude this time. Interesting.

"Sorry, man. I think you're barking up the wrong tree."

"You don't hear me barking, do you? I bet I could make you purr." He gave a shrill meow.

Snickering, I fastened my seatbelt. "Tell ya what— I'll make an exception this time. You pick up a pizza, I'll get the beer. Meet me at my place in thirty minutes."

Several beats of silence followed as my prank caller processed the fact that I'd called his bluff.

How sad was it that I kind of hoped he'd say yes? That I was willing to hang out with a complete stranger

12

because I was so desperate for company? Anything sounded better than going back to my empty condo.

"I'll even chip in for a pay-per-view," I added to sweeten the deal. "What'll it be? UFC, hockey, porn...?"

I heard frantic whispering on the other end, catching snippets here and there.

...actually wants me to come over.

Are you fucking serious...?

...he said porn...

Hang up! Hang up!

They didn't bother responding to my invitation and the line went dead.

Sighing, I dropped my phone into the cup holder. Guess it was time to change my number again.

At first the prank calls, sexual offers, and the occasional dirty pic had been flattering. But after a while it became annoying.

They didn't really want to talk to *me*.

They wanted the guy I played on TV, just like all the women I'd tried to date since starting the show. Back when I was literally scooping shit for a living, girls weren't exactly fighting for my attention. The instant fame from the show had made me a sex icon overnight.

And I'd dated them all—vapid, shallow, greedy, desperate. Some wanted my money, others wanted bragging rights.

All I wanted was someone I liked talking to. Someone to come home to at night. Someone who wanted me for me.

I'd always preferred the comfort of a relationship over the excitement of a passing fling.

I couldn't seem to find it.

Maybe my standards were too high. Or maybe dating was just awful in general.

First, you had to meet someone. Then you had to be mutually attracted to each other. And that was the easy part. If, by chance, you hit it off, then you had to get to know each other.

Then came the questions.

Is she nice? Is she honest?

What if I come on too strong? What if she's too eager?

When can we hang out at my place instead of going to a fancy restaurant?

Does she like cats? If the answer is no, automatic deal breaker.

And after jumping through all those hoops, what if we figured out it still wasn't working?

So after a year of models, groupies, and reality stars trying to get to the top, I gave up on trying to find the emotional connection I craved. Decided to concentrate on my career instead. I was fine on my own. Besides, I traveled too much to maintain a relationship.

And the best part about keeping to myself? The tabloids had no scandals to report. A while back, one magazine falsely claimed I was doing steroids to stay in shape, but compared to some of the stories they made up about people, that was nothing.

My condo building came into view in the distance, the shiny black exterior extending fourteen floors up. The last glimmer of daylight reflected off the pristine glass windows.

When I drove into the parking garage beneath the building, I got the same feeling of unfamiliarity I always did. The fancy high-rise had been home for almost a year, but it seemed like I would never get used to the luxurious lifestyle.

The bowtie-wearing concierge greeted me with a nod as I walked through the lobby.

"How's it hanging, Charles?"

"Very good, sir," he replied the same dry response as always.

Maintaining the utmost professionalism was his thing, but it didn't stop me from trying to get him to crack. I'd been trying to get a reaction—any reaction—out of my doorman for months and, so far, I'd failed miserably.

I swung my keyring around my finger and stopped in front of the marble countertop. "What do you say? Drinks after your shift? I've got a bottle of Jack and Netflix. I'll even let you pick the show."

Not even a ghost of a smile. "Sorry, sir. I'll have to politely decline."

"All right, all right. I'll break out the big guns, just this once—I'll chip in for some pay-per-view porn," I joked.

It was the second time in less than thirty minutes that I'd tried to entice someone to my place with the promise of porn. I had officially reached a new low.

Apparently, Charles didn't think my joke was funny because the frown lines around his mouth deepened. "I'm afraid I have prior obligations."

Aaaand also the second time getting turned down.

"You're a tough crowd." Tapping the counter twice, I strolled away and called, "But one of these days, Charlie, you won't be able to say no."

The elevator took me up to the fourteenth floor,

opening into the penthouse.

Gleaming stainless-steel appliances and black granite countertops greeted me in the kitchen. The floor-to-ceiling windows along the living room wall offered a priceless view of the darkening sky. Fluffy orange clouds floated just above the horizon, throwing some much-needed color onto my bare white walls.

I'd meant to add some decorations after I moved in, but never got around to it. The neutral color scheme of whites, grays, and dark tones made the open floor plan feel masculine, yet terribly impersonal.

My keys landed on the island with a clank as I headed for the fridge. I popped open a beer, then sat down on the black leather couch with the client profile to do some research and preparation for the upcoming job.

Taking a long drink, I scanned the front page.

In bold letters, the main issue was listed: Cat hoarder (owner of nine cats)

The second page was a questionnaire we had clients fill out to get a good feel for who we were dealing with. The messy chicken-scratch handwriting was just barely legible.

Name: Estelle Winters

Occupation: Owner/seamstress at Estelle's Costume Shop

Hobbies: Working, reading, and spending time with my cats

Fears: Flying on planes. Ending up alone.

It sounded like this woman didn't get out much. I pictured a little old lady curled up on her recliner on a Friday night, hiding from the world under a pile of books and cats. If you asked me, that was no way to live.

I made a note in the sidebar to have a therapist on hand. Sometimes the owners were a bigger problem than the cats.

During the two seasons we'd filmed, I'd dealt with all kinds of feline problems. Aggression. High anxiety. Going to the bathroom in all the wrong places.

But we'd never had a cat hoarder. Rhonda was right. This was a whole different ballgame, and I wasn't equipped to handle human mental instability.

I flipped to the next page and almost choked on my beer when my eyes landed on the location at the bottom: Remington, South Carolina.

No fucking way.

Excitement made my heart pound as I read it again in disbelief. Turning the page over, I scanned the detailed itinerary to make sure there wasn't some mistake.

No mistake.

I was going home.

I knew the name of that costume shop sounded familiar. When I was a kid, I used to get all my Halloween gear from Estelle's. That was many years ago, but I faintly recalled the eccentric elderly woman who owned it. She loved clowns and always smelled like lemons.

I sent a text to my sister.

> **Me:** Hey, looks like I'll be in town for a few weeks on a shoot.

Her response was immediate.

> **Nikki:** Omg!!! No way! Lizzie is going to be so excited to see you.

I smiled when I thought about my five-year-old niece.

> **Me:** Tell her Uncle E will be there in three days.
>
> **Nikki:** Eek! Text me as soon as you get here.
>
> **Me:** Will do. Have you seen Dad lately?
>
> **Nikki:** Last weekend.
>
> **Me:** And?

While I waited for her to respond, I flipped through some old pictures on my phone.

There were several from last Christmas. Lizzie on my shoulders while she held a red stocking. My sister and her husband, Tom, opening the new dinnerware set I got for them. My dad wearing his blue ballcap and a faraway smile.

All the pictures had one thing in common—the background of the assisted living home where my dad lived in the dementia/Alzheimer's unit.

He'd been at Windsor Lakes Retirement Home for six years now, and it was worth every penny.

And I'd given them *a lot* of my pennies.

Using my college fund to pay for the upscale medical facility wasn't a decision I'd made on a whim. Neither was getting a shitty job and moving into the shitty studio apartment where I lived for three shitty years.

To say Nikki had been pissed about my sacrifice was an understatement, but I didn't regret a thing. The decision had been simple for me—I was able to help him, so I did.

Luckily, money wasn't something I had to worry

about anymore.

> **Nikki:** He was having a bad day. The nurses were talking about starting him on a new medication. I'm visiting him tomorrow.
>
> **Me:** Don't mention me coming back.
>
> **Nikki:** You know I won't. So have you applied for vet school yet?

I rolled my eyes because she was always hounding me about that. No matter how old we got, she couldn't seem to snap out of big-sister mode.

Every year she gave me a calendar with certain dates filled in. Important birthdays, days she thought I should ask off for vacation—which I usually didn't do—and all the cutoff dates for class signups.

It was obnoxious, but as much as I liked to complain about her nitpicking ways, I didn't mind it. Felt nice to have someone care about me, even if I didn't get to see her very often. What she didn't seem to understand was that I couldn't just walk into a college, even if I was somewhat famous. There were prerequisites and an application process. I had to get accepted first.

> **Me:** That's not until next fall. As in, almost a year from now. I think I have time.
>
> **Nikki:** Just making sure you don't forget.
>
> **Me:** I'm a grown man who happens to own a kitten calendar, thanks to you.
>
> **Nikki:** Ha-ha. You love it. Text me when you get settled. We can meet for dinner and you can

tell me all about vet school. Vet school. VET
SCHOOL.

Me: Relentless.

Shaking my head, I drained the rest of my beer.
Another text came through.

Nikki: I just want you to be happy.

Me: I am.

It wasn't a complete lie.

My life hadn't turned out the way I'd imagined, but
I couldn't say I was *un*happy. For me, working with
animals and successfully resolving difficult situations was
what gave me satisfaction. Contentment had become
about being good at my job, providing for my dad, and
rebuilding my college fund.

And I was totally kicking ass in all areas.

Satisfied and content—that was good enough. True
happiness was rare for me, but as I thought about the
hoarding case and the challenge it would bring, I felt a
flicker of the emotion.

I was going to kick ass at this too.

Going back to my pictures, I kept scrolling and
paused when I came to the sunset on the beach—the
one I'd taken the day before I moved to Chicago. Before
I realized I was making the best decision of my life.

Filled with uncertainty, I sat on that beach for hours,
letting the sand slip through my fingers while I wondered
if I was doing the right thing.

It was the right thing.

I took a chance, and it paid off. If knowing my dad was healthy and cared for came at the price of missing home, I'd choose it every time.

But I guess I wouldn't have to miss South Carolina for much longer.

Chapter 2

Emery

THE RENTED LUXURY RV cruised down familiar streets as we made the ten-minute drive to the filming location.

Remington was a nice city. Big enough to avoid town gossip or unfortunate run-ins with old acquaintances. Small enough that heavy traffic and crowded streets weren't a problem.

We passed through the business district and I caught a glimpse of the vet clinic where Steve had found me. I wondered if Dr. Carson ever got more comfortable in his position there or if he was long gone. I would've bet good money on the latter.

Looking down at his phone, Steve made a sound of distress in the seat across from me in the booth-style dining table. As always, he was impeccably put together in a crisp black suit and tie. The rectangular black-framed glasses gave him a hipster vibe, but the graying combover gave away his age.

"What's wrong?" I asked. "Didn't get the result you wanted on your horoscope today?"

He glanced up at me and shook his head. "I took one of those quizzes again. The one about which Disney princess I would play in a movie."

I held in a snort, because the guy was dead serious. "And? Don't leave me hanging here."

Unsatisfied, he sniffed. "Aurora from *Sleeping Beauty*."

These pointless tests could ruin his entire day. Yesterday it was what kind of coffee beverage he was, based on his birth month. He got the latte and fretted about it for a good half hour at the airport while we waited for our flight. Because he was a *cappuccino*.

It was ridiculous. It was entertaining as fuck.

Honestly, it was one of his few redeeming qualities.

You'd think being an animal lover would've been a requirement for working on the show, but it wasn't. There was no love lost between Steve and the cats we worked with. This was strictly business to him—a fat paycheck that gave him the lifestyle he wanted.

Just like I knew he would, Steve had booked himself and the crew the best hotel in the area.

I stayed there last night because our flight got in late, but I would be spending the duration of our time on the job in the RV outside the client's home. I liked being nearby in case any problems arose, day or night. Plus, it was convenient for the crew to have a place to lounge around during breaks.

Although I barely fit in the tiny bathroom, the bed in the back was a good size and there was a kitchenette stocked with food and beverages. Not much else a man could ask for.

I shot off a quick text to Nikki that I was in town. We'd made tentative dinner plans, depending on how much work the hoarder needed, but I was assuming it was going to be complicated. Quite possibly the most difficult situation I'd ever dealt with.

Steve let out another muttered curse and something about his life motto results. We spent the rest of the ride in silence.

Five minutes later, we came to a stop in a parking lot.

As I stepped out of the RV, I studied the four-story apartment complex. It wasn't fancy, but not a total dump either. My guess was that the units had either one or two bedrooms. Possibly three, but from the narrow size of the building, that was a stretch.

There was no way a cat hoarder could live comfortably in such a small space.

The white-sided exterior was lined with patios on the ground floor and balconies on the upper levels. Most had chairs or potted plants outside.

All except for one.

My eyes lingered on the chicken wire that caged in the entire second-level balcony. I spied a carpet-covered cat tower and some peacock feathers dangling from the wire.

Yep, there's our hoarder.

The vans full of stage hands, camera crew, and other staff pulled up behind us.

Everyone started piling out, and I smiled at the cowboy hats some of them wore as part of their disguise. 'Meemaw's Rodeo and Cattle Show' decals were slapped all over the vehicles, including the RV.

As the popularity of The Pussy Tamer grew, keeping our filming location a secret had become increasingly difficult, especially if we were in one place for longer than a few days.

And we were definitely going to be here for a while.

Glancing back at the caged-in balcony, I imagined we were about to walk into some pretty crazy shit, and my biggest concern was overwhelming the cats.

"All right." I whistled to get everyone's attention. "You know how it goes. Joel, you come in with us first. Everyone else can wait outside in the hallway until we've assessed the situation. Then get in, set up your cameras, and get out. We need to limit the number of people to keep the environment as stable as possible."

Having a few people on set during any given time was pretty much inevitable. I mentally calculated myself, a camera man, at least one producer, possibly a medic, occasionally a caterer, the hoarder, and nine cats. Tight fit for such a small space.

"You ready for this?" Steve asked skeptically as he peered up at the balcony.

"Don't doubt my abilities now." I smirked. "This is my moment to shine."

He just grunted in response, and we made our way to the entrance. He dialed a code number into the panel.

"Hello?" A soft voice came through the speaker.

"NTT for Estelle Winters," Steve announced.

"Come on in."

The door buzzed, and we headed up to apartment 210 with a small filming crew following close behind.

I glanced at Joel, our best camera man.

He was the one who followed the action, and he was

the coolest dude I worked with. We weren't great friends, but he went with the flow and laughed at my jokes, even when I gave him shit about his '70s porno 'stache. I'd tried to convince him to shave the thick mustache at least a dozen times, but he wouldn't budge.

Joel hoisted the large camera on his shoulder and gave me a thumbs-up, signaling that he was ready.

Then I knocked.

The white door opened a crack, only about six inches or so, and the person peering at us through the small gap took me by surprise.

I wasn't looking at an old lady. She was a blond-haired bombshell. Tiny thing, about five foot two. The curled ends of her hair hung around her collarbone, and the scoop-neck shirt she wore displayed a good amount of cleavage and tanned skin.

She gazed up at me with big, doe-like eyes the color of molasses, framed with smoky eyeliner and dark lashes.

Those eyes.

They got wider, flaring with recognition—something I was used to. They also held a hint of lust, pupils dilating as they roamed my face. Women looking at me like that wasn't uncommon, but usually my body didn't respond to the attention.

It was responding now. My cock twitched. My heart beat faster.

I glanced down at her lips, pink and shiny from lip gloss. Button nose. High cheekbones. Her face was stunning, somehow managing to be cute and elegantly beautiful at the same time.

I looked at the numbers over the peephole again. We were definitely at the right address. Did the hoarder have a granddaughter?

"We're here for Estelle Winters?" I spoke up, sounding as confused as I felt.

"You're lookin' at her," the bombshell replied.

Holy shit.

The twang in her voice did something to me. I'd grown up with that drawl, so it shouldn't have affected me the way it did. Hell, I used to talk that way too, but I'd forced myself to lose the accent for the show.

I'd heard people talk about this moment. When they were so captivated by someone, time seemed to stop.

That happened to me, right there in the middle of the hallway.

The whole world would get to witness the first time I ever felt weak in the knees from one look. One simple sentence. One set of perfect plump lips.

I just hoped Joel had the decency to avoid recording the stiffy I was suddenly sporting.

Estelle was still staring up at me, but I couldn't speak. It felt like the wind had been knocked out of me and I had to remind myself to breathe.

Apparently, she didn't have the same effect on Steve.

"Are you going to let us in?" he snapped impatiently.

Whipping my head in his direction, I glared. Who pissed in his Cheerios? Putting up with his crankiness had become second-nature for me, but lately he'd been on another level.

Frowning, Estelle replied, "Sorry. One of the cats is a runner and I don't want him to get out again."

"It's not a problem." I gave her a reassuring smile. "And that's good to know. We'll definitely want to hear about that soon."

"Can you give me a minute?" She glanced at the crew behind me and all the equipment they had to bring in. "I'll put the cats in their room so they won't be in the way while you're setting up."

Ignoring Steve's huff as he made a big show of looking at his watch, I nodded. "Sure thing."

A minute later, the door opened wide and Estelle smiled.

The apples of her cheeks were round and rosy, making her appear even more youthful. Her black shirt had shoulder cutouts and when she turned away, I caught a peek of a large tattoo on the back of her right shoulder blade. Colorful roses and other various flowers burst together, and I saw the words 'at a time' in the tail-end of a script woven through the design.

I followed her into the kitchen, which was just a few steps to the left of the entrance. The aroma of breakfast sausage filled the air and my stomach rumbled, unsatisfied with the bagel I'd grabbed from the hotel.

"I made breakfast for y'all," she offered, motioning toward the kitchen counter.

Y'all. So fucking cute.

A cast iron skillet on the stove was filled to the brim with steaming gravy, and a basket of biscuits sat next to it. Paper plates, plastic silverware, and a stack of napkins completed the elaborate spread. My mouth watered.

"Thanks, but we hire caterers," Steve rudely declined before walking away to bark an order at one of the assistant producers.

Looking at all her hard work, Estelle's face fell, that perfect mouth turning down at the corners.

Fuck him. No way in hell was I missing out on

homemade biscuits and gravy.

"I'll have some," I said.

She smiled and my heart gave a hard thump. "Just help yourself. I'm pretty sure I made enough to feed an army."

Grabbing a plate, I piled a massive amount of food on top of more food. Meanwhile, Rhonda and one of the sound technicians hooked Estelle up with a mic.

Pretending to fiddle with a napkin, I watched out of the corner of my eye like a dirty perv, waiting for a peek of her skin as they connected the wires under her shirt. Much to my disappointment, I only saw a two-second sliver of the curve of her hip.

It was a good two seconds, though.

After they were done, the second wave of the crew came through to set up the permanent cameras. Estelle and I moved off to the side in the kitchen, which seemed to be the only area of the apartment that wasn't pure chaos.

I still hadn't taken a bite of my breakfast yet.

I couldn't take my eyes off Estelle as I tried to wrap my head around the shock I was still experiencing. She was supposed to be old. Not… this.

She didn't fit the profile at all.

There was something about her that screamed innocence and sweetness, all while projecting an air of badassery. Her graceful movements were confident, her hips swaying and shoulders squared as she fussed with the breakfast no one else wanted.

As she pointlessly rearranged the napkins for the third time, she surveyed the activity around her with curiosity instead of nervousness, which was unusual for people who were about to be filmed.

"Let's get set up over here," Steve said to Joel, stepping into the living room. "We'll do the interview on the couch. Get the lighting guys to put spotlights here and here."

Tuning him out, I turned to Estelle. I needed to say something. Anything. It was unlike me to be tongue-tied, especially when I was supposed to be making the client feel at ease.

"Hi," I said lamely, then I wanted to slap myself.

That's the best you could come up with? Get it together.

Her lips tipped up. "Hi."

"Your name is Estelle Winters?" I asked, needing clarification again.

"Yes. And you're Emery Matheson," she stated, holding out her hand.

Balancing my full plate in one hand, I placed the other against hers, trying to ignore the softness of her skin and the fact that I didn't want to let go.

"You're a seamstress?" Fighting the urge to keep touching her, I took a bite of my breakfast. I groaned, closing my eyes as I tasted the best thing I'd had in years.

Estelle was talking a mile a minute, but I didn't even hear it because I was too busy having a foodgasm.

"I'm sorry," I interrupted her, my mouth half-full. "But this is so good, I think I just blacked out for a second. What did you say?"

She laughed. "I said, I do a lot of sewing at the costume shop I own. And that's my great aunt Estelle's recipe, so I'll be sure to tell her it was a hit with at least one person."

"Great aunt Estelle," I repeated slowly, still confused.

She nodded. "She passed the shop down to me before she retired and moved down to Florida to live out the rest of her life as a beach bum. She taught me everything I know about sewing and sausage gravy. She's the original Estelle."

The puzzle pieces finally fell into place. She wasn't the old woman who smelled like lemons. She was her niece. Her young, hot niece.

"How old are you?" The curious question escaped before I could stop myself.

"Twenty-three." A knowing grin spread across her face. "You thought I was my aunt."

"Yeah," I confessed, shrugging. "I knew her, sort of. I used to go to Estelle's every year for my Halloween costumes. Did you know I grew up here?"

Nodding, she admitted, "I might've done some Google searching on you."

I grinned, unable to hide how flattered I was by her mild stalking confession. "And what else did you find out?"

"You went to Remington-Central High, where you played on the baseball team and you were nominated for homecoming king, but you didn't win. After that, you worked at the vet clinic where I take the cats, and now you live in Chicago."

Maybe her stalking levels were a little beyond mild. She would've had to dig pretty deep to get back to my high school days.

And she wasn't even guilty about it. Chin up. A small smile on her lips. She was owning that shit.

"But you're not from Remington," I stated. It wasn't a question. Unless she was homeschooled, there was no way I wouldn't have at least heard of her before. This city only had three high schools, and with sporting events and other social activities, kids in the same age bracket crossed paths at some point.

"No," she confirmed. "Chesterville, born and raised. I even went to college there."

I knew of the place—about an hour away, with a population that ranged from middle-class to downright wealthy. The private college within the town wasn't cheap. Because of the quaint shops and restaurants in the area, it was a tourist attraction. Many of the historical plantation houses had been turned into bed and breakfasts. I'd heard a rumor once that if you wanted to live there, you had to go through the mayor just to get permission. I didn't believe it, but the exclusivity made the town even more attractive as a getaway destination.

"What happened to the man bun?" Estelle blurted out, gesturing toward my head. "I'm a fan. Of the show, I mean. And your hair…" Her confession tapered off and her cheeks pinked, some of her boldness slipping away.

I raked my fingers through the strands on the top of my head, and they got caught on all the mousse and gel.

"My producers got a lot of requests for me to chop it off. It's a pain in my ass, though. Too short to tie up, but so long that it falls in my eyes. They said keeping it longer gives me 'animalistic appeal,'" I said, putting air quotes around the words.

Estelle laughed and agreed, "That it does."

"I had long hair for years, so now I just feel naked without it."

Swaying closer, Estelle's eyes flitted down to my

chest before going lower, lingering below my belt. A subconscious action. Was she picturing me naked?

I resisted the urge to fidget, because I was getting hard. Again. If she kept staring at me like that, she was going to notice the bulge growing behind my zipper.

She was less than two feet away from me now.

During our conversation we'd slowly gravitated toward each other, and I caught a whiff of something flowery and sweet. Like Jasmine and honey. I wondered if it was coming from her.

If I buried my face in her hair, would the scent be stronger? If I licked her neck, would I be able to taste it?

Steve clapped his hands, jarring me from my inappropriate fantasy and saving me from scaring off our client before we even got started. The room went quiet as he spoke.

"All right. We've got a long day ahead of us. It'll take about two hours to get all the permanent cameras in place. We'll start things off with an interview now, then we'll get a tour and meet the cats."

Finally showing a hint of nervousness, Estelle nibbled her lip as she glanced around. "I want to thank everyone for coming here and giving me this opportunity. I'm just way in over my head, and I'm so grateful for your help."

Such heartfelt praise was enough to warm even the coldest of hearts, but all she got from Steve was a sharp nod as he said, "It'll make for good television."

"You'll do great," I reassured her. "Just pretend we're all friends who are very interested in your cats. Forget about the cameras."

Giving me a grateful smile, she blew out a breath. "Thanks."

After getting situated on the middle cushion of her yellow and white striped couch, a calico jumped up onto Estelle's lap and made herself comfortable.

"This is Alice." She scratched the top of the cat's head. "I must've missed one when I was putting them away. Is it okay if she stays out? She's a sweetheart and it might help me to be less nervous."

"Sure." Steve gave a non-committal shrug.

On the wall behind her, there were nine yellow picture frames in a zigzag pattern. Each one held individual portraits of the cats. Now that I looked around, I noticed splashes of yellow all over her apartment, brightening up the drab white walls and beige carpet.

My attention was drawn to a gray vase full of Yellow Jasmine on the white end table by the sliding glass door that led out to the balcony. It was the South Carolina state flower, but also toxic to cats if ingested.

Concerned, I leaned down to sniff them, recalling the flowery scent from earlier. But they didn't smell like anything. When I touched the trumpet-shaped petals, I was relieved to find that they were fake.

As if Estelle read my mind, she offered, "They're plastic. I know better than to own real plants. Can't keep them alive for anything. Plus, they're poisonous to cats."

I was proud of her. "You've done your research."

She smirked. "It's a good thing I don't have the same problem with animals as I do with plants."

"Ready," Joel announced, throwing a thumbs-up from behind his tripod.

Steve sat on the metal folding chair on the other side of the coffee table. Looking down at his phone, he started asking questions.

"Estelle, can you tell us a little bit about how you came to own so many cats?"

"I didn't mean to become a crazy cat lady." Laughing, she held up her hands. "It all started a little over a year ago when my boyfriend broke up with me. We'd been living together for several months when he had a quarter-life crisis and suddenly changed his mind about us, about his job, about everything. One day I came home to find him packing, and he told me he was moving to California to become a professional surfer." She scoffed. "The guy couldn't even put his pants on without falling down, so it was quite the surprise—"

Steve loudly cleared his throat. "We really just want to know about the cats."

"Well, I was getting to that before you interrupted me." She gave him a sweet smile that contradicted the edge in her voice, and I had to stifle a laugh behind my hand. "Anyway, within two hours, he was gone. I'd always had a roommate in college, so I was living alone for the first time in my entire life. I was lonely."

"So, the cats...?" Steve prodded.

"Some asshole in 102 abandoned Alice." Estelle's nostrils flared and cute little wrinkles formed between her eyebrows as she scowled. "He was going to get evicted, so he moved away without a word. She was pregnant and he left her in that fucking apartment for days with no food and—"

"Try to keep the swear words to a minimum," Steve cut in again. "We're already in enough trouble with how many times we say 'pussy' on this show."

"Sorry," she drawled, not looking all that sorry. "I have a bit of a potty mouth sometimes, especially when it comes to motherfuckers who leave knocked-up cats to die alone."

Making a sound of distress, Steve waved his hand. "Please continue."

Estelle shrugged. "I begged the landlord to let me keep Alice. It saved him a trip to the shelter, so he agreed. But it didn't take long for me to figure out she was pregnant with how big her stomach was. And two weeks later, kittens started popping out. Eight kittens, to be exact."

Distracted by a text, he didn't look up as he asked, "Why didn't you take them to a shelter? That would've been the easiest thing to do."

A horrified expression appeared on her face. "And let them sit in cages for months waiting to get adopted? Or even worse, risk them getting euthanized? No way. I love them. I'd keep them all if I could."

Finally looking up at her, he sighed. "So why are we here then? Why don't you keep all your cats and live happily ever after?"

Estelle's face flushed again, only this time I could tell it was from anger, not embarrassment. Seemed her nerves had been replaced with feistiness.

Good.

Pursing her lips, her eyes narrowed, and I got the feeling we were all about to find out just how much of a potty mouth she really was.

"Why don't you let me conduct the rest of the interview, Steve?" Giving him a pat on the shoulder, I didn't wait for him to respond before grabbing a nearby folding chair and sitting on it backward.

Client interviews weren't part of my job criteria, but

Steve's rude comments were pissing me off. He thought he ran this show—and technically, he did—but that didn't mean I was going to sit by and watch him be an ass. He didn't understand southern hospitality. Politeness was a way of life here, but that charming drawl could turn into a quick-witted bite at any moment, manners be damned.

And we were here to help Estelle, not piss her off.

Leaning my forearms on the back of the chair, I grinned. "So, Estelle. You were saying…"

Biting her lip, she fought a smile at the way Steve sputtered in disbelief beside me.

"I guess he's right—I could've brought them to the shelter. But like I said, I was a little lonely. I don't like being alone," she admitted quietly.

I was reminded of the questionnaire she'd filled out. One of her biggest fears was ending up alone. I hadn't thought much of it because that's not an unusual fear.

But at the time, I'd assumed she was someone else. Someone completely different.

Someone like Estelle didn't need to worry about ending up alone.

"I wanted to keep Alice after the kittens were old enough to find homes," she continued, lovingly petting the calico on her lap. "Some of the babies had a rough start. I had to bottle-feed Cindy every two hours. She was born with a cleft lip and she had trouble latching. Bobby was the runt, so he had to have formula too."

A warm sensation spread through my chest at the thought of this woman working around the clock to make sure helpless kittens survived.

"That's really amazing of you," I told her. "In a big

litter like that, there's bound to be some eating issues."

She nodded. "Marcia and Jan were bullies when it came to meal time."

Amused, I held up a hand. "I'm sorry to stop you again. But did you name them after 'The Brady Bunch?'"

"Yeah." Her lips tipped up. "I mean, I had to come up with eight names that went with Alice."

I barked out a laugh, startling her companion. Raising her head, Alice gave me the stink-eye before snuggling deeper in Estelle's lap. Suddenly, I was a little envious, wondering what it would feel like to be in her place, nuzzling those soft warm thighs…

"Anyway," she went on, forcing my attention up to her face. "My plan to find them homes didn't quite work out, and now my landlord has given me an ultimatum— get rid of seven of them by Thanksgiving, or move out. My lease says I can only have two pets. Besides, it's not fair to keep so many animals in such a small space. They need more than what I can give them."

"But when the time came, you just couldn't cut the cord, huh?" Steve filled in.

She cut him hard look. "No. All the cats have…" She stopped, seeming to think about her word choice. "*Unique traits* that make them somewhat unadoptable."

My eyebrows furrowed in confusion. "Can you elaborate on that?"

"For example, Greg is a hair chewer. He got adopted by a family with a seven-year-old girl, and overnight he chewed a huge bald spot on her head. It was so bad she had to have her head shaved."

"No shit?" I breathed out, earning a stern grunt from Steve.

"Swear words, Emery."

We ignored him.

"Yeah, they were really upset. That poor kid…" Estelle cringed. "Marcia and Jan refuse to be separated. They go everywhere together. Someone tried to adopt Jan and they both went crazy when he put her in the carrier. Marcia attacked the guy."

"Yikes. So, he walked?"

"No, he still took Jan. I'm pretty sure it was the worst three days of his life. Both cats spent their time apart pacing and meowing incessantly. Neither of them slept, so it was awful for everyone, including me."

I got out a notepad to write all this down. "Okay, so we've got a hair chewer and some separation anxiety. I think I can work with that. What else?"

"Mike is the runner. He's the reason for the chicken wire on the balcony. He needs outdoor time or he goes nuts. A nice family adopted him a couple months ago, and he got out. He went missing for a week and somehow made his way back here. They weren't interested in keeping him after that."

"Wow, that's pretty crazy."

"Then there's Carol. I'm not kidding when I say she's the most annoying cat in the world. She shreds the toilet paper, which is why I have to keep it in a container. If there's a cup on the counter or the table, she knocks it off, and that's why all my dinnerware is plastic. Most people just don't have the patience for her. I understand it, but it still sucks."

As I made the notes, my head started to spin. This was a bigger mess than I'd originally thought. "That's five. What about the others?"

"Well, Peter..." She shrugged. "Peter's just a dick."

"Peter equals dick," I muttered while scribbling the words. "Got it."

"I'm serious—he's really aggressive. No one in their right mind will want him."

I grinned because that sounded like a challenge. "Three more to go."

Estelle nodded.

"I want to keep Alice and Bobby. I know I'm probably not supposed to pick favorites, but"—cupping her mouth, she lowered her voice to a whisper—"I love them the best. That leaves Cindy. Her lip—it's purely cosmetic. She doesn't have any health issues, but people don't like the deformity." She frowned, her sad eyes becoming misty. "I've overheard the whispers when they see her. They call her ugly, but she's not. She's going to make someone so happy someday."

Again, her deep affection for the cats caused my heart to clench. I knew all too well how the birth defect could put people off.

It obviously meant a great deal to Estelle that Cindy found a home where she was loved. I put a star next to her name, marking her as priority.

"I've got an idea," Steve interjected, rudely interrupting Estelle's emotional moment. "I'd like for you to look directly into the camera and say, 'I've got ninety-nine problems and seven of those are pussy cats.'"

She raised a skeptical brow. "Seriously?"

"It's genius, right? I just thought of it," he boasted over his self-perceived cleverness.

"Okay, um..." She focused on the lens and cleared her throat. "I've got ninety-nine problems and seven of those are pussy cats?"

"Exactly, but say it as a statement this time, not a question. Add a little pep to your voice. I need to *believe* it."

She blinked at him, like she couldn't figure out if he was serious or not. "But I don't have that many problems. I doubt I could even name twenty."

"It doesn't matter how many problems you really have." He gave an exasperated sigh. "Just try to pretend."

Her eyes narrowed and she pinned him with her gaze. "I think I just thought of another one."

"Fantastic," he responded, oblivious to the witty jab.

Highly amused, I covered my laugh with a cough. Estelle straightened her shoulders and recited the line one more time, delivering it perfectly.

"Okay, cut it," Steve said. "Let's take a short break."

Gently removing Alice from her lap, Estelle stood up.

"If anyone wants sweet tea, I made a fresh batch yesterday. I know you said y'all have caterers, but I just don't get company very often. It's even made with organic sugar…" She trailed off, a hopeful expression on her face.

I recognized that look. Because I had it too. Of course she was starved for social interaction. She'd been holed up in her apartment for months trying to manage her situation.

Most of the crew shuffling around us murmured a polite '*no, thank you,*' and went about their business.

"I'd love a glass," I spoke up. "You can't beat homemade."

Once again, that smile lit up her face, almost knocking me on my ass. And in that moment, I knew

I'd drink her sweet tea by the gallon if it made her happy.

Just as she poured my beverage into a plastic mason jar, Steve came into the kitchen. "The camera crew needs access to the cat room."

I nodded, taking a long sip before setting my cup on the counter. Damn, that was good tea.

"It would be a good time to let the cats become acquainted with the changes," I said to Estelle. "And I'd love to meet them."

Unable to contain her excitement, Estelle did a little happy dance with her feet.

"You're going to love them. Well, most of them. Be right back." She pranced out of the room, and a minute later several cats sauntered out of the hallway. Estelle was close behind, and she pointed at the two calicos similar to Alice. "That's Marcia and Jan. The three gray tabbies under the table are Greg, Mike, and Carol. The light orange one is Cindy, and this little guy is Bobby."

I looked down to see a small black furball winding around her ankles. Estelle's enthusiasm was infectious, and I found myself grinning like a fool.

Taking out my phone, I started snapping pictures so I could make sure I learned to recognize everyone. A dark-orange tabby hopped up onto the counter next to me and sniffed at my arm.

"Careful," Estelle warned. "That's Peter."

"Right. The dick." I pointed my phone at him and snapped a pic. "What would happen if I pet him or tried to pick him up?"

"I can't say I recommend it," she responded apprehensively. "But this is your show."

When it came to aggressive cats, part of my job

was pushing the boundaries and finding out what their limits were. The best way to do that was to have as much contact as they'd allow.

If I could just sit down with Peter, I could fully explore his tolerance for human contact.

He squinted his green eyes at me as if he knew my plans.

"Hey, buddy," I said softly, letting him smell my hand before scratching the underside of his chin. "Let's go see what's going on in the living room."

His body tensed as I picked him up, and he let out a low growl. The vocal warning was actually a good sign. He wasn't flying off without communicating that he was unhappy with the current situation, which showed a semblance of self-control.

The quiet grumbling became louder with every step I took, and the other cats started showing signs of distress. Throwing a quick glance behind my shoulder, I saw several of them pacing anxiously, as though they anticipated catastrophe.

I was almost to the couch when the gates of hell opened in the form of claws and teeth. Peter screeched while digging all four sets of his razor paws into my skin.

"Oh, shit," I grunted as the ungodly sound reverberated throughout the apartment. "All right, all right. Message heard loud and clear, buddy."

Wincing at the sharp claws still attached to my chest and stomach, I gently let Peter go, making sure he made it safely to the ground. At lightning speed, he scampered down the hallway out of sight.

"Well, it's safe to say he means business," I joked, noticing the concerned expressions around me.

Rhonda looked ticked, probably because I put myself in danger. Joel was franticly grappling with the camera, even though it was too late to catch the incident on film. And Estelle looked horrified, one hand covering her mouth and the other over her heart.

"Dammit, Emery. We were on a fucking break," Steve whined. "You should have waited until the cameras were rolling."

Shaking my head, I clucked my tongue. "Go easy on the swear words, Steve."

Chapter 3

Estelle

EMERY MATHESON was actually in my home.

When my assistant at work said she'd submitted me for the show, I laughed. I didn't think they'd pick me.

They fucking picked me.

Maybe that should've been a sign that my predicament was severely messed up.

October was the worst month for me to be taking a vacation, but I was pressed for time and I needed professional help.

I'd had to hire two extra employees to make up for my absence at the shop. Julia was just about the best assistant ever, but there was no way she could handle it on her own. Not this close to Halloween.

And it wasn't that I was emotionally attached to my apartment—I could've found another place that would let me have more pets. But moving was such a pain in the ass. Plus, I was serious when I said the cats deserved a better living environment. One with a larger space and more attention to go around.

So far, it'd been a really weird day. With the cranky producer being a douche and my uncharacteristic jitters, I was thrown for a loop.

Stage fright was a completely foreign concept to me. I wasn't shy or bashful, but I'd been having hot flashes all day.

And now, less than three hours into filming, Emery had been attacked by Peter.

I brought my hand up to my cheek. My face felt fire-engine hot. What the hell was wrong with me? I never blushed. I wasn't easily embarrassed. And I was too young for menopause.

Maybe I was coming down with something. I touched the back of my hand to my forehead. Yeah, that had to be it. I was sick and feverish.

It was a bad time to be hit with a virus. Between busy season at the shop and being on the show, I didn't have time for the sniffles.

I'd just take some medicine and push through. The show must go on, and all that jazz.

Red spots began soaking through Emery's gray T-shirt.

"Oh my God. You're bleeding." I pointed at his chest. "I'm so sorry."

He just laughed. "Occupational hazard. We have a medic on hand for that very reason. Besides, it's not like you didn't warn me."

His words summoned a brunette carrying a first aid kit.

"You know the drill," she said, grinning at him while she opened the case and started lining up her supplies on the kitchen table.

Emery grabbed the back of his T-shirt and pulled it over his head, being careful not to disrupt the wires from his mic.

Suddenly, it felt like all the air had been sucked out of the room. The thin material had done little to hide the muscle definition underneath, but at least then I couldn't see his smooth skin.

His nipples.

The ridges of his abs and that highly coveted V by his hips.

A thin smattering of hair covered his chest, traveling down the center of his abs and below his belly button. The light brown trail disappeared into the waist of his jeans.

I wanted to run my fingers over it. All of it. Even the parts I couldn't see.

I was looking at the most magnificent torso ever—not just in real life—in the entire damn universe. He had movie stars and models beat. I remembered watching a video of Charlie Hunnam training for an upcoming role, and I'd been in awe of the amount of work it took to look that good.

Regular people didn't just go walking around in that kind of shape. Apparently, Emery didn't fall into the category of 'regular people.'

And God bless him for it.

Feeling weak in the knees, I leaned my hip against the counter and wondered if I was the only one affected. Everyone else went about their tasks as usual. Well, everyone except for the medic.

After taking a seat, Emery said something to her about not using bandages this time, and her response was a nervous giggle. She quickly cleaned the area with disinfectant, then put cream over the scratches.

Red-faced, she slowly backed away as Emery slipped a new shirt on.

A different kind of heat flared through me, but this one was familiar and much more unpleasant than the virus I was fighting off.

Jealousy.

I was jealous that she got to touch him.

I made a face, because that was ridiculous. Emery was here to work, not get eye-fucked by the crazy cat lady.

The hot-and-bothered medic taped a sign to the wall by the door. In big letters, it said, 'Do not leave door open. Mike will run.' It made my sudden desire to claw her eyes out diminish.

She was just doing her job.

Psycho much, Estelle?

Opening my cabinet, I grabbed the bottle of Tylenol and choked down a couple pills along with my sweet tea.

I extended the medicine toward Emery. "Want some?"

"Nah," he replied. "It doesn't hurt that bad."

"That happens a lot, doesn't it?" I lightly accused.

"Getting mauled by cats?" He laughed. "More times than I can count."

"No." I tipped my head toward the flushed woman retreating from my apartment. "People losing their shit every time you take your shirt off."

Glancing away, Emery blushed a little, surprising me by the shy response. I wasn't trying to flatter him. I was just telling the truth.

Hmm. Maybe he was getting sick too.

Instead of answering me, he ran his hand through his hair again, causing some of the brown strands to stick up at odd angles, his look going from 'animalistic appeal' to 'crazed maniac.'

I laughed.

"Oh, here. Let me…" Rising up on my tiptoes, I reached up to smooth it down. My fingers combed through the wild mass, sculpting it away from his forehead and off to the side.

He was so much taller than I thought he'd be. With my short height, I barely made it to his shoulder. I tipped my head all the way back to look up at him and had to stretch my arms to get to his hair.

Awareness hit me when I realized my body was pressed against his, my breasts grazing his abdomen with every rise and fall of my chest.

I froze.

Emery opened his mouth like he wanted to say something, but no words came out.

And holy shit, he smelled good. Something woodsy and clean and gloriously masculine.

Faintly aware of the way my fingers were still buried in his hair, I stared at the perfect features on his face. His bottom lip had a slight indent in the middle, matching the cleft in his chin.

My eyes roamed his cheekbones, the five o'clock shadow on his jaw, and his straight nose until I landed back on his eyes.

Then there was eye contact. Earth-shattering eye contact. I had no idea how so much could pass between two people in just a few seconds, but my entire body came alive.

My nipples tightened, my hair stood on end, and it felt like my skin was tingling everywhere.

As I studied the blue flecks in his irises, he studied me back. He licked his lips.

And then the moment was broken.

"Hi." A middle-aged woman with short red hair sidled up next to me and extended her hand. "I'm Janice."

Untangling my fingers from Emery's hair, I tried to hide how flustered I was as I accepted her handshake. "I'm Estelle."

"I can't tell you how great it is to be here on this project—"

Emery suddenly looked panicked as he shook his head and cut in with, "Thank you, Janice, but I don't think we'll be needing your services this time."

Her eyebrows pinched together. "Are you sure? I don't mind sitting down with Estelle for a chat—"

"No, I'm positive."

"I cleared my schedule for this."

"And you'll be compensated for your time, regardless."

"I don't understand." She glanced at me. "Isn't this why I'm here?"

Emery's hand assaulted his hair again—a nervous habit I was picking up on—ruining my efforts to tame it. "It's my mistake. I think I came to the wrong conclusion."

"I'll be the judge of that," she argued, giving him an effective warning glare. "Let me do my job."

They entered a stare-down. As the seconds ticked by,

things got awkward.

"If Janice wants to talk, I'm more than willing to do it." My voice got higher at the end because I was confused. Who was this woman and why didn't Emery want me talking to her?

She handed me a business card. "Dr. Janice Hudson, psychiatrist at your service."

"Psychiatrist?"

Nodding, she beamed. "I'm thrilled to be working with the show on this project. I specialize in hoarding tendencies, but this is the first time I'm dealing in the subject of live animals."

"Hoarding tendencies…" I parroted, then it clicked. As a self-proclaimed reality show junkie, I'd watched those extreme hoarding episodes. How many nights had I spent on my couch surrounded by my cats wondering why these people couldn't just get rid of their stuff? My gaze swung to Emery. "Y'all think I'm crazy? Like, legitimately bat-shit crazy?"

"I did," he admitted, sheepishly rubbing the back of his neck. "But I don't think that anymore. We hire Dr. Janice if we think our clients might need counseling."

I just shrugged. Given the situation, I guess I couldn't blame him for making that assumption.

Janice turned to me with a pleasant smile. "I'm here if you need me. If not, I guess I'll just enjoy an impromptu vacation."

Just as she walked away, the douche producer waved his hand around and announced, "We're rolling again. We'll have time to socialize later. Let's get that tour."

"Is he always this much of an asshole?" I muttered quietly to Emery.

He grimaced. "Unfortunately, yeah. But the good thing is, he won't be around all the time. If you can get through today without strangling him, you'll be fine."

"I make no promises," I deadpanned before turning toward the hallway. Stopping at the first door on the right, I grinned and made a sweeping motion with my arm. "This is the cat room."

The crew had done a good job of working around the cats' belongings, because the only difference I spotted was one small camera mounted to the wall by the closet. Joel moved stealthily into the room after us and shrank back into the corner, trying to look as inconspicuous as possible.

"Whoa." Emery turned in a circle. "You really went all-out in here, huh?"

The small bedroom was devoid of any human furniture, but it was every feline's dream.

A kitty castle, made from an upcycled TV entertainment center, was the main focus of the room. I'd painted it with pastel colors and glitter. Not like the cats cared, but I thought it was pretty. Then there were eight little round beds, two carpet-covered towers with scratching posts, and four litter boxes.

Oh, and a sink.

Emery pointed at the porcelain pedestal sink with a confused look on his face. "Why is there a sink bolted to the wall?" He bent down to look under it, and I took the opportunity to check out his amazing ass. "There's no running water in here."

My eyes snapped up to his face when he stood. "Right. Remember how I told you Carol is the most annoying cat in the world? Well, she'll only sleep in the sink. I had to put one in here so I could use the one in the bathroom."

"That's an interesting quirk." Emery walked by me and sniffed. I tried to ignore the adorable wrinkles on the bridge of his nose—I really did—but he was *so* fucking cute. "You've got a pisser," he stated bluntly. "That ammonia smell is really strong in here."

"Yeah." I sighed because it'd been a source of frustration for months. "Someone is peeing outside of the boxes, but I can't figure out who's doing it."

"It could be a behavioral issue," Emery supplied. "The other possibility is a urinary tract infection. How many litter boxes do you have in the apartment?"

"Ten in total. There are five more in the living room and one in the bathroom. My bedroom is off-limits to the cats. I need to have my own space, and they all sleep in here at night anyway."

"That's understandable, especially with Greg's hair-chewing habits."

Emery took me by surprise when he reached out to toy with the ends of my hair. I'd already had my fingers all up in his, so maybe the hair touching was a thing now.

But the way he looked at me was… affectionate.

I felt my face heat again. We were stuck in another one of those moments—the second one of the day already—where an invisible connection sizzled between us. Only this time, we were being filmed.

Clearing his throat, Emery let his arm fall awkwardly to his side.

"Okay, so what we'll do today is start an isolation process." He turned to Steve, who seemed very bored out in the hallway. "Can someone get me a crystal box?"

Then his eyes swung my way again. "Will any of the cats be opposed to staying in the bathroom overnight?"

I anxiously chewed my lip. "Only Marcia and Jan. But as long as they stay together, they'll be fine."

He nodded. "We can keep them together. That'll rule out two cats at once, so that's good."

"I'm sorry, can you explain what a crystal box is?"

"It's just a litter box with non-absorbent litter. We'll be able to take urine samples and test them for a UTI." He wrote something down before sticking the notepad in his back pocket. "Now, tomorrow we're going to start bringing in possible adoptees."

"Already? Wow…"

"And we'll probably need to do a light sedative for Peter when we have visitors. We don't want him scaring people off or injuring anyone."

"Like, drugs?" I asked, slightly alarmed.

"I'll do a natural approach first." Emery must have been able to read the panic on my face because he looked concerned. "Are you okay?"

"Everything's just moving so fast." I didn't even realize I was wringing my hands until Emery put his big palm over them, but as soon as he did, I was effectively distracted from my anxiety.

His skin was warm and rough, just like a man's hands should be.

Why did he have to keep touching me? If he kept this up, I'd be in serious danger of literally throwing myself at him.

"Estelle," he said low. Placing a hand at the small of my back, he steered me out into the hall away from the cameras. He leaned in close. "We're very good at what we do. The process might feel rushed at times, but all the cats will find good homes. I promise you that."

I believed him. This was a man who kept his promises, I could tell. My mom had always told me I was an impeccable judge of character.

But why did he smell so good? And why did he have to be so hot? Literally hot. I could feel the warmth radiating from his skin.

Between Emery's intoxicating scent and the close proximity of our bodies, I was having trouble forming a complete thought.

Giving him a small smile, I just said, "Okay."

Like a total airhead.

He returned my smile, flashing those straight white teeth before stepping back. "Do you want to meet with Janice? Not because you're crazy, but just because?"

"It couldn't hurt." I shrugged. "I think everyone needs counseling."

He chuckled. "I'm sure she'd like to feel useful. I think she's mad at me for dragging her all the way to South Carolina for nothing."

"I'll even act like a nutcase just to make her feel like her time is worthwhile," I joked.

APPARENTLY, I DIDN'T have to try very hard to act like a nutcase. All Janice had to do was ask me how I felt about going from nine cats to two, in less than three weeks, and I lost it.

I blew my nose into the tissue she handed me. "They were there for me during a time when I really needed them. They're my friends, you know? That sounds weird, but it's true."

"It's not weird at all. Pets become our companions, especially when we live alone."

"I'll still have Alice and Bobby." Silently willing the tears away, I picked at a loose thread on my shirt. "But the apartment will feel so empty."

"What about your social life? Maybe you could spend more time with friends," she suggested.

I nodded, although I was unsure about that.

The cats had basically taken over every aspect of my life. If I wasn't at work, I was home taking care of them. I saw Julia at the shop, but we weren't really friends. Everyone I knew from college lived too far away for frequent visits.

"To be honest, I've never been very good at having friends," I divulged, relaxing in the chair as I went full-on patient mode. We'd chosen to have our session in an alcove at the end of the apartment complex hallway, and the two plush armchairs presented the perfect setup. "I've struggled with fitting in for as long as I can remember. When I was a kid, I got left out a lot. Some of my classmates told me their parents didn't want me at their birthday parties or sleepovers because I was too wild."

"Children can be harsh. Parents too, unfortunately. What do you think they meant by 'wild?'"

"I was just really creative, and I had a lot of ideas. Sometimes those ideas got messy. Like when I was six, I thought raiding the refrigerator meant you stole everything out of it." I laughed at the memory I was about to share. "So one time at a sleepover, I convinced my friend to help me get all the items from the fridge and hide them in her bed. Stuff got everywhere. I'm pretty sure the pancake syrup ruined her mattress. All the food went bad because it'd been sitting out all night. Needless to say, I wasn't invited back."

Janice chuckled. "That sounds like normal childhood mischief to me."

My smile faded. "Where I grew up, appearances and manners are everything. My parents are great people, but they just didn't know what to do with a wild child like me."

"And what about romantic relationships?" she asked, switching topics. "I understand you had a bad breakup about a year ago."

"It wasn't a bad breakup. Just unexpected." I tried to think about how to explain that my ex and I were never right for each other. I decided to start at the beginning. "I had a rebellious streak in high school, but I calmed down once I got to college. I met Brian my freshman year and he was everything I *thought* I needed. You know, studious and stable. And I tried to be what he wanted." I sighed. "My mom really loved him. After he left, you would've thought someone died the way she cried for days."

"What did your parents like most about him?"

"They thought he 'stabilized' me," I replied, using air quotes.

"And did he?"

"Yes. A little too much, I guess. He stifled me—my quirks, my creativity, my independence. I shouldn't have been surprised when he broke things off. He disapproved of everything I did, from the nail polish I wore to my plan of running the costume shop."

"And how did that make you feel?"

"It sucked ass. No one wants to feel like they're constantly being judged by the person who's supposed to love them unconditionally."

"What a douche," she deadpanned, and I laughed.

I had a feeling we were going to get along just fine.

"I might not be a hoarder, but I can see why someone would collect pets and never want to let them go."

"Oh, really?" Janice's eyes sparked with interest. "Now you're speaking my language. Tell me about that."

I smiled. "The best thing about animals? If I want to walk around the apartment naked, they don't bat an eye. If I want a bowl of ice cream for breakfast, they want to share it with me."

"And do you eat ice cream for breakfast?"

"Well, yeah." I laughed. "Isn't that the best part about being an adult? You can do whatever you want, within reason. After my ex and I broke up, I made a promise to myself that I would never try to change for someone ever again. This might sound heartless, but when that door shut behind him, the strongest emotion I felt was relief."

"Did you argue often?"

"Not really. He just used to make this face a lot." I pursed my lips, puffed out my cheeks, and furrowed my eyebrows. I didn't have to look in the mirror to know I resembled the love-child of a monkey and a blowfish. "That was his displeased face. But that wasn't the worst part."

"I'm almost afraid to ask what was." Janice chuckled.

"Things were just very… *comfortable* in our relationship."

"Comfortable?"

"Boring," I clarified, huffing out a laugh. "He was a total bore, okay?"

"Are you talking about your sex life?" she asked hesitantly.

"Let's just say I've been DIY-ing it for a looong time."

"Ah. Well, nothing wrong with that." Fiddling with the top button of her blouse, Janice looked uncomfortable, and I was reminded that sometimes my bluntness caught people off guard.

"Are you blushing, Janice?" I teased. "Surely you've had people talk about this before."

She snickered. "I told you I specialize in hoarding tendencies. I'm not a sex therapist. Now, if you're hoarding sex toys, then we can talk."

Holding up my hands, I laughed. "I only have one, I swear."

A quiet knock drew my attention, and Emery poked his head around the corner. "Sorry to interrupt. Steve wants to get another interview before we pack it in for the day."

Janice glanced at her watch. "Our time is just about over anyway. Estelle, would you like to meet again tomorrow?"

I grinned. "I would love that."

Much to my relief, Emery conducted the evening interview instead of Steve. We did a basic recap of the day, where I got to voice my thoughts about how much progress we'd already made.

My overall feelings? Everything was moving so fast. It was great, but my mind was having trouble keeping up with the changes.

Then I watched in fascination as Emery did a quick exam for each of the cats on my kitchen table—except Peter. He listened to their hearts, checked their teeth, and felt their lymph nodes. They hadn't been to the vet in a few months, but all of them were up to date with their shots and spayed or neutered.

After it was over, my apartment quickly cleared out until it was just Emery and me. And the cats, of course.

Marcia, Jan, and Bobby circled my ankles, alerting me that it was mealtime. God forbid I be fifteen minutes late on serving their dinner.

Opening the bottom cupboard, I got out nine nameplated bowls and the large food container.

"Can I help with anything?" Emery offered.

I glanced down at my arm full of bowls, then lined them up on the table. Doling out two scoops of kibble, I handed him the ones belonging to Marcia and Jan. "These go in the cat room."

As he carried the food, the hungry cats followed, weaving through his legs. I snorted out a laugh when they almost tripped him.

When he came back, I'd already set most of the containers in their designated spots around the kitchen. I pointed at the last two on the table. "Cindy and Bobby eat by the balcony door." Then I whispered, "They get an extra half-scoop, but it's our secret."

Grinning, Emery took the bowls and both cats were hot on his heels.

"Thank you for all your help today," I said as the room filled with a chorus of crunching sounds from all the ravenous cats.

"That's what I'm here for. If you need me, day or night, I'll be right outside in the RV. Just call this number." Emery pulled out a business card. He crossed out the number on the front and scribbled one on the back along with something else. Holding it up, he pointed at what he wrote. "Make sure you say this code phrase."

I read over the words and my eyes got wide. "Are you serious?"

"Yep."

"You want me to say *these exact words* to you?" I squeaked.

Seeming amused, he nodded. When he handed me the card, our fingers brushed, sending tingles up my arm. The sensation traveled through my chest until it settled in my stomach, morphing into a violent fluttering.

I could've lied to myself some more. Could've blamed it on nausea from the so-called virus.

But I had to face facts—it wasn't a virus.

It was unbridled sexual attraction. The feeling had grown throughout the day, and that wasn't a good thing.

I bit the inside of my cheek hard enough to snap myself out of it. Attraction couldn't happen.

Not here. Not now. Not with him. I needed to reel that motherfucker in.

I was a lot of things, but a celebrity groupie was *not*

one of them.

Of course, it didn't help that Emery had basically just propositioned me for a booty call.

I'd been out of the dating game for a long time, but I wasn't too rusty to realize I was being hit up for a hookup. I mean, he gave me his personal number and basically asked me to talk dirty to him on the phone.

Maybe I wasn't so rusty after all.

Score one for Estelle.

For a split-second, I considered taking him up on his offer.

No. That was a bad idea. I had too much class for that.

Who was I kidding? No, I didn't. But that didn't mean I had to make an already-odd situation any weirder.

Cats. Focus on the cats.

Emery was typing out a text, and I zeroed in on his hands. Such long, masculine fingers. How was it possible for someone to have sexy knuckles?

My sexual depravation bubbled to the surface. A steady throb started between my legs and I resisted the urge to fan myself. Rubbing my thighs together, I hoped my flustered state wasn't too obvious.

But Emery wasn't paying attention.

Putting his phone away, he seemed completely oblivious to my raging hormones as he had a powwow with Peter, who had jumped up onto the counter next to him.

"I forgive you, buddy. You might not realize this now, but you and me? We're gonna be super bros. Let's pound it out." Emery held out a fist, and much to my surprise, Peter gently headbutted it.

And damn if that didn't make him even sexier.

It was going to be a long couple of weeks.

Chapter 4

Emery

I CANCELED DINNER with my sister.

The variety of issues Estelle's cats had was tricky, and I needed to brainstorm. Not only would I have to individualize my strategies, but I would also need to work with the prospective owners once the cats found homes to make sure they were adjusting to the move.

It probably would've been easier if this had been a hoarding problem.

Estelle wasn't mentally unstable—she just had a really big heart. She'd completely rearranged her life for these animals. Hell, she bolted a damn sink to the bedroom wall for Carol.

She hadn't just provided a suitable living environment. She'd created a home. And yes, there was a big difference between the two.

Sifting through my notes from the day, I looked at

the star next to Cindy's name. Fortunately, I already had plans for her.

> **Me:** How do you feel about Lizzie having a cat?
>
> **Nikki:** Seriously Emery?
>
> **Me:** Yes, seriously.
>
> **Nikki:** We told her no pets until she's old enough to take care of it.
>
> **Me:** She's old enough. And you might change your mind once you see Cindy. Come tomorrow and just meet her.
>
> **Nikki:** Ugh. Okay, but don't tell Lizzie we're there to adopt. I don't want her getting her hopes up. Will we have to be on the show?

I had a feeling she was going to ask that. Steve would have a conniption fit if I made him stop filming, especially for the first successful adoption.

> **Me:** I'm afraid there might not be any way around it. I won't let them interview Lizzie, but they might want you to say a few things.
>
> **Nikki:** That's fine.

Next on the list: Peter. I didn't want him going apeshit tomorrow while my niece was around. Luckily, I had local resources to help me.

There was a guy in the vet med department at the university who specialized in calming cats without using conventional sedatives. Evan was wicked smart, and I believed he was going to change veterinary medicine someday. The clinic I used to work at had been in contact with him on a regular basis, and I still kept his number on hand just for these special occasions.

> **Me:** Hey, man. I know this is short notice, but I'm in the area and I need something to make this cat chill out.

He responded right away.

> **Evan:** What are you dealing with? Anxiety or aggression?
>
> **Me:** Aggression, mostly. But it could be stemming from anxiety.
>
> **Evan:** Ok. Swing by the lab tomorrow around 7am. I'll have something for you.

I had just set my phone down on the small dining table when I spied Estelle walking across the parking lot, her blond hair glowing under the tall lamppost.

Before I could second-guess what I was doing, I was cracking the window and yelling, "Hey, Estelle!"

Smooth move, ass-wipe.

She stopped and waved.

Trying to recover from my unrefined attempt to talk to the hottest woman ever, I exited the RV. In a fitted black leather jacket and knee-high fuck-me boots, Estelle looked even more badass than earlier as she spun her keyring around her finger.

"Where are you going?" I asked, panting from trying to get to her so fast. God, I was only making things worse.

Grinning, she motioned toward the pink Jeep Wrangler ten feet away. "I'm heading to Target. The cats are getting low on food, and believe me, you don't want to be around them if they've missed breakfast."

I laughed and shuffled my feet. "Gotcha. Okay, well, I just wanted to say hi…"

You awkward son of a bitch.

"Do you want to come with me?" she offered, kindly throwing me a bone. "That is, if you need anything…"

"I could use some beer." I was already nodding my head before she could finish her sentence. Never mind the fact that the RV was already stocked with every kind of beverage a guy could possibly want.

I fell into step beside her. The fuck-me heels made a distinct *clack* on the concrete with every step as she made her way around to the driver's side.

"I hope you don't mind a windy ride," she said as we got in. "I like driving with the top off if weather allows, and it's a nice night."

It was a perfect night. The sky was clear, showcasing the stars and the nearly full moon. At almost seventy degrees, the air felt good. The black interior of the vehicle looked old, but clean. Judging from the faded leather seats, my guess was she left the top off a lot.

"What happens if it rains?" I asked.

She grinned. "I get wet."

Holy mother of fuck.

Biting my lip to the point of pain, I had to look away while I willed my instant erection to go away. *Rain.* She was talking about rain. I asked an innocent question and got an equally innocent answer. When did I become such an uncontrollable pervert?

Clearing my throat, I tried to distract myself by flicking the bobble head cat stuck to the dash. "Cute."

"Thanks. Buckle up." Smirking, she pulled her seatbelt across her chest. "How about some music?" She opened the middle console and shuffled through some CDs. "What do you like?"

"Anything, really."

After starting the ignition, she put a disk in the player and pressed a few buttons. "Hot in Herre" by Nelly came on.

"Hold onto your tits," Estelle announced before jamming the vehicle into reverse.

Any amusement I had over the fact that she said *tits* died as soon as we started moving. The tires squealed as we tore out of the parking lot, and I gripped the roll bar so hard my knuckles turned white.

When we got out onto the road, she cranked the music up to deafening levels while haphazardly weaving through traffic.

I glanced at the speedometer and noticed it wasn't working. In fact, none of her gages were. The only thing on her dash that was correct was the lit-up 'check engine' light.

Estelle started dancing and rapping along with the song, her body bouncing up and down, arms waving through the air. It would've been one of the cutest fucking things I'd ever seen if I wasn't scared for my life.

"Shouldn't you have both hands on the wheel?" I yelled over at her.

"What?" she shouted back.

She shifted toward me and started to swerve into the

wrong lane. Someone honked their horn as we sped by.

"Nothing." I frantically pointed out the windshield. "Keep your eyes on the road."

Shrugging, she went back to singing about taking off her clothes as the wind whipped through her hair.

She was fucking crazy. We were going to die.

But even through the sheer terror, I couldn't help being drawn to the uninhibited smile on her face. She was beautiful. Completely lost in her own world.

For a second, I wanted to get lost with her, and I almost forgot how close we were to ending up in a head-on collision.

Almost.

A horn blared behind us when Estelle switched lanes without checking her blind spot, and self-preservation kicked in.

In the three-mile trip, I prayed for my life, making all kinds of bargains I probably couldn't follow through with: I'd go to church every Sunday, donate at least ten hours of volunteer time at the shelter each week, and I'd even start helping dogs, because canines need love too.

Pretty sure I screamed like a girl a couple times, but it must've been drowned out by the loud music.

Making a sharp left, Estelle ran over the curb as we turned into the parking lot, but I was too relieved to care.

We'd made it alive.

Once the car was safely in park, I finally let go of the grip I had on the door.

"Whew!" Looking in the rearview mirror, Estelle smoothed her windblown hair. "That was fun, right? It's been way too long since I took this thing out. My work is less than two miles from my place, so I usually ride my bicycle. Knocks out cardio and saves the environment. Two birds, one stone," she rambled, oblivious to the heart attack she'd almost given me.

"Uh-huh," was all I could manage as I tried to slow my racing pulse.

Once she was satisfied with her appearance, her gaze finally made it to me. "Oh, wow. Your hair is an epic disaster."

Leaning over the middle console, she reached for my head, just like she'd done earlier in the day. She paused, her hand hovering an inch away from her destination.

Estelle looked conflicted, with a crease between her eyebrows as she seemed to debate whether or not she should fix my hair. I had no idea what she was waiting for, but I craved her touch.

"I could probably use a little help," I encouraged.

Finally, those delicate fingers softly threaded through the mess on my head. My eyelids drooped at the sensation. Stylists for the show did my hair all the time, but it never felt like this. Goosebumps broke out over my scalp, spreading down my neck and arms.

My heart was still beating fast, but for a completely different reason now.

That sweet scent lingered in the air again, and it mixed with the smell of Estelle's leather jacket. Fighting the urge to grab her, I clenched my fists in my lap.

I wanted to pull her closer.

She pulled away.

Satisfied with the work she did, Estelle gave a nod. "Much better. We should be out of here in, like, five minutes."

W E SHOULD BE *out of here in five minutes.*

Famous last words coming from a woman who was about to walk into Target. I should've known better—I had a sister.

First, Estelle got reeled in by the clearance rack in the clothing section. That resulted in her needing to try on at least five outfits; I lost count after she came out of the dressing room in a black dress with an open back, her tattoo on full display. The high neckline had see-through lace that went from the top of her breasts up to her collarbone, and the hem fell to about mid-thigh. It took an enormous amount of strength to close my mouth once I realized it was hanging open.

She decided to buy the dress. And a mustard-yellow throw blanket because it was so *soft.* And a set of plastic wine glasses because they were *so cute.*

Only needed cat food, my ass.

Now I was stuck in the vortex known as the makeup aisle, helping her pick out lipstick shades. As I stared down at all the pink and red lines she'd drawn on the back of her hand, I had a surreal, almost out-of-body experience.

How did I get here? How did I end up in my hometown at Target, debating if Pink Champagne was better than Roseberry Red? The biggest shock of all was that it didn't feel uncomfortable or unnatural. And I didn't hate it. In fact, I hadn't had this much fun in years.

Maybe because this wasn't a date. Maybe because Estelle was a client, which basically made her off-limits.

Didn't matter anyway. I was positive that playing makeover planted me firmly in the friend zone. Hell, maybe she thought I was gay.

It was for the best.

"Well, which one do you think I should get?" She shoved her hand closer to me.

My gaze bounced between the colors and her face, trying to decide what would suit her best. I didn't know anything about this shit, but I pictured the deepest red on her full lips. The shade would look stunning against her sun-kissed skin.

"That one," I replied, pointing to it.

She gave me a brilliant smile. "Good choice. That's what I was going to pick."

I paused. "If you already knew you were buying that one, why did you ask me?"

Shrugging, she tossed it into the cart and it landed on top of the dress. "I was just curious. Now onto the cat food."

Grinning like a fool, I resumed pushing the cart because, apparently, at some point there had been an unspoken agreement that it was my job.

Women were a mystery I would never solve, but tonight I was okay with that.

THE TRIP BACK to Estelle's was just as terrifying as the first, but at least I knew what to expect this time around.

As she slammed on the brakes, we came to a halting stop in her designated parking spot.

I tried to control my breathing when she shut off the ignition. I didn't want to look like a wuss in front of her, but shit. That was the scariest thing I'd experienced in a while.

Estelle dropped her keys into her purse, then turned to me.

"I know I'm a terrible driver," she said, shrugging like she wasn't even embarrassed. "I'm still surprised they passed me at the DMV."

I didn't want to lie to her, but I felt bad agreeing. So I just nodded and said, "That was… different."

"I've had my license for less than two years," she went on as we got out and grabbed our bags from the backseat. "And like I said, I usually ride my bike."

"Less than two years? How is that possible?"

"In high school, my parents used the possibility of a car and a driver's license as a reward for being good." Smirking, her red lips twisted to the side. "I couldn't stay out of trouble long enough to get it."

"Why am I not surprised by that?" I teased.

"And I didn't need a car in college because the campus was so small." As she talked, I followed her up the sidewalk to the front entrance. She stopped by the bike rack and pointed at the only transportation chained to the metal. "Besides, The Flying Purple People Eater gets me from point A to point B." She gave the lavender, adult-sized, three-wheeled contraption a loving pat on the handle bars.

I laughed because of the ridiculous nickname she'd given her bike and also because it wasn't a bike at all.

"Estelle, that's a tricycle."

She gaped at me. "It is not. Okay. Well, technically, it is. But calling it that makes it sound like a toddler toy. This beast is way too badass to be for kids."

My grin was so wide my cheeks hurt. "You ride a trike."

"Speaking of sweet rides," she continued, tilting her head toward the RV, "that's a pretty nice setup you've got."

"You want to come in?" The question was out of my mouth before I could stop it. "I mean, just to see it. There's a flat screen TV and a standup shower. Not that you want to see the shower. It's actually really small."

Her lips twitched at my offer and subsequent bumbling. "Sure."

When we got inside, she gasped and dumped her shopping bags on the bench seat.

"This place is amazing." She turned in a circle. "My parents used to have a popup camper because my mom refused to sleep in a tent. I thought it was huge but this… it's almost as big as my apartment."

I laughed. "Too bad I don't get to keep it."

I followed behind her as she admired all the special features—the booth-style dining table, the extra bed above the driver's seat, the miniature appliances that lined the small kitchen.

"This is so cute," she said, running her fingertips over the laminate countertop next to the oven. "It's like everything is fun-sized."

The appliances weren't the only thing that was fun-sized.

I had a foot of height and probably a hundred pounds on Estelle. As I took in her petite frame, I imagined what it would be like to have her fragile body beneath mine.

"Except my bed." My voice came out huskily. "It's pretty big."

Whipping her head in my direction, Estelle's eyes were wide, her lips parted.

Damn it. That didn't come out right.

The cozy space suddenly felt impossibly tiny. I could smell her. My hands itched to grab her around the waist, to squeeze her ass, to set her on the counter and peel off every article of clothing.

I wanted to kiss her lipstick right the fuck off.

It'd been a mistake to invite her in. A big mistake. I needed to get her out before I did something stupid.

"Well, I should probably get some sleep," I rushed out. "Long day tomorrow and it's getting late."

It wasn't late. The clock on the microwave showed 8:17.

"Oh, okay." Estelle looked disappointed. "Thanks for braving it with me to the store. It was nice to have human company for once."

Before she could turn away, I blurted, "Do you want me to give you driving lessons? I don't mean that in a condescending way. I wouldn't mind teaching you if you want."

She shook her head and gathered her bags. "That's nice of you, but you're already doing enough for me as it is. And I might not be the old woman you were expecting, but I'm a big girl."

After following her out, I walked her to the front

entrance of the apartment building.

Like the gentleman I was, I offered to help her carry her bags up to her place. With the two bottles of wine she'd added to her merchandise, it was a heavy load.

"Thanks, but I got it," she responded, reaching for the code panel. "Good night."

"Good night, Estelle."

I was almost to the door of the RV when her voice stopped me.

"Hey, Emery?"

I turned.

"Thanks again for coming with me tonight. Really. You're the sweetest."

The sweetest.

Yeah, she definitely thought I was gay.

As soon as I got inside, I popped open a beer and got back to work. Well, I tried to anyway. But as my eyes scanned over my notes from the day, the letters blurred. I was having trouble concentrating. Not because of the beer—I'd only taken one sip. No, it was because it seemed that all the blood in my body had rushed to my lower half.

I'd spent most of the day alternating between full-blown hard-on and half-mast.

And spending more time with Estelle hadn't helped. I was unbelievably attracted to her. She was funny, bold, honest. Gorgeous. Compassionate. A terrible driver and a compulsive shopper.

So fucking sexy.

As my dick pressed uncomfortably against my zipper, I had trouble remembering why I'd sworn off women in the first place.

It wasn't just any woman, though. It was *her*.

Estelle was a temptation and she didn't even know it. I never messed around with clients or coworkers. Ever. I prided myself on adhering to that cardinal rule.

But I felt unleashed. Like something inside of me had snapped—something I didn't even know was restrained in the first place.

Desire.

I couldn't want her.

I shouldn't want her.

But adrenaline from the near-death experience in the pink Jeep still pumped through my veins. That, combined with the knowledge that Estelle was nearby, made me feel an uncontrollable hunger.

We were literally separated by this RV, one hundred feet of space, and a wall.

My mind went back to earlier when I'd overheard Estelle talking to Janice. I shouldn't have listened in on their conversation. Not only was it a violation of Estelle's privacy, but it didn't do me any favors.

Hearing her say she'd been 'DIY-ing it' gave me all sorts of mental images. Thinking about her touching herself, what noises she made, what her face looked like when she came.

Although, in all honesty, I'd been listening in on their conversation long before any masturbatory talk. Long enough to hear Estelle talk about her ex and how he made her feel like she couldn't be herself. I wholeheartedly agreed with Janice's sentiment: What a douche.

There was nothing wrong with Estelle. Yeah, she was kind of a mess—a wild, perfect mess.

Groaning, I unbuttoned my jeans and pulled the

zipper down, giving much-needed relief to my erection.

I gave my dick a tug as I thought about her red lips. The black dress. What kind of panties did she have on? I took her for a thong type of girl.

Unable to stop it, the fantasy took control of my thoughts, and suddenly, I had her cornered in the Target dressing room.

I imagined bending her over, flipping the dress up, and pulling her panties down. Running my fingers through her slickness before lining my tip up at her entrance. Thrusting hard, plunging into her heat.

My hand moved up and down my shaft, squeezing the head with every pass.

Estelle moaned, and I covered her mouth with my palm to keep her quiet. Didn't want to get caught.

My fist pumped faster.

Removing my hand from her face, I rubbed circles over her clit as I pounded into her. Palmed her tits. Spread her ass cheeks. I wanted to touch every inch of her body.

She whimpered again. *Bad girl.* Bringing my palm back to her mouth, I smothered her increasingly loud cries. And although I couldn't understand what she was saying, it sounded like she was chanting my name.

My balls drew up tight.

Body shaking, she exploded around my cock, her snug walls clamping down as she let out a muffled scream behind my hand.

Then I came. Hard.

I let out a hoarse shout as I coated the front of my T-shirt with the strongest orgasm I'd ever had.

My eyes slammed shut. My head tilted back. My

fingernails dug into the leather of the bench seat.

Ripples of pleasure raced through my body with every jet of cum shooting from my cock.

When it was finally over, I sat there trying to catch my breath for a few minutes with my softening dick resting on my stomach.

"What the fuck was that?" I whispered to myself, still astonished at the intensity of the moment. I'd never come that hard, especially not from jacking off.

Physically drained, my head lolled to the side and I peeked through the crack in the curtain. I had a good view of Estelle's balcony and her living room light was on. Suddenly, the sliding glass door opened and Estelle came outside with Mike.

I jerked away from the window.

Even though she hadn't seen me, I felt a little guilty. Technically, I hadn't done anything wrong, but I was reminded that I was here for one reason—find homes for seven cats so Estelle didn't get evicted.

I didn't have time to date, and fucking a client was unethical. Not to mention if the tabloids caught wind of an onset romance, they'd have a field day with it, and I couldn't let her get dragged into that.

I can't have her.

But even as my mind tried to rationalize why getting involved with Estelle was wrong, I knew that if she wanted me, I was fucked.

Good thing she didn't think of me that way.

I'd be 'DIY-ing' it a lot over the next couple weeks.

After getting cleaned up, I went back to my notes and started thumbing through the cats' medical records. Now that I was sexually sated, I could focus on the task at hand.

It was only the first day and I was already making good headway. We might even be able to wrap up filming early and I could spend a few days at the beach before going back to Chicago.

Confidence filled me, and I gave myself a mental pat on the back.

I was so fucking good at this job.

Chapter 5

Emery

SOMETIMES I WAS really fucking bad at this job.

The morning had been a disaster, and it wasn't even 9 a.m. yet. Mike had gotten out when I held the front door open for too long, so Estelle and Janice were searching the halls for him now. Joel had technical difficulties with his camera, which was going to delay filming for at least two hours. And Steve was being a jackass, per usual.

"Son of a bitch," he whined, glaring down at his phone.

"What?" I asked, concerned.

"I took a quiz. 'Where will I be in five years based on my pizza topping preference?'" He violently tapped the screen. "Shearing llamas in Peru? The creators of these tests are way off. How can they sleep at night?" he asked incredulously.

"Steve, on top of everything else that's happened

today, I don't have time for your drama llama." I snickered at my own joke. He wasn't amused.

On the plus side, the urine sample we'd collected from Cindy came back fine, so she was in the clear to be adopted. Also, we were one step closer to finding the pissing culprit.

A knock sounded at Estelle's door and I opened it to find Nikki and Lizzie.

"Sorry we're late," she said, grappling with her oversized mom-bag. She leaned in for a hug. "Like, ten things went wrong before we even got out the door."

"No worries," I assured her. "Same here. We're behind schedule, but that means you'll have time to meet the cats without so many people around." Looking down at my niece, I ruffled her strawberry-blond curls. "How's it going, squirt?"

"Good." She giggled down at her feet with her usual shyness, hiding behind her hair. "Where are the kitties?"

I'd already administered the sedative to Peter, leaving him calm and pleasant. Evan had given me a special mixture of liquid catnip drops that he'd concocted, and they were like magic. It'd been way easier than I thought—all I had to do was mix it with a little tuna and Peter ate it right up.

"Down that hallway, first door on the right," I told her. "That's where a lot of them like to hang out."

"I found Mike," Estelle announced, coming through the door with the gray bundle in her arms. "He was trying to eat the plastic leaves on that fake plant down the hall, so we might need to watch him for diarrhea—" Stopping short, she smiled at Nikki. "Oh, hi."

I did a brief introduction. Not that I needed to,

because within fifteen seconds, Estelle and Nikki were chatting about lipstick like old friends.

I backed away, because I had absolutely nothing to add to that conversation. Instead, I headed for the cat room to check on Lizzie.

I was just about to the door when I heard her little voice call out, "I think this one's dead, Uncle E."

What? Shit.

Quickening my pace, I made it to her side and my eyes followed her pointing finger. Peter was lying on the top level of the kitty castle on his back, upside down, with his head and front paws hanging all the way off.

"Peter?" I scratched the underside of his chin. "You okay, buddy?"

He laughed—I kid you not—he actually laughed like a person. That was some creepy shit. I picked him up and cradled his limp body. Resting my head on his chest, I heard his steady heartbeat and felt the rise and fall of his breathing.

Then I sent a text to Evan.

Me: What the hell is in that catnip?

Evan: It's just concentrated catnip that's been genetically modified.

Me: What does that mean exactly?

Evan: Why? What happened? How many drops did you give him?

Me: Only two. Peter is tripping the fuck out. He's damn near comatose.

Evan: Can you send pictures and a documented time log of his activities?

Me: What the FUCK, man?

Evan: It's still in the experimental stages.

Me: Experimental stages??

My mind raced as I tried to think of what to do. If we had a cat die on this show, we were going to be in deep shit. We might even get canceled by the network. Estelle would be devastated, and I'd never forgive myself.

As if Evan read my thoughts, he sent another text.

Evan: I'm totally kidding! Don't panic. We've had this happen a couple times, but it's not harmful. Some cats react strongly. Let me know if he doesn't snap out of it within an hour.

Evan: And sorry he's catatonic. Get it? Cat-atonic? Haha I love making that joke.

Me: Not funny.

A gasp drew my attention to the doorway.

"What's wrong with Peter?" Estelle hurried over, concern etched on her face. Nikki wasn't far behind.

"He's having a strong reaction to the sedatives," I told her. "The pharmacist said it's not dangerous, though."

"Oh, poor baby," Estelle cooed, her sweet voice going straight to my cock. She hesitantly reached for Peter. "Can I hold him?"

Nodding, I placed him in her arms. "Yeah. He's yours, after all."

"This is the first time I've ever gotten to hold him like this. He never lets me cuddle." She softly stroked his fur while rocking him like a baby. Her serious eyes shot up to mine. "How pissed do you think he'll be later if I take advantage of the fact that he's high?"

I laughed. "It's probably best if we keep him in our sights, so, cuddle away."

"Momma!" Lizzie's screech caused panic to shoot through me.

What now? I really didn't want anything else going wrong today.

All three of us approached where she sat in the corner, petting the peach-colored cat sleeping in one of the beds. My heart warmed. She'd found Cindy all on her own.

"Look. This one's just like me." Kneeling down next to Cindy, she positioned herself so their faces were side by side. She looked up at us, letting her hair fall away from her face. A rare, unguarded moment for her.

"Oh," Estelle breathed out, barely managing to stifle her gasp of surprise when she saw Lizzie's scar.

What I hadn't told Estelle was, Lizzie had been born with a cleft lip too. A simple cosmetic surgery had fixed it, but a scar on the left side remained, becoming more prominent when she smiled. And she was smiling now. A big, exuberant smile.

I didn't tell Estelle on purpose; I wanted an honest, unfiltered reaction. The way people responded to Lizzie's birth defect said a lot about their character.

A test.

And she passed with flying colors, just like I suspected she would.

I don't know why I cared. Why was her reaction so important to me? Knowing she was a good person only made it ten times more difficult to stay professional, made me want her more than I already did.

Swallowing hard, Estelle gave me a grateful grin as she mouthed, "Thank you."

I returned a smile that said, 'you're welcome.'

Gently placing Peter in his bed, she kissed his head before turning back to Lizzie. "Look, your hair color matches. Cindy's a strawberry-blond, too. Twinsies, for sure."

"You hear that, Mom?" Lizzie beamed. "We're twinsies."

"Would you like to see her favorite toy?" Estelle sat on the floor next to them and grabbed a wicker basket full of feathers and strings. "She can fetch like a dog."

Pulling out a spongy ball, she waved it in front of Cindy to get her attention, then threw it out into the hall. The cat sprang after it and returned less than ten seconds later with it in her mouth. Cindy dropped it by Lizzie's feet. My happy niece clapped like it was the best trick she'd ever seen.

Nikki pinched my forearm and hissed, "You're such an awful sneak."

"What are you talking about?" I feigned innocence.

She made a rude noise. Glancing down at the pair becoming fast friends, she didn't say anything else. She didn't need to.

She was going to adopt that cat and both of us knew it.

Letting out a resigned sigh, she joined the girls on the floor in their game of fetch. Even though the day had started out shitty, it was times like this when I loved my job.

Chapter 6

Estelle

WHEN I BOXED up Cindy's things, I did a pretty good job of keeping my emotions in check. I collected her foam balls, her bed, a litter box, and scooped several days' worth of food into a sandwich baggie.

I decided to keep the framed picture. It was mine. And in a few minutes, it was the only piece of Cindy I'd have left.

For some reason, letting go of her monogramed bowl was the hardest part. Emery had to practically pry it from my fingers.

With a sympathetic expression, Nikki offered to let me visit any time. After all, they were less than fifteen minutes away.

"I would like that," I told her honestly. Struggling with the lump in my throat, I bent down to give Cindy one more scratch on the head before shutting the metal door on the carrier.

She looked confused and a little scared. I wanted to tell her it would be okay, that she would be happy at her new home. But I was afraid if I tried to talk, I'd burst into tears, and I didn't want her to see me cry.

And then she was gone.

I went out to the balcony to watch them leave. Curling my fingers around the chicken wire, I gripped it tighter than necessary, hoping the sting would stop me from becoming a weepy basket case on camera.

Nikki carefully placed the carrier in the backseat while Lizzie danced around like she was the happiest little girl in the world. Then she clamored into the car with her new pet. Within a minute, the vehicle was zipping away, along with the cat I'd come to love so much.

Emery softly touched my shoulder. "You okay?"

Nodding, I swallowed hard.

Dammit. I hated crying, especially in front of people.

"I didn't realize it was going to be this difficult." My voice broke. My nose burned and my chin trembled. Clearing my throat, I struggled to get my shit together as I looked up into kind blue eyes. "All the sleepless nights. Setting my alarm every two hours to feed her. It was worth it."

"I'm really proud of you," Emery praised. "For taking care of Cindy and for letting her go."

Oh, geez. Was he *trying* to make me cry?

"She couldn't have gone to a better home, Emery. Thank you so much."

"You're welcome," he said with a smile.

"I don't know what's wrong with me. I should be happy right now." Despite my attempt to blink away the tears, they escaped anyway, spilling down my cheeks. One ran to the corner of my mouth.

"Estelle," Emery whispered, automatically bringing his hand up to my face to brush the wetness away.

His thumb swept over my lips and I held in a gasp.

Suddenly, I forgot about the cameras and crew surrounding us. I forgot about the bittersweet sadness.

For a few seconds, we were the only two people in the world.

In person, Emery Matheson wasn't anything like the man on TV. He was so much more. On the surface he was incredibly sexy, but underneath his good looks and charisma, he was compassionate, patient, and kind— that was more attractive than anything else.

Something was happening between us. Lust slammed through my body, my chest tightening, my heart pounding. Emery was making me feel a kind of connection I'd never had before.

The boys I dated in high school were just that—boys. And my ex… Well, I wasn't kidding when I told Janice he was a bore. Missionary position, all the way. And only in the bed at night with the lights off. He wouldn't even take a shower with me. In fact, I was pretty sure we never saw each other fully naked during our relationship.

Even in broad daylight, he looked right through me. He never *saw me*. The real me.

But Emery did.

And it was impossible to miss the hunger in his eyes as he rubbed his thumb back and forth over my bottom lip, wiping away the remainder of my tears.

"Okay, cut it," Steve said with a clap, and I almost growled at him for interrupting the most sexually charged moment of my life. "Let's pack it in for the day."

Without breaking eye contact, Emery and I both took a step back. And as much as I felt the loss of his warmth, I knew I needed the distance. I needed time away from him to get my head on straight.

And alcohol. Lots of alcohol.

Chapter 7

Estelle

I took three huge gulps of my wine as I watched a rerun of The Pussy Tamer.

"*The house smells like a dumpster,*" the distraught woman cried. "*We're going to have to replace all the carpets. I can't tell you how many puddles I've stepped in. We love Mr. Boots, but it's just not sanitary! Do you know what it's like to slip a foot into your new Louboutins, only to have a cat turd squished between your toes?*" Her voice rose to near shrieking.

"*I can't say that I do,*" Emery responded, running a hand over his mouth.

I suspected he was trying not to laugh.

Draining the rest of my glass, I rubbed my thighs together to quell the ache between my legs. Subjecting myself to Emery on TV wasn't exactly giving myself the distance I needed. But he sure was nice to look at.

It was an episode from the first season, and Emery was helping a cat get over his irrational fear of balls. Not balls as in testicles. Actual balls. You wouldn't think eliminating all round objects in the house would be that hard, but with three young children, the family had been having a lot of trouble.

Mr. Boots expressed his fear by going to the bathroom anywhere and everywhere.

"We just can't live like this anymore. We need your help." She sighed.

"Don't worry, Mrs. Franklin," Emery assured her. Then he turned his eyes straight into the camera, and it almost felt like he was looking right at me when he said the next words. "I'm going to tame your pussy."

Equal parts amused and turned on, I rolled my eyes at the cheesy line.

Ever since the show started, I'd been a fan, making sure I watched every episode. The perfect mix of perverted and heart-warming, it was extremely entertaining. I'd even made a drinking game out of it: Every time someone says pussy, take a shot. Or a sip.

Which reminded me, I was due for a refill.

Dizziness hit me when I stood up too fast, and I stumbled my way to the kitchen. I decided to grab the whole bottle because there wasn't much left anyway.

I got back to the couch in time to see a slow-motion segment where Emery was tying his hair up. Once it was secured at the back of his head, the camera zoomed in on his face and he smirked.

"Here, kitty kitty."

The hot flashes were back.

Before him, I'd never thought the man bun thing was

sexy. But damn.

It was a shame they chopped it off, but I had to admit his new style really worked for him. Also, it gave me a reason to touch him when it got all messed up, and I had no complaints about that.

No wonder cats responded to him the way they did. The man was half-animal himself. During his time on the show, Emery had been hailed a hero. The healer of family feuds. Some had even called him an exorcist.

After seeing what went on behind the scenes, I could say with complete certainty that Emery was the real deal. I had always assumed the show was staged. No one could be *that* good with animals.

But Emery was.

In just two days, he'd worked his magic. Thanks to him, Cindy was snuggled up at her new home. We still had six more cats to go, but I was confident he could help me find a good match for every one of them.

As Emery started making a game plan for the family—something about positive reinforcement with treats and introducing round-shaped cat toys into everyday playtime—I tried to concentrate on what he was saying.

But every time he said *playtime*, I couldn't stop myself from thinking about all the ways I wanted to *play* with him.

Tipping up the wine bottle, I took a swig.

Does he like having his hair pulled?

Another swig.

Why does he have to be so good-looking and nice?

I chugged the rest and set the empty container on the coffee table with a thud.

And why do I have to be so pathetic and horny?

I was a woman in my prime, yet here I was, getting drunk by myself, fantasizing about a man on TV while trying to remember when the last time I'd had an orgasm was.

It'd been a long fucking time.

Hitting pause on the show, I made my way down the hall to my room. I shut the door behind me; I didn't want any of the cats to witness what I was about to do.

I was severely overdue for a session with my battery-operated-boyfriend, and a few minutes was all I needed.

Sitting on the side of my bed, I opened the second drawer down on my nightstand and took out my vibrator. The pink cock was equivalent to the average penis size, complete with a clit stimulator and three rotational speed settings. Oh yeah, and it glowed in the dark.

We'd been through some hard times together—pun intended. It was everything men weren't: reliable, always erect, and got the job done every time.

Turning off the lamp, I got comfortable under the covers, held up the glowing rod, and hit the on switch.

And... nothing. No buzzing. No vibrating. No glorious rotating.

"Oh, come on. Don't fail me now," I groaned, slapping it a few times. Still nothing. Apparently, it'd been so long since I used it the batteries had gone bad.

Sitting back up, I shuffled through my drawer and found an unopened pack of batteries I kept on hand for this very reason. Because of my uncoordinated fumbling, I ripped the package harder than I'd meant to, and batteries scattered to the floor, rolling in all directions.

"Son of a bitch," I muttered.

I nearly fell off the bed when I reached down to snatch them up. After grabbing the closest three, I decided not to bother with the rest. It took some serious concentration, but eventually I got the new ones in.

I lay back to try again and… still nothing.

Disgruntled and sexually frustrated, I glared at the useless rubber wand. Maybe it wasn't the batteries. Maybe my vibrator's lifespan had come to an end.

So much for being reliable.

I tossed the traitorous device at the open drawer, but I missed by a long shot. Like, I didn't even hit the nightstand. The vibrator bounced off the closet door with a loud clatter and rolled underneath the bed.

Shit. I didn't even have the energy to retrieve it. I fell back onto the pillows and let out a huff.

What was I supposed to do now? I couldn't use my own hands—that had never worked for me. It was like trying to tickle yourself. Not possible.

I was more turned on than I'd ever been in my life and the one thing I could count on had let me down. I wanted to weep at the injustice of it all.

The ache between my legs made me feel irrational and desperate.

Throb. Throb. Throb.

Emery was such a gentleman. So fucking wholesome. Level-headed. And it wasn't an act—that was just him.

Ache. Ache. Ache.

Desperation coursed through me. I wanted to get under his skin, to make him lose his cool.

Want. Want. Want.

What the hell was in that wine?

I spied a rectangular piece of paper on my dresser.

Ambling over to it with unsteady footsteps, I picked up the business card, remembering the way Emery had emphasized the fact that he was putting his personal number on the back.

I'd never had a fuck-buddy before, but I could make an exception.

Just this once.

Okay, maybe not just once. Maybe, like, ten times. A dozen, tops. That would definitely be enough to get Emery out of my system.

I went back out to the couch and as I plopped down onto the cushion, I looked around my feline-filled living room.

The wine bottle had been knocked to the floor. Carol swatted at it, causing it to spin in a circle. She got spooked when it clanked against the leg of the coffee table, and she ran into the kitchen.

One set of boots sat next to my door. One jacket hung from the hook on the wall. My singular plastic glass mocked me.

I could blame my reclusive ways on the cats all I wanted, but honestly, my social life had been nonexistent long before I adopted Alice.

What happened to me? I used to be fun.

Picking up my cell phone in one hand and holding the business card in the other, I made an impulsive, alcohol-induced decision. My uncoordinated fingers tapped over the number keys.

The other end of the line rang twice, then a deep voice came through the phone. "Hello?"

Suddenly, I couldn't find the words. There were no words. *What happened to my words?*

I heard Emery clear his throat. "Heavy breathing is pretty much the most unoriginal prank call ever," he deadpanned. "Just saying, you might want to up your game next time."

"Wh-what?" I stammered.

"Estelle?" he asked, immediately sounding concerned.

"Um, yeah." I said, taken aback. "How did you know it was me?"

"I, ah, I recognized your voice when you spoke just now. That's not creepy, is it?"

I huffed out a laugh. "Surprising, but not creepy."

"What's wrong?"

My smile faded, his question reminding me of why I'd called in the first place. Using the code words on the back of the business card, I cringed at what I was about to say next.

"I have a pussy emergency."

Chapter 8

Estelle

Because I was an overeager, sex-crazed, half-drunk maniac, I didn't even give Emery time to say hello before I grabbed him by the neck of his T-shirt and dragged him into my apartment.

As soon as the door slammed shut, I pushed him up against it. Rising on my tiptoes, I pressed my lips to his.

Fireworks exploded in my belly. To hell with butterflies—this was some good shit. His lips were so soft, a sharp contrast to the two-day scruff scraping against my chin. My tongue swept out, tasting him.

Mmm. Beer and a hint of something minty.

It took me about three seconds to realize Emery wasn't reciprocating. At all.

Opening my eyes, the first thing I noticed was his shocked, wide-eyed expression.

I immediately stepped back. His hands were splayed

against the door behind him—hands that should've been on my waist, my ass, my *anything*.

Confusion and rejection rang loudly in my mind, extinguishing those sparks until it felt like my stomach was filled with heavy, wet sludge.

"Emery, I—" The explanation died in my throat, my head swimming from all the wine.

What could I possibly say? My vibrator broke and I need your dick?

Not exactly the best pickup line in the book.

And I wasn't too drunk to realize he just wasn't into me. Clearly, I'd read him wrong. The flirtation, the eye contact, the sexual tension. All the signs were there. How could I have been so off?

"Estelle?" He swallowed hard, still flat against the door, looking at me like I was a wild animal that had escaped from the zoo. "What's going on?"

"The—the secret code," I stuttered. "I said the pussy emergency thing."

His eyebrows knitted together and he stepped toward me. "Yeah. Are the cats okay?"

"So that's… not a booty call thing?" My voice got smaller as my embarrassment grew to epic proportions.

Laughing, he ran a hand over his jaw.

"No. I get a lot of prank calls if my number gets out. I have people say some kind of catch phrase so I know they're calling me for a reason. I switch it up now and then, just in case people figure it out. Pussy emergency is the latest one…" he trailed off awkwardly, hiking a shoulder.

I could've died from mortification right then and there.

He was trying to avoid sexual harassment, and I'd assumed he just wanted to get into my pants.

That damn blushing thing was happening again. I covered my burning face with both hands. I couldn't look at him.

"I am so sorry." The apology came out muffled. "You can go now. Please just forget this whole thing happened."

"I'm not in the habit of mixing business with pleasure. I don't get involved with coworkers or clients," he kindly explained.

Most polite rejection ever.

Without removing my hands, I nodded. "Got it."

"And I'm not into casual sex," he added.

"Very admirable of you."

Could this moment get any worse?

I felt ridiculous. The dress I'd bought at Target the night before wasn't super short, but I was suddenly very aware of the fact that I wasn't wearing pants.

Thinking I was getting lucky tonight, I'd thrown it on and fluffed my hair. I had even touched up my makeup and quickly swiped a coat of red fast-drying nail polish on my toes.

The vinyl kitchen floor was cold beneath my bare feet. I wished a hole would just open up and swallow me so I could escape the unbelievable awkwardness that was my life.

Several moments of silence ticked by, and the only sounds in the apartment were our breathing and one of the cats using a scratching post in the other room.

"But I'm not saying no," Emery added quietly. So quiet, I almost didn't hear it.

I peeked through my fingers. "You're not?"

100

Warm hands wrapped around my wrists and gently pulled down. Braving a glance at his face, I looked up.

He licked his perfect-as-fuck lips. "I want you."

"I thought you said you don't get involved with clients."

"I don't. Usually, I have a lot of self-control." Prowling toward me, his hands landed on my hips. He backed me up until my ass hit the edge of the table. His face was just inches from mine. "You've taken away my ability to give a fuck, Estelle. Right now I don't care about what's right or wrong." He sounded pissed and sexy as hell.

"I'm sorry?" I squeaked, and my apology ended up sounding like a question. I wasn't really sorry. In fact, I was pretty damn proud of myself.

Up until now, Emery had seemed surprisingly shy, sometimes awkward, and even a little submissive. It was incredibly endearing.

But that wasn't the man in front of me now. This man was hungry. Predatory.

It was exactly what I wanted.

I wanted both sides of him. The gentleman and the animal. Honorable and depraved.

His eyes zeroed in on my face, focusing on my mouth. He brought his hand up and brushed his thumb over it, just like he'd done earlier when he wiped away my tears. Only this time he pulled down, opening my lips.

Without hesitation, he moved in on me. His mouth descended over mine, hot and wet, his smooth tongue pushing past my teeth. A surprised moan resounded in the back of my throat because I hadn't expected him to be so vigorous.

First kisses tended to be tentative—I'd had plenty of

them. First kisses were meant to test the waters. They were supposed to be brief and gentle.

Nothing about Emery's kiss was quick or apprehensive.

I'd waited my entire life for a kiss like this—I just didn't realize I'd been waiting for it. Until now. Adrenaline surged through my body, kicking my heartrate into overdrive.

Technically, it was our second kiss, but the first one didn't count because I'd obviously shocked the hell out of him.

Picking me up, Emery set my butt on the edge of the table before moving between my legs.

The hand that had been gently cradling the back of my neck came up and fisted the strands at my scalp, tilting my head back while he continued the assault on my mouth. Sucking at my bottom lip, he bit down.

I was panting. I couldn't seem to get enough air. Clutching Emery's shirt, I tried to pull him closer, even though it wasn't possible.

"I think we have an audience." His voice pulled me out of the lusty haze.

"What?" My heart was pounding so hard, I could barely hear anything over the rushing of blood in my ears. "Oh, shit. The cameras."

I started scooting away from him on the table, but he chuckled before grabbing my ankle and dragging me back. "No cameras. These are turned off at the end of the day. The only one that's on right now is in the cat room. I was talking about them."

He nodded his head toward the living room, and I followed his line of sight. Eight pairs of curious eyes were focused on us.

"I think they're judging us," he said, amused.

"They definitely are."

"Bedroom?"

I nodded.

A surprised noise left me when he picked me up, hands on my ass, and started carrying me down the hall.

Laughing, I looped my arms around his neck and linked my ankles behind his back. "I can walk, you know."

Shaking his head, he grinned before grappling with the doorknob. "More fun this way."

As soon as we got into my room, he pinned me up against the door. The sound of it slamming shut echoed through the apartment. Then there was silence and darkness. I moved forward to kiss him again, but he pulled back.

"I feel like I need to tell you that I'm not in a good place to be starting a relationship," he stated.

"I appreciate the disclaimer, but it's not needed. And that's perfect because I'm not looking for one."

"What are you looking for?"

I nipped at his lips. "What does it look like?"

"I'm gonna need you to be more specific."

Palming the front of his jeans, I rubbed at the thick length beneath. "How's this?"

"That's pretty specific." He let out a sexy grunt before asking, "We going all the way?"

I appreciated his straightforwardness. "Fuck yeah, we are."

Sliding his fingers up my thigh, his hand slipped under the dress. His thumb grazed the sensitive skin on my hip before he grabbed the waist of my panties and pulled. Hard.

Aaaand wedgie city.

"Ow!" I yelped.

"Sorry! Shit, are you okay?"

"Yeah," I said, rubbing my ass. "What are you doing?"

Seeming caught between concerned and embarrassed, he said, "I was trying to do a thing."

"What kind of thing? Seduction by wedgie?" I squirmed as I tried to dislodge the fabric from between my ass cheeks.

He laughed and leaned his forehead against mine. "A sexy thing. I thought they'd just rip off. And I was impatient." Giving them another light tug, he growled. "It's—wow, they're really on there. These things are pretty durable, huh?"

Giggles bubbled up as I attempted to respond.

"One hundred percent cotton and elastic... So, yeah." Laughing so hard I couldn't breathe, I dug my fingers into his muscular shoulders. "I think... I—have a... rug burn on my butt."

"Oh, God. I'm sorry." He started to put me down.

"Wait." I tightened my legs around his waist and pressed my back against the wall for leverage. The humor died away as I blinked, my eyes adjusting to the lack of light in the room. I ran my fingertip over the indent in Emery's bottom lip. "We don't have to stop. Here—like this." Taking his hand, I brought it to my center. Both of our fingertips grazed the inside of my thigh as I helped him move my soaked panties to the side. "There."

He sucked in a breath as he slid through my wetness. "You shave?"

"Wax, actually. Hurts like a bitch, but gets the job

done."

"I like it," he breathed out, dipping two fingers into me before circling my clit.

Gasping, the back of my head fell back with a dull thud.

Light from the hallway glowed under the door, casting shadows over the awe-filled expression on Emery's face.

With heavy-lidded eyes, he moved his fingers in and out of me. Slid over my smooth, slick skin. Took his time exploring me, relying on his sense of touch to memorize my anatomy in the dark.

When his thumb brushed over my clit again, I lost my patience, bucking against him while making an unattractive grunting sound.

I needed more.

He laughed, pushing away from the door. Fucking tease. Connecting his mouth to mine for a much-too-quick kiss, he carried me over to the bed, set my butt on the edge, and dropped to his knees on the floor.

Emery Matheson was on his knees.

On his knees *for me*.

"Take off your dress," he commanded huskily, his fingertips lightly grazing my knees.

My fingers went to the buttons at the back of my neck, but I was trembling so badly I couldn't get them undone. Frustrated, I let out a huff.

"Fuck it—leave it on. These, though…" Sliding his hands under the skirt, he grabbed my panties and started tugging them down. "These need to come off."

"I don't normally wear panties," I admitted.

He stopped, the red lacey material at my knees. "Ever?"

"No." I shook my head. "I'm not a fan of fanny floss."

"You mean to tell me you've been going commando for the past two days?"

Nodding, I kicked my legs a little, trying to get the damn underwear off already.

"During the interviews?" he asked gruffly.

"No panties."

"At Target?"

"Nope," I confirmed. The thong slid down my calves and got caught around my ankles.

"Then why did you wear them tonight?"

"I was trying to do a thing," I teased, repeating the words he'd said just minutes before. "A sexy thing."

He chuckled.

"Well, I think we can both agree that these aren't needed from now on." Finally removing the panties, he tossed them over his shoulder. He pushed my knees apart. "I want to taste you."

"Can you do me a favor first?"

His eyes bounced up to mine. "Be careful what you ask for. I'd say yes to pretty much anything you want right now."

I laughed. "Turn on the lights."

His eyebrows shot up. "Really?"

"Yeah." I pointed to the wall. "That switch right there. I know that's an odd request," I said as he got up. Bright light flooded the room and in one smooth move, he whipped his shirt off. My eyes roamed his chiseled torso, memorizing every indent of his abs, the sharp lines of his pecs, the V leading down into his jeans. "I just want to see everything. And I want you to see me."

"I see you." Smirking, his gaze raked over my body

before his eyes landed on mine.

That face… That was what I really wanted to see. The muscles were great, but it was his expression that got me.

I knew what I must've looked like—a horny, tipsy mess. My hair mussed up, my dress bunched around my waist. My lipstick was probably smeared.

But he looked at me like I was precious and beautiful. Perfect and important.

And my room was a disaster. While I kept the rest of my apartment clean and clutter-free, my bedroom was my safe space of unorganized madness. The closet door was halfway open, showing the tightly packed dresses and clubbing tops I never wore. Clothes were overflowing the hamper in the corner, and half of the contents of my makeup bag were scattered on the dresser. My yellow comforter was crooked, only covering half of the bed.

But Emery didn't seem fazed by any of it. His eyes were focused only on me.

As he closed the distance between us, he nimbly undid his belt and the button on his jeans, but he didn't pull his pants down. Instead, he let them hang open, giving me a view of his black boxer briefs and the bulge underneath.

My core clenched.

I started scooting back because I expected him to get on the bed with me, but he grabbed my ankle and dragged me back to the edge of the mattress like I weighed nothing. Any trace of the gentleman I'd gotten to know was gone. Then he knelt on the floor again.

"Lie back," he ordered.

"Um…" Propping myself up on my elbows, I went for complete honesty. "Since we're doing disclaimers tonight, I feel the need to tell you that I can't get off this way. Going down on me is *nice* of you, but maybe we should just skip it."

Raising his eyebrows at me, the lower half of his face disappeared between my legs. "We'll see about that."

"Okay." Lying back down, I shrugged. "Just don't be disappointed when nothing happens."

The heat of his breath on my center sent a pleasant jolt through my body.

It wasn't that I didn't enjoy oral sex. Just like I'd told him, it was *nice*. Like sinking down into a hot bubble bath is nice. Like being given extra meat on your Subway sandwich without paying for it is nice. Like reading the last page of a book is—

All my thoughts fled when he pushed two fingers inside me, curling them up in a 'come here' motion, while also sucking on my clit. No build up—he went from zero to sixty in less than a second.

Totally intense, just like his kiss.

I moaned. "That feels—that's good. Ohmigod."

My thighs tightened around his head, but he nudged me back open by bringing his other arm between them.

His fingers continued to move inside of me, while his other hand rubbed my lower belly in a circular motion before pressing down. The pressure from the outside and the inside at the same time stimulated some place deep inside me in a way that had never been done before.

"Oh, shit. Fuck, fuck." I let out a guttural groan, my eyes rolling back at the extreme combination of sensations. "What—*whatareyoudoing*?" The words all ran together.

Emery lifted his head, a knowing smirk on his face.

"Getting you off."

Then his mouth was on me again and his hands went back to work. Those long, thick fingers curled up again while he rubbed my belly, just above my pubic bone.

My G-spot. That was what he was getting at. And it was beyond intense. It obliterated every sexual experience I'd ever had, and that included time with myself. Suddenly, I was very happy that my vibrator kicked the bucket.

My heels dug into the mattress. I fisted the sheets. Panted heavily. Moaned loudly.

I had completely lost control of my body. All my awareness was centered on the quickly building orgasm. My vision blurred, spots exploding in front of my eyes.

What kind of extraordinary talent did this man possess? It was like a three-ring circus down there. What he was doing required coordination and the ability to multitask. No one had ever touched me with this much enthusiasm. Emery wasn't half-assing it. He was giving it everything he had.

He'd successfully gone from awkward and clumsy one minute, to a magical vagina wizard the next. I liked his contrasting sides. Liked that he was multi-dimensional and so damn real.

Threading my fingers through Emery's hair, I gripped a handful and pulled.

He growled against my clit before sucking it back into his mouth.

The hand on my stomach pushed down harder, increasing the pressure on my G-spot. Wetness gushed onto his hand and face, but I was too lost in the sensations to be embarrassed.

"When's the last time someone made you feel like this?" He lifted his head long enough to ask.

"Never," I choked out.

"Good."

His tongue flicked my clit, and a violent tremble worked through me, my pussy clenching around his fingers.

My stomach muscles tightened and fluttered. My thighs shook. My toes curled.

Achieving an orgasm had always been so much work for me. It took a huge amount of effort to get there.

But like a runaway train, I couldn't have stopped it if I tried.

My entire body quaked as I came, my inner muscles spasming so hard my shoulders lifted off the mattress and a scream ripped from my throat.

Emery didn't speed up or slow down. He just let me ride it out, waves of ecstasy rippling through me. A long moan tapered off into a series of whimpers as I tried to catch my breath.

Then his fingers slowly slipped from my sensitive core.

Stuck in some euphoric state, I was slightly aware of strong arms scooping up my body, moving me until my head rested on the soft pillows.

I felt the bed dip and I cracked an eye open to find Emery sitting on the side of the bed, watching me while licking his fingers.

Licking his fucking fingers.

"How do you know how to do that? Maybe you watched a shit-ton of online tutorials? Lots of practice probably," I mused. "And I don't know why I said that.

Your sexual history is none of my business. Actually, I take that back. It's kind of my business since we're about to fuck, but I still don't want to know the answer. Besides, if you feed me some cheesy line about being the pussy tamer, I might be tempted not to sleep with you. And I can't let you ruin this for me."

Climbing up my body, he chuckled at my rambling. "Truth is, I haven't so much as kissed someone in over a year."

It was difficult to hide my shock, but I tried. "Well, that makes two of us then."

His face softened. "I meant it when I said I don't do casual sex."

"Then what are we doing?"

"I don't know. I just want you so bad I can't think straight."

"Good enough," I responded with a nod. Gripping the back of his neck, I pulled him down for a kiss. I tasted myself on his tongue and it made me hot all over again.

Grabbing his wallet from his back pocket, Emery pulled a condom out before tossing the leather to the floor. Taking the package between his teeth, he ripped it open.

I pushed his boxers down far enough for his thick cock to bob out.

When my hand wrapped around his hard length, the throbbing in my center came back with a vengeance.

I thought I would've been satisfied after the orgasm of the century, but I felt like I could come again just from the sight of his gorgeous dick.

Long, straight, and thick. I stroked him from base to

tip, loving the feel of his velvety skin.

"Oh, fuck," he rasped, watching me jack him off.

His cock twitched when I flicked my thumb over the bead of precum at his tip.

He reached between us and rolled the condom on in one graceful movement. The underside of his erection tapped my clit and a new surge of heat flooded my center.

This was it. I was going to have sex with Emery.

"Ready?" he breathed out, and I wasn't sure if he was asking me or himself.

Rocking my hips, I nodded. "Now."

Any hesitation Emery had vanished as he drove into me with a powerful thrust. I cried out at the sudden stretch. I was already sore from his fingers, and the pain heightened the pleasure.

He groaned against my neck, loud and long, but he didn't stop the rolling rhythm of his hips. That was the only way I could describe how he moved—he wasn't just grinding against me, he was *rolling*.

I could feel the wave undulating through his stomach, traveling down to his pelvis, ending with a smooth rocking motion, his cock plunging deep.

A high-pitched gasp left my mouth every time he pushed all the way in, my body struggling to adjust to his size.

Missionary position had never felt like this before.

Nothing had ever felt like this before.

With every pump of Emery's hips, his belt clanked and jingled. There was something erotic about the fact that we both still had some of our clothes on. He palmed my breast over my dress, finding my nipple and plucking it with his fingers.

"Fuuuck, Emery." I grabbed the headboard, wrapping my hands around the thick iron bars. Needing something to hold on to. "Your dick is huge." It sounded like a complaint, even though I was pretty happy about it.

Emery let out a half-laugh, half-grunt. "Estelle, I'm not gonna last long, especially if you keep talking like that."

"Ohhh, your massive rod of steel feels so good." Now I was just fucking with him, and he knew it. "Fuck me with your big, hard—"

Reaching between us, he pinched my sensitive clit and I squeaked.

"I'm serious, Estelle. I don't want it to be over yet." His thrusting slowed and I grinned up at him.

"Good thing we've got all night."

Chapter 9

Emery

I WASN'T GOING to last. As much as I tried to fight it, I knew the orgasm building in my balls was coming, whether I liked it or not.

And Estelle wasn't helping the situation.

She wanted to push me over the edge. Wanted to make me lose control. It made me want to fuck her harder, but if I sped up I'd definitely be done for.

Peppering kisses along my jaw, she latched onto my neck and sucked at my pulse point. Chills and heat simultaneously raced through my veins.

She rocked her hips in time with mine, and her pussy squeezed my dick every time I retreated from her body, like it was trying to suck me back in.

It felt so fucking good.

I tried to think about un-sexy things: cleaning litter boxes, Steve's recent freak out over a virtual fortune cookie, the latest men's fashion craze known as the romper.

It was no use. Estelle bit down on my earlobe, bringing me back to the moment.

Against my own will, my hips bucked faster. Estelle spread her thighs wider, welcoming me into her body, even though I could tell it was hurting her.

I knew my dick was above average in size, but hearing her say it turned me on. One of the things I liked most about Estelle was her blunt way of speaking.

But right now I needed her to stop talking about my 'massive rod of steel' so I could last long enough to make her come again.

I kissed her, pouring all of my unexpected feelings into the hard press of my lips. Without slowing my pace, I circled her clit with my thumb.

"Mmm," she moaned into my mouth. "Touch me there. So close."

"That's it. Come on my cock," I panted as her inner muscles began pulsing around me.

"Don't stop," she begged. "Please, please. Oh my God. I'm gonna—"

Throwing her head back, she didn't finish the sentence. Feeling her pussy squeeze my dick, watching her face contort with ecstasy, hearing her call out a string of profanities—it was the best moment of my life.

There.

There was that unadulterated happiness I'd almost forgotten about. Making Estelle come was my new favorite hobby.

And now it was my turn.

Spreading her legs wide, I drove hard, rooting myself

as deep inside her. I didn't think it was possible to come harder than I did the night before in the RV. But I was wrong. So very wrong.

Tingling started in my spine, my balls drew up tight, my abs clenched. I felt something powerful building as I quickened my pace. Shudders wracked my body, and I tightly gripped Estelle's thigh, anchoring her to the bed. Or maybe I was the one who needed the anchor, because it felt like my entire body was going to implode.

Pieces of me were going to shatter, splinter, and break. And I wasn't sure if I was ever going to be the same.

Raking her nails down my shoulder blades, Estelle cried out as my cock swelled inside her. I could tell she was going to leave marks.

I liked it.

The sharp sting pushed me over the edge and I buried my face in her neck, groaning as my dick pulsed, filling the condom with cum.

I thrusted deep two more times, breathing in the scent of her sweat combined with jasmine and honey.

For a second, I feared I would always associate this feeling with that smell. That, for the rest of my life, I'd never be able to come again without thinking about Estelle.

"Goddamn," I gasped as the orgasm ebbed away, but I didn't pull out yet. I wanted to stay inside her for as long as she'd let me.

She breathed out a satisfied moan and I lifted my head to find a small smile on her face. Eyes closed, features relaxed.

I kissed her slowly—first her top lip, then her bottom lip, then her whole pouty mouth. The flesh was puffy and pink from our aggressive kisses and the scruff on my jaw.

"Goddamn, Estelle," I said again, my lips brushing against hers with every syllable. Resting my forehead on hers, I tried to control my ragged breathing. "I think you might've just ruined me."

She laughed lightly, but I wasn't joking.

Our physical connection was intense, but it was the emotional thread between us that scared me the most. I'd only known Estelle for a couple days, but I already felt like I *knew* her. She was so open. When I looked into her eyes, she didn't hide anything. Didn't hold anything back.

She let me see her—all of her. I was such a lucky motherfucker.

Having the lights on was an uncommon request for a woman. Bold, just like Estelle. I wanted to take advantage of the opportunity while I had the chance.

After leaning over the bed to dispose of the condom in a nearby trashcan, I rolled Estelle onto her side. "Let's get this dress off."

I unhooked the clasp at the nape of her neck, before undoing three little black buttons. Sliding the fabric down her left arm, I kissed her shoulder—the one without the tattoo. I wanted to turn her all the way over so I could study the art on her back, but the material fell open in the front, revealing her perfect breast.

Estelle shrugged her arm out of the dress, and a breath whooshed out of me at the sight of her creamy skin. Her nipple was hard and rosy. My mouth watered at the thought of sucking on it.

Starting at her hipbone, I trailed a finger up her side, bumping over her ribs, then tracing the underside of her tit.

Goosebumps pebbled her skin, the bright light from the ceiling fan above spotlighting everything from the hitch of her breath to the four freckles on her collarbone.

I didn't stop there. I continued my path down her spine until I reached the curve of her ass. She shivered, and I pulled the covers up around us.

Turning her head, Estelle speared me with those big eyes. "I don't want tonight to be over yet. I don't want to stop."

"Neither do I," I responded before nipping at her neck. "But I'm gonna have to go to the RV to get another condom."

"Get two," she demanded, making me chuckle.

"Okay, I'll get two."

But before I left, I needed to do something. I pushed Estelle onto her back and sucked one of her stiff peaks into my mouth. My tongue circled her nipple. She moaned, arching up, offering more of herself.

"Emery," she panted. "Hurry."

Scrambling to get her other arm out of the dress, she sat up and gave me an irresistible view of both tits as she wriggled it down over her hips.

The thought of seeing her completely naked was all the motivation I needed.

After delivering a swift kiss to her lips, I said, "I'll be right back. Less than three minutes, I promise."

"Make it two," she demanded again.

"Greedy." I grinned. "Two minutes. You can even time me."

I almost tripped up the stairs of the RV once I got through the door, but I went full speed ahead. I hadn't even bothered to put a shirt on and my belt still hung undone around my waist.

Not wasting any time, I went straight to the bathroom and began frantically searching the cabinet for the condoms. Rhonda was in charge of stocking everything from Advil to toilet paper. Surely safe sex was taken into consideration when making the list of necessities.

But I didn't find any.

The bedroom was next. I dove onto the mattress and yanked the bedside drawer open. Staring back at me was an unopened box of Magnums. Thank God for Rhonda. I hadn't asked for condoms in a long time, but she remembered the kind I preferred.

After tearing into the box, I ripped two off the long chain. Fiddling with the little square packages, I contemplated the possibilities.

I had no idea if tonight was a one-time thing. Maybe this was the last chance I'd ever get to be with Estelle. If that was the case, two more condoms wouldn't be enough.

Feeling overly optimistic, I dropped the two back into the drawer, then grabbed the whole box instead.

I was ready for a long night.

Chapter 10

Emery

ESTELLE WAS FUCKING wild.

Everything about her was unexpected, but her sexual appetite was the biggest shock of all. It was a good thing I'd decided to bring the entire box of condoms; we used five of them last night.

Sex with Estelle wasn't just sex. It was a life-changing experience.

She used every single part of her body when we were together—teeth, nails, tongue. Squeezed my hips with her thighs, rubbed my calves with her feet, raked her fingers through my hair.

I learned that her toes curled right before she was about to come.

She was all-consuming.

Even now, as I staggered out of her apartment in a daze before sunrise, I could smell her. Feel her lips on my skin.

And the sounds she made—they still ricocheted in my mind. I loved that she wasn't shy about asking for what she wanted, where she wanted it, how hard she wanted it. There was no guessing when it came to Estelle.

Fuck me harder, Emery. Please, please. Right there. Right fucking there.

It wasn't until I got to the RV that I realized my shoes were on the wrong feet and my shirt was inside out.

I caught my reflection in the bathroom mirror and laughed.

I'd done the walk of shame before, but shit. I'd never looked so disheveled in all my life. Muscles I didn't even know I had were stiff and sore from overuse.

Last night had presented an interesting turn of events. When Estelle called me, I thought something was seriously wrong. Then she basically attacked me. To say I was surprised didn't even scratch the surface of how I felt.

And as soon as her lips touched mine, I'd forgotten all the reasons why I didn't do casual hookups.

Why did I ever think one night with Estelle would be enough?

Now that I'd had her, I craved her. I'd just left her place and I already wanted to go back. The short distance between the RV and her apartment suddenly seemed much too far.

Today's schedule was set aside for networking, so I wouldn't even have a reason to see her until tomorrow.

What would happen next time we saw each other? Would she pretend like last night never happened? Would she want me again or would she move on?

Shaking off the unpleasant hollowness in my chest, I began stripping off my clothes.

I'd just stepped out of the shower when my phone buzzed.

Nikki: Are we still on for breakfast?

Shit. I'd totally forgotten about our plans. Scrubbing my hair with a towel, I typed out a short reply before quickly getting dressed in a long-sleeved Henley and jeans.

Me: Yep. Be there soon.

Ten minutes later, I was hopping into the rented minivan for the crew and driving the short distance to the 1950s style diner where Nikki and I usually met up. It was surprisingly busy, but I spotted the back of her blond head in a booth by the window.

Walking across the black and white checkered floor, I slid into the seat and picked up a menu.

"Sorry I'm late," I said, swiping my still-wet strands away from my forehead.

"Uh-huh." Smiling at me over her coffee mug, she asked, "Have a rough night?" Then she grimaced. "I probably don't want to know the answer to that."

"Ah, kinda." I gave her a questioning look, because how did she know these things?

She gestured toward my neck. "You might want to cover that hickey with some concealer before filming. Might not be a bad idea for the dark circles under your eyes too."

122

Well, shit. I just shrugged, sheepish.

"So how's Estelle?" she went on. "You might as well spill it."

"What are you talking about?" I played aloof.

"You think you can fool me?" She waggled her finger through the air. "Even a stranger would be able to see the way you look at her. I've known you your whole life. I wiped your butt when you were a baby."

I made a face. "Why do you always have to remind me of that?"

"I was a six-year-old changing diapers. I did you a huge favor. The least you can allow me is some good-natured ribbing."

Shaking my head, I huffed out a laugh. The waitress came over and I put in an order for the biggest coffee they had and the pancake breakfast platter. An Elvis song played through the overhead speakers.

"How did Cindy do on her first night?" I asked, veering away from the topic of Estelle.

Nikki's blue eyes went soft. "The first couple hours she hid under the bed, but after she got comfortable, she spent the night curled up with Lizzie. They've been inseparable."

"That's what I was hoping for."

"You were right. I think they need each other."

Cupping my ear, I leaned closer. "I'm sorry, what was that?"

"I said you were right." She laughed. Then her face got serious as she played with the corner of her napkin. "I take it you probably haven't had time to visit Dad yet?"

I shook my head. "No, but I'm going later today.

How's he doing?"

She shrugged. "The same. Good days and bad days. On Saturday, he knew who I was," she said, smiling. "It was really nice."

I smiled back because I knew how great that felt. "And they're treating him well?"

The question wasn't necessary, because I already knew the answer; the place was the lap of luxury. Windsor Lakes Retirement Home was the best assisted living facility in the area.

But that wasn't where Dad started out. Before becoming a resident there, he'd spent one month at a state funded nursing home where he shared a room with two other patients, the food was shit, and they were constantly short-staffed.

He might not have known what was going on all the time, but I could tell he was miserable. I couldn't leave him there.

"They always treat him well." Nikki frowned as she peered at me over the rim of her coffee cup. "You were right about Windsor Lakes too. I'll never be able to repay you for what you've done for him."

I frowned back. "You don't have to repay me. We're both his kids. We're in this together."

"When Mom died, and with Dad's medical condition, you were practically an orphan—"

"I was eighteen," I cut in. "Legally an adult."

"Bullshit, Emery. You were still in high school. When I was eighteen, I thought I knew everything there was to know about the world, but I was wrong. Hell, I'm thirty and I still don't know shit."

I sighed. Not this again. Same argument, different

day. "We can't go back and change anything now, and I don't want to."

"I know, but you gave up everything to take care of him."

"And it all worked out, didn't it?"

Glancing down at her lap, her voice came out quiet. "But at what cost, Emery?"

"He's my dad, Nik. I couldn't let him rot in that nursing home."

"If I could've done more to help—"

"You would've done it in a heartbeat. I know that," I told her. "But there wasn't much you could do. Not on a teacher's salary and with a family to support."

"It shouldn't have fallen on you," she whispered, her guilt transparent. "It's just so unfair."

I couldn't argue with that. Nothing about Alzheimer's was fair, but we were more fortunate than some. At least I was able to give my dad the best life possible, even if it meant sacrificing my dreams.

"Sometimes plans change, and things are pretty good for me now," I said, because I had money and a job I enjoyed.

And maybe—just maybe—I had a fun, crazy, beautiful woman, even if it was temporary.

Chapter 11

Emery

I SPENT THE rest of the day networking and trying not to think about Estelle's pussy. And no, I didn't mean her cats.

I contacted a few local shelters and vet clinics to let them know about our project and the urgent need to find homes for the cats. Most of them were more than willing to help.

When I called Remington Animal Medical Center, Christine answered the phone. We chatted for a good twenty minutes, catching up and talking about old times.

Then she told me something that could be a game changer for Estelle; more specifically, for Peter.

Apparently Twinkle Star Snowy Nose Tickle Toes (AKA Arnold) had been hit by a car six months prior and his injuries were too severe for him to pull through. Marty Miller was devastated.

But…

He was open to adopting another cat.

And who loved asshole cats? Marty Miller.

It was late afternoon by the time I made it to Windsor Lakes. The winding driveway was meticulously landscaped on both sides, and a big fountain sat out front by the parking lot. Behind the brick building there were gardens, a courtyard, and two large ponds.

There were reasons why it was so expensive.

It was nicer than any place I'd ever lived, and that included my fancy-ass condo. Whoever designed it had purposely made it feel more like an all-inclusive resort instead of a medical facility.

Complete with a barber shop, a library, and an eating area that was more like a nice restaurant than a cafeteria, most of the residents didn't even have to leave. The lounge was cozy, with leather couches, a flat screen TV, and a billiards table. There was even an onsite gym with physical therapists who created individualized workout plans for the residents.

All the staff members were medically trained, and because they were paid so well, the turnover rate was extremely low.

But the best part? Every patient had their own living quarters, with their own bedroom and bathroom. There was something to be said about having your own space with your own personal belongings—it made people feel normal and in control.

Automatic sliding glass doors welcomed me into the entryway. The floors were paved with dark laminate flooring, the walls a soft beige. Framed prints of famous art lined the hall.

The receptionist flagged me down as I walked past the front desk. "Hey, Emery. Long time, no see. I'm glad you stopped in. I think one of the nurses would like to talk to you."

I nodded. "Who's on duty today?"

"Gretchen," she replied before getting up to find her.

A minute later, Gretchen came around the corner in her usual uniform of jeans and a cartoon-covered lab coat. It was unconventional, but most of the staff wore casual outfits to make the patients feel more at ease. Her salt and pepper hair was tied in a neat bun, and she smiled when she saw me.

Gretchen was the best nurse at Windsor Lakes. She'd been here long before my dad became a patient. She was the one to show me around the first day I checked out the place, and ultimately, the one who convinced me it was the right fit for my dad.

"It's been a while," she said. "How are you?"

"Busy, but good," I replied. I didn't waste any time getting to the issue. "What did you want to talk to me about? Is my dad doing okay?"

"Oh, he's fine." She lifted a bowl in her hands. "I couldn't get him to eat his tapioca this afternoon. Thought maybe you could give it a try. He always does so much better for you and Nikki. It has his medication in there because he was having trouble swallowing the pill."

Taking it from her hands, I nodded. "I'd be happy to try."

"You're such a good boy," she praised as if I was still that scared kid she'd met six years ago. "You'll find him watching the ball game."

"Wait." I stopped her before she could walk away.

"Nikki said Dad's on some new meds. What's that for?"

"Arthritis pain, mostly in his hands," she replied before giving my shoulder a gentle squeeze. "He's doing okay, Emery. Try not to worry so much. Oh, and I can't wait for the next season of your show," she whispered. "You've even got my husband hooked."

All the staff knew who I was and what I did for a living, but I was grateful that they were discreet about it. Confidentiality was important here. They didn't blab to people outside of work about my occupation or that my father was a patient.

"Thanks." I smiled. "Tell your husband I appreciate the male fans, too."

Stirring the creamy contents of the bowl, I headed for the lounge.

I spotted his blue ballcap first. Dad was sitting on the brown leather couch in front of the TV, tapping his knee like he was listening to a song I couldn't hear.

Taking a deep breath, I sat next to him. Then I waited—for acknowledgement, for recognition, for some glimpse of the man I used to know.

The tapping slowed. His brown eyes slowly turned to mine, and he smiled. "How's it going, son?"

I let go of the breath I was holding and grinned.

It was a good day.

"I'm great, Pops."

"That's what I like to hear. How's work? You know the nurses in this place watch your show all the time. They can't believe you're my boy." He chuckled. "Sometimes I think they give me extra pudding, hoping I'll get them a date with you or something."

Snickering, I raised the bowl. "Speaking of pudding,

how about eating some of this?"

Seeming agreeable to the suggestion, he reached for the spoon but his hand shook so badly that he couldn't get a good grasp on it.

"I can do it," I said, picking up the spoon. "Here, like this."

I fed him a bite, and he made a sound like it was good. I gave him another. We went on like that until I was scraping the bottom of the bowl.

"Last one," I told him.

After he was done, I handed him a napkin and he wiped at his trembling lips.

It was painful, seeing someone you love in this condition. Seeing them helpless and dependent. Never knowing if they would recognize you.

When I was a kid, Robert Matheson had seemed like an indestructible giant, but now I was two inches taller than his six feet.

He'd aged quite a bit in the last few years, but on the outside, he looked mostly the same. Khaki pants. Reebok tennis shoes. The hat he'd worn for as long as I could remember.

On his bad days, I felt like I was trapped on the other side of a two-way mirror; I could see him, but he couldn't see me. And I could bang on that glass and yell as loud as I wanted to, but he'd never hear me.

I missed him so much. Even at almost twenty-five, sometimes I just needed my dad.

"So," he started, "tell me something great."

Tell me something great.

I loved it when he said that. Because that was the dad I used to know. It was what he'd said to me after the first day of kindergarten, after my SAT test, and after Mom died.

And the day after we moved him here, I'd tried so hard not to get choked up as I sat on this couch and answered him. I'd told him I was going to make sure he was taken care of—that was the only good news I had for him at the time.

Scratching my jaw, I wondered if I should tell him about Estelle. It'd been a long time since I talked about women with my dad, and I didn't want to confuse him.

Fuck it. He was *himself*, and I had no idea when another opportunity like this would come up.

"There's this woman I met on the job I'm working on right now. I like her." I paused, trying to think of how I could describe Estelle. "She's kinda crazy, in a good way."

Laughing, Dad slapped his knee. "That's the best kind. The very best. What does she do?"

"She owns a costume shop."

"An entrepreneur. Impressive."

"And she has nine cats."

He guffawed. "Sounds like she's perfect for you."

Loud cheering from the TV pulled his attention away. We sat together and watched the game for several minutes before he spoke up again.

"If I drop my bag over the railing, will they let me go get it?"

I turned my head toward him, my stomach sinking. "What do you mean?"

"My backpack," he said, getting more distressed by the second. "My baseball glove is in there. Will they let me go onto the field to get it?"

"Where do you think you are right now, Dad?"

Finally glancing at me, he blinked twice. "I don't know."

Closing my eyes, I swallowed around the rising lump in my throat and told myself to be thankful for those few lucid minutes I got with him.

"Yeah." My voice was raspy. "They'll let you go get it."

He gave me a lopsided smile. "Oh, good. Wouldn't want to lose my glove."

"No," I agreed. "I wouldn't let that happen."

"Thanks." He studied me for several seconds before grinning again. "You know, my wife has the same color eyes as you. Do you know my wife?"

"Yeah," I replied sadly. "I know her."

"Where's Mary? I'd like to see her now."

"You'll see her tonight."

I knew from the hospital staff that he dreamed of my mom often, and I was glad. I was glad he had that one thing left. At night when he closed his eyes, they were together—he was young and in love. He got to experience the best days of his life over and over, moments frozen in time.

"I can't wait to see Mary. She's the best part of my day." Dad reached over and patted my arm. A subconscious fatherly gesture.

His hands were still callused from years of working as a handyman, playing sports with his kids, and gardening with his wife. The life he'd once lived was etched in every wrinkle on his face and every gray hair on his head.

And somewhere in his mind all the memories were jumbled, but they weren't gone. Simply misplaced, but not missing.

"Tell me a story," I requested, as I often did. If there was one thing Dad loved, it was regaling everyone with tales of his youth.

"Oh, I've got a bunch of good ones. Which one do you want to hear?"

"The one about the boy and the thumbtack."

Slapping his knee again, he laughed.

"That's the best one I've got. So," he started, "I believe I was in the second grade. And there was this kid named Billy who used to torment all the girls. Real ornery. He used to put thumbtacks on their seats when the teacher wasn't looking. Poor things got quite the unpleasant surprise when they sat down."

"No way." I acted shocked, even though I'd heard this story so many times that I could've recited it word for word.

"Yes way. One time, the teacher caught him in the act and sent him to the principal's office. And do you know what the principal did?"

I hid my smile behind my hand. "What did he do?"

"He put a thumbtack down on the chair in his office. Turned to Billy and said, 'Well, go ahead and sit down.'" His voice got deep, and I laughed at his impression of the old man he used to describe as a wet blanket.

"And did he sit down?"

Dad nodded. "Nowadays, schools would never get away with that kind of punishment. Keep in mind, this was the '60s. So Billy sat down, expecting to get a sharp tack on his backside." He paused dramatically. "But Billy just sat there and smiled. The principal pushed down on his shoulders, just to make sure he was down all the way. Still, Billy smiled. Eventually, he got sent back to class and the principal was baffled. Can you guess what happened?"

"Tell me."

"When he sat down, that sharp point went right between his ass cheeks! Right in his crack. He couldn't feel a thing."

I laughed. "That's a great story."

"It is. Just too bad Billy didn't learn his lesson."

"That is a shame," I agreed.

We went back to watching the game. I stayed until Dad dozed off and one of the nurses came to get him ready for bed. He didn't say good night to me as he shuffled away.

My heart was a little heavy as I made my way out of the building. Leaving was always difficult because I knew my dad's condition would only get worse over time.

But then my phone pinged with a text, and when I checked it my mood instantly lifted.

Estelle: I have a pussy emergency.

I grinned.

Guess I knew how I'd be spending my night.

Chapter 12

Estelle

THE CREW HAD just arrived, bright and early, and even from the other side of the apartment, I could hear Steve bitching about the low quality of the continental breakfast at the hotel.

Serves him right for snubbing my biscuits and gravy.

Leaning against my closed bedroom door, I took a moment to enjoy a minute of alone time. I had no idea how Emery did it all the time. Smiling for the camera, the hustle of the staff, the twelve-hour days. I thought owning my shop was exhausting, but this took it to a new level.

It had been one of the longest weeks ever. Also one of the best weeks ever.

At least there were no cameras in my room. Heat rushed through my body when I thought about all the things they would've seen in here over the past couple days.

Reveling in the pleasant soreness between my legs, I changed into skinny jeans and a flowy black T-shirt. I'd gone a little heavier on the eyeliner today, hoping to look my best on the show. Sometimes standing next to Emery made me feel like a plain-Jane.

I had just applied some lipstick when I realized I wasn't alone in the room. Peter meowed and scratched at the door.

"When did you come in here? You want out? I'm glad you're finally being more social. We have plans for you today."

Just as I opened the door, Peter picked something up in his mouth and dashed out. It looked a lot like…

Something pink. Something much bigger than a regular cat toy.

No. Oh, fuck no.

I had no choice but to chase after him, and his fluffy tail disappeared into the second bedroom. My suspicions were confirmed as I cornered him by a scratching post—my vibrator was dangling from his teeth.

"Where the hell did you find that?" I whispered.

My mind flashed back to the night of too much wine and how the sex toy had rolled under my bed after it gave out on me. I'd forgotten all about it, and now my cat was ready to show it to the entire world.

"Drop the vibrator," I hissed quietly, glancing at the doorway. "Drop it now, mister."

His gaze stayed pinned on me, but his body language said he was going to make a run for it. My eyes flitted to the red light on the camera facing our direction. This room was being filmed 24/7 so we could catch the pisser.

At the time, I'd thought that was a brilliant idea.

Now? Not so much.

Grabbing a nearby stick with feathers on the end, I waved it at Peter and cooed, "Come on, Peter. Be a good boy and give me the dick."

Oh, that did not sound right at all.

A deep, booming voice sounded from the living room. Distracted by the possibility of everyone getting an eyeful, I looked toward the door again.

Big mistake.

Peter took the opportunity to zoom past me. I threw the feather stick in his direction, cutting him off from running into the living room. I followed him into the bathroom and shut the door behind me.

Breathing out a sigh of relief, I glared at the traitor hiding behind the toilet. "This is the most uncool thing you've ever done. I've forgiven you for a lot of shit, Peter, but *this*? This is crossing the line."

His response was a low growl.

I crouched down on the floor. The cumbersome object was still hanging from his jaws. Backing farther away, the hair on his back stood and his tail puffed out.

I could tell I was going to have a fight on my hands.

Chapter 13

Emery

Day four of filming. Today's objective was to introduce Marty to Peter and hope for a love connection. Or something.

Love was a long shot, but maybe they'd hit it off. Marty had just arrived, and Rhonda was getting him hooked up with a mic when I heard a commotion from down the hallway.

"Damn it, Peter!" Estelle's voice was muffled. "Put it down!"

In the short time I'd known Estelle, I'd become familiar with that warning in her tone. The one that said, 'I'm about to lose my shit.'

I had no idea what was going on, but it didn't sound good. I followed the ruckus to the bathroom and knocked. "Estelle? Everything okay?"

"Yes," she replied, sounding panicked. "I'm naked.

You don't want to come in here."

I smirked.

"If you're naked, I'm pretty sure I do," I said quietly into the wood. If she was trying to keep me out, that was a bad strategy.

I heard some scuffling and hushed whispers from the other side of the door. Just then, Joel came into the hallway, camera at the ready. I tried to get the shit-eating grin off my face as I knocked again.

"Are you sure you're okay?"

"I'm fine!" she shrieked. "Everything's just fine."

"Okay. The man who wants to meet Peter just got here."

"Sounds great," she chirped. "Be out in a minute."

Shrugging, I started to turn away when I heard a pained, "Ow!" from inside. My protective instincts took over and I turned the knob. It wasn't locked, so I opened the door far enough to peek my head in.

Estelle wasn't naked, but everything definitely was not okay. On all fours, she looked up at me with wide eyes and I spotted blood running down her arm.

She held up her uninjured hand. "Don't come any closer."

I frowned. "You're hurt. Let me get the medic. Can we get a medic in here?" I called over my shoulder.

"Oh, for fuck's sake," Estelle huffed.

As I stepped inside the bathroom, the situation became even weirder. She'd corralled Peter into the corner under the toilet, and I craned my neck to see what kind of trouble he was causing.

"Emery, can you please shut the—"

Suddenly, Peter jumped up onto the counter and

flew through the doorway with a large phallic-shaped object in his mouth. Naturally, Joel followed him, intent on getting the scoop. Estelle wasn't far behind as she scrambled by me—still on all fours.

"Was that a...? Um, it really looked like a—"

"A huge dildo? Yep," she replied, out of breath from the encounter as she crawled over my feet.

Out in the hallway, Peter and Estelle entered a face-off, with Joel at one end to document it and me at the other, gaping as I watched the chaos unfold.

Intent on keeping his new toy, Peter covered it with the length of his body. But his weight must have been enough to press the 'on' button because it began moving.

Startled, he jumped three feet in the air.

And there it was in plain sight—a pink dildo twisting and jittering around on the floor, hopping down the hall like a giant caterpillar on meth.

Crawling forward, Estelle made a swipe for it, but Peter beat her to the prize. Batting at it with his paws like it was his mortal enemy, he knocked the wiggling object against the wall a few times until it stopped moving. Then he picked it up in his mouth and took off again, zig-zagging between Joel's legs out into the kitchen.

"I give up." Plopping down on the floor, Estelle sagged back against the wall and covered her face with her hands. "Everyone's already seen it anyway. Oh my God. I'm never gonna live this down."

"Shit." I was torn between running after them and staying with Estelle, who was now lightly banging her head on the wall. Each impact made a dull thud. I decided to stay with her. "Stop," I said softly, cradling the back of her head. "You're already injured. It'll be fine."

Picking up her hand, I inspected the scratches. They weren't too deep and had already stopped bleeding.

"That's easy for you to say," she retorted. "You're not the one who just had your sex toy recorded on national television. I don't give a fuck about what the rest of the world thinks, but my parents—oh my God, my parents. They're conservative people who live in a very pretentious neighborhood. When everyone sees this, they're gonna be horrified."

"Hey, I'll talk to Steve about deleting the footage, okay?" I rubbed my thumb over her cheek.

Estelle's hopeful eyes were filled with hero-worship as she stared up at me. "You'd do that?"

"Of course."

Loud laughter rang through the apartment and Estelle cringed while turning an even deeper shade of pink.

"Take a minute if you need it," I told her. "I can just say you're not feeling well."

"A minute?" she asked incredulously. "It's going to take a lot longer than sixty seconds to recover from this. And 'not feeling well?' Like suddenly I'm incapacitated because everyone saw my vibrator? What would we call it, the dildo flu?"

I barked out a laugh. "It doesn't sound so great when you say it out loud. Maybe I could do something really embarrassing to distract everyone."

A small smile played on her lips. "Like what?"

"I could spill sweet tea on my jeans and tell everyone I peed my pants."

Shaking her head, she sighed. "I appreciate the offer, but we don't need to make a bad situation worse. I might go hide in my room for a few minutes. Tell Janice I'm definitely gonna need some extra time with her today."

"Will do." Giving her a reassuring smile, I turned away to go do some serious damage control.

The laughter I heard before continued, and I was about to tell whoever it was to fuck off. But when I turned the corner, I realized the humor had nothing to do with what had just happened.

Marty was on the couch, his big frame looking oversized in the small living room. Greg was perched on his round stomach while licking the hell out of his beard. Apparently, Marty thought it was hilarious.

"Uhh, Marty, meet Greg." I did the introductions while turning in a circle, looking for a cat with a giant dildo in its mouth. Shouldn't have been hard to spot it, but Peter and the vibrator were nowhere to be found.

Not under the coffee table, not behind the couch, not in the kitchen.

The leather-clad man was still chuckling as Greg made a tangled mess of his facial hair. "This one. This is the one, Emery."

"Really?" My eyebrows went up. "I should warn you that he does that a lot. In a couple days, you might not have a beard anymore."

"That's okay," he said, petting the cat who was grooming him. "I was thinking about shaving it off anyway. Just saves me the trouble."

Okay, then.

Not the original plan, but it was great news.

Smiling, I glanced around the room, still searching for the orange-striped devil. "I'm really glad to hear that. I wanted you to meet Peter, but I think this is a good match."

A *psst* sound came from around the corner, and I turned to find Janice beckoning me into the kitchen.

"I think I might have something you're looking for," she whispered.

"Did you get it from him?" I whispered back, reaching under my shirt to unplug my mic.

She nodded.

"How did you manage that?" I asked, perusing her arms for any scratch marks.

She shrugged. "Easy. He just hopped up onto the counter, dropped it, and ran away."

Of course he did. "Where is it?"

"I wrapped it in a dish towel and threw it under the sink," she replied, her face beet-red.

Every time Janice said '*it*' her voice dropped and the blush deepened. Maybe Estelle wasn't the only one traumatized by this event.

While Marty and Greg were bonding on the couch, I pulled Steve out into the hallway to ask him to delete the footage of the dildo debacle.

"Are you kidding?" He laughed. "This is reality show gold! You can't make this stuff up."

"You can't show that on TV, Steve. I'm gonna need you to erase it."

"What? No way," he said, aghast. "We'll probably get two full episodes out of this deal. Do you have any idea what this will do for our ratings?"

"Fuck the ratings." Clenching my jaw, I tried to reel in the impulse to punch him in the face. "Estelle is embarrassed."

"Well, of course she is. That's what makes it great."

"You can't do that to her."

Steve's smile faded away, his lips pressing into a flat line. "You don't make the rules here. I'm not going to lessen the quality of this show just because you have a soft spot for this chick. Do you want to keep your job or not?"

I jerked back like I'd been hit. "You'd fire me just because of this?"

"No. You don't get it." Huffing, he threw his hands in the air. "We're in hot water with the network. They're making demands, wanting to make changes. They want more sexual content, but less profanity. More drama, more humor, less heart-warming. It doesn't make any sense, but I'm not in the position to challenge it."

So that was why he was being such a prick lately. Suddenly, the short temper and bad moods made sense. And he'd probably been provoking Estelle on purpose, hoping for tears or angry outbursts.

I didn't know why the network was putting so much pressure on him, and the last thing I wanted was for the show to get canceled. Still, I wouldn't allow him to make a fool of Estelle.

"I won't let you do it," I insisted, crossing my arms over my chest.

"She's under contract, Emery. We have permission to show anything we film. You think I picked her at random? You think I chose this project because of the unique situation?" Shaking his head, he scoffed. "She's fucking hot, that's why. Again, think about the ratings. It's not my responsibility to make everyone look like a saint on this show. I'm doing my job. You do yours."

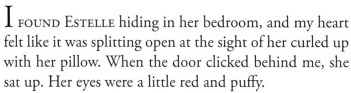

I FOUND ESTELLE hiding in her bedroom, and my heart felt like it was splitting open at the sight of her curled up with her pillow. When the door clicked behind me, she sat up. Her eyes were a little red and puffy.

"The universe hates me," she said vehemently. "Fate, destiny—whatever you want to call it—it's a twisted bitch."

Taking a seat next to her, I ran my thumb over the pink splotches on her cheeks. "It was just bad luck. And Peter's kind of a dick. We know that."

She shook her head. "Three days ago, that dildo was dead as a doornail, Emery. *Dead*. I couldn't get it to work for anything. The fact that it chose *that* moment to have a resurrection? Un-fucking-believable."

"I'm sorry." I wanted to tell her it would be okay, but I didn't want to lie. "So, the bad news is that I couldn't get Steve to agree not to show what happened."

"Shit." She sniffled. "What's the good news? Please tell me there's good news."

I wrapped my arms around her. "I think Greg found a home."

A genuine smile stretched across her face. "Really? That's great."

"Come out and meet Marty. He was so distracted by Greg giving him a complimentary beard trim that he didn't even notice the stuff with Peter."

"Okay." Drawing a deep breath, she wiped the remainder of the smudged mascara from underneath her eyes.

Standing up, I held out my hand. She linked our fingers like it was the most natural thing in the world. I kissed her knuckles before letting go.

"Do you have a copy of your contract with the show?" I asked, because no matter what Steve said, I wasn't willing to accept defeat just yet.

She nodded. "Yeah. Why?"

"Can I have it? I'm going to have my lawyer look over it to see if we can find a loophole or something." I smoothed my hand over her hair. "Until then, try not to worry about it."

"It'll be hard to think about anything else," she said glumly.

Smirking, I touched my forehead to hers. "I bet I can help you with that."

Chapter 14

Estelle

INCESSANT RINGING WOKE me and I blindly reached out for my phone. I hit the nightstand several times before I felt the bed dip behind me and a masculine hand gently placed the noisy device in my palm.

Without opening my eyes, I mumbled a 'thank you' before answering, "Hello?"

"Hi, dear. I hope I'm not catching you at a bad time."

I squinted at the clock. It was only 8 p.m. "No, Mom, it's fine. I must've fallen asleep a little early."

Truth: After the excitement of the day, Emery made it his mission to make me forget all about the 'dildo debacle.' And damn, did he make me forget. Then he took it a step further and did things to my body until I couldn't keep my eyes open. Sometime after orgasm number three, I'd passed out.

But I wasn't about to say that to my mother.

"Oh, okay," she responded pleasantly. "Well, I don't want to keep you. I was just wondering how the kitty show is going?"

Fact: She refused to call the show by its rightful name. The word 'pussy' wasn't in her vocabulary, even if she was referring to cats.

"It's great," I half-fibbed. "Cindy and Greg already found homes."

"That's wonderful. My little girl is famous. I'm going to arrange a block party for the neighborhood for the season premier. We can't wait to watch it."

"Fantastic," I choked out.

Reality: She was going to have an aneurism when it aired. And in front of all her hoity-toity friends, no less.

Warning her ahead of time was probably a good idea, but not now. I'd cross that bridge when I came to it.

As the only child of a technical engineer and an accountant, I was spoiled—there was no other way to put it. Growing up, they'd doted on me, given me the best education money could buy, and tried their best to instill the manners and etiquette every perfect southern belle should have.

I still felt bad about the fact that their efforts to make me ladylike were futile. They meant well, but it had only exacerbated my rebellious streak.

They were horrified when I died my hair pink at age fourteen, when I got drunk at my debutante ball at sixteen, and when my high school almost suspended me for the senior prank I pulled. Was it really so bad to change out all the staff pictures with characters from the cast of Grease? That was a damn good musical. And it wasn't my fault that our principal was a dead-ringer for

Rizzo.

Nonetheless, my parents loved me something fierce, and that was the most important thing. I knew they were proud of me and the life I'd built for myself as an entrepreneur.

And that was why the events of the day were so devastating. I didn't want to be an embarrassment to them. *Again*.

Rubbing my temple, I told my mom something that was 100 percent true. "I love you."

"I love you, too. Call me when your kitty situation gets resolved, and we'll get together for brunch to celebrate."

After saying our goodbyes, I rolled over to find Emery sitting up in my bed, holding a stack of papers.

"What are you doing?" I asked sleepily, placing my head in his lap.

His free hand went to my hair, soothing me with every gentle sweep of his fingers. I scooted up a little and he wrapped an arm around me.

"Going over the profiles for the cats." He shuffled with some papers, turning to the next page. Even as he worked, he didn't stop holding me.

I snuggled closer. "Profiles?"

"Yep. It's all about finding the right match. I don't believe there are bad cats," he said. "Being called a tamer indicates I somehow train them, but anyone who's ever owned a cat knows you can't *make* them do anything. Cats aren't wired that way, so it's more about changing their environment to make it work for them."

I liked Emery like this. Shirtless. Hair wild from my hands running through it. The scratch marks on his chest from his encounter with Peter were still red, but healing.

"What's up with your fear of flying?" he asked, changing the subject. "You've never been on a plane?"

"Oh, I've been on a plane. It was awful."

"But you made it out alive. The chances of a plane crash are really slim. You're more likely—"

"To die in a car wreck less than five miles from my house," I interrupted, finishing the line I'd heard a hundred times.

"Especially with the way you drive," he muttered.

"Hey!" I pretended to be offended as I twisted his nipple, but it wasn't like I could deny his claim. "I'm not afraid of the plane going down."

"What else is there to fear?"

"The thing is, crashing is highly unlikely, so I'm not very worried about that. But you know what's not unlikely? There is a 100 percent chance that someone is going to fart on that flight. Probably several people. And then I'm stuck with it for hours."

He laughed. "That's kind of ridiculous."

"Yeah, if you don't mind breathing in smelly stranger gas."

"You're a piece of work," he said, affection evident in his voice.

"So how did you become the pussy tamer?" I asked, curious about the man who seemed to have it all.

Looking thoughtful, he set the papers down on the nightstand and shifted down on the pillows. "You want me to start at the beginning?"

"Well, yeah," I responded. Flipping onto my stomach, I propped my face in my hands and grinned. "Tell me the whole story."

"Okay. But you have to promise you won't feel sorry for me."

My eyebrows scrunched together. "Okay…?"

"Promise me."

I held up two fingers. "I promise. Girl Scout's honor."

"That's a peace sign."

Letting out an exasperated noise, I shook the mattress next to him. "Okay, I promise. Just tell me."

He chuckled. "My parents were in their early thirties when they got married. They wanted kids right away, but struggled with infertility for several years. By the time they had my sister, they were forty. So five years later, when my mom got pregnant with me, it was a shock, to say the least."

Wide-eyed, I snickered. "Yeah, I bet."

His face became serious while he toyed with a strand of my hair. "When I was a senior in high school, my mom suddenly passed away. I remember she'd been tired for weeks, with muscle aches and a cough that wouldn't seem to go away. She thought it was a respiratory virus and tried to ignore the symptoms. One morning, she didn't wake up."

Swallowing hard, I asked, "What happened?"

"Heart attack," he stated, struggling to keep his voice emotionless. "After she was gone, I started noticing things about my dad and his mental condition. He was older, so at first I thought it was normal, you know? But it was more than just confusion. Sometimes he forgot where he was, sometimes he didn't recognize me. After taking him to the doctor, we figured out he had early-stage Alzheimer's."

I just barely held in my gasp.

"Mom had been hiding it from us," he went on. "She didn't want my sister and me to know. The signs had been there for years, but I was a self-absorbed teenager. And Nikki didn't notice because she was in college, getting married, and buying a house. I remember one time when I was about sixteen, Dad asked the neighbors if they'd seen our cat…" He trailed off, as though he was lost in the memory.

"What's weird about that?"

"Fuzzy had been dead for two years."

"Oh."

"Yeah. Mom laughed it off like he was joking, but now I realize she was just covering for him." Emery took a breath. "The spring after Mom died, Dad and I moved in with Nikki, but she and her husband were teaching full-time. I was in school. We tried to take care of him, but we didn't know how."

I had no idea what to say. I couldn't imagine going through something like that at such a young age. So instead of saying anything, I ran my fingers through his hair, smoothing the strands away from his face.

He closed his eyes and sighed before continuing. I stayed silent as he told me about the time his dad got lost and wandered the neighborhood for hours. How afraid Emery was that something had happened to him. How his dad cried like a child when they found him. How painful it was to make the decision put him in a nursing home.

My heart hurt at the thought of Emery not having parents. I didn't see mine very often, but at least they were just an hour-drive or a phone call away.

"I couldn't stand to see him in that nursing home.

The living conditions—they weren't ideal. Not for someone you love," he added quietly. "Priorities changed for me. I was on track to attend college, and hopefully become a vet someday. Instead, I found an assisted living home, and I used my college fund to set him up there for two years."

"Emery," I breathed out.

Although he didn't smile, he playfully tweaked my nose. "You're doing it."

"Doing what?"

"Feeling sorry for me. I've worked too hard to have anyone's pity."

"There's a difference between sympathy and pity," I argued, but I could tell he wasn't having it. I schooled my features to a neutral expression. "Please, go on."

"That summer, I looked around for jobs and found one at an animal hospital. Cleaning kennels isn't glamorous, but it was the closest I was going to get to doing what I loved. Plus, it was a paycheck. Nikki and I started a savings account together for Dad's care. We scrimped and saved every spare penny. I was eighteen years old, working a dead-end job, living with my sister and her husband. They would've let me live with them for as long as I wanted to, but when she got pregnant with my niece, I decided it was best for me to move out."

"Where did you go?"

"Moved into a cheap studio apartment. The only furniture I had was the mattress on the floor. If it wasn't a necessity, I didn't buy it." A small smile pulled at his lips as though he was recalling a pleasant memory. "Nikki was so pissed at me when she saw how bare it was. That afternoon, she went to the Dollar Store and bought the most heinous decorations. I'm talking teacup curtains and Disney-themed throw pillows."

I snorted, absentmindedly tracing his abs. "I would've loved to see that. Your sister is awesome."

"She is. After she stocked my fridge with enough food to feed an army, I made her promise not to buy me any more stuff. Not because I didn't appreciate it, but she couldn't afford it either."

I tried not to frown. "That's tough. I got my business management degree because I always knew I wanted to run the costume shop. But if it hadn't been for my parents' support and the fact that the business was basically handed to me, I don't know how I would've done it. Honestly, I owe most of it to Aunt Estelle. She came from a family of accountants and lawyers, so it was hard for her to go against the grain. But eventually, she proved her success and earned the respect she deserved."

"She paved the way for you."

I nodded. "I was so in awe of her when I was a kid. She sewed this amazing Marie Antoinette dress, and I just remember staring at it for hours. When I asked her how she did it, she just said 'one thread at a time.'"

"Your tattoo." Emery's fingertips traced the words written on my skin. "I like how the petals are stitched together in some places."

"That was pretty much her life motto. She said that was how anyone did anything—builders lay one brick at a time. Authors write one word at a time. Eventually, it adds up to something amazing." Poking my chest, she grinned. "You make the world better, one cat at a time."

"Hey, that's not a bad slogan. Maybe you should pitch it to Steve," he teased. "I'm glad you have your aunt and get to do what you love. This city wouldn't be the same without Estelle's Costume Shop."

"Thank you. She and I were always kindred spirits because we're both odd ducks."

"My favorite kind of duck," Emery said, giving me a soft smile before getting back to his story. "I was twenty-two when Steve found me at the vet clinic, elbow deep in litter boxes and dirty kennels. There was this cat named Twinkle Star Snowy Nose Tickle Toes—"

I giggled. "You're not serious."

"Oh, I am. And this cat was the biggest asshole in the world, may he rest in peace. He was probably worse than Peter. Guess who he belonged to?"

"Who?"

"Marty Miller."

Surprised, I leaned up on an elbow. "The guy who adopted Greg?"

"That's the one. For some reason, he just called his cat Arnold."

I was laughing so hard my stomach muscles hurt. "I can't… I can't. That's the worst cat name in the history of cat names."

"I know." Emery grinned.

Then he went on to tell me about his encounter with Arnold that day, and the mysterious suit-wearing man in the corner.

"Steve," I concluded, finally getting my laughter under control.

"That's right. He was there to check out the vet, but Dr. Carson was terrified of cats."

I cocked my head to the side. "That's weird."

"Exactly. I think he was hoping to get into showbiz

instead, but there was no way he could've handled this role. After I diffused the situation, Steve gave me his card and said to show up for an official audition if I was interested."

"And you were interested," I stated.

"This show was my way up the ladder. They paid for my vet tech certification, and now I have a college fund for myself. I have to look to the future—I won't be doing this forever. I still want to be a doctor someday," he said quietly, his words heavy with hope and vulnerability. "Someday I'll be more than just a guy who says 'pussy' a lot on television."

"You're so much more than that, Emery." I sighed. "You're…" *Everything a woman could possibly want? Kind. Caring. A real winner in the sack?* "You're not anything like I thought you'd be."

"What did you think I'd be like?"

I thought it over before going with the most honest answer. "Kinda douche-y?"

He huffed out a laugh. "Well, I thought you were an old cat hoarder, so we're even."

As his blue eyes flitted about my face, I wanted to tell him thank you—for caring about my pets, for not laughing at my occupation, for making me feel like I could be myself, rough edges and all.

I didn't say any of those things, though. Instead, I let the unspoken feelings hang between us.

But words didn't matter anymore once his lips connected with mine.

My legs automatically fell open for him as he moved on top of me. After quickly rolling on a condom, he slid into me. I hissed at the intrusion, my body still sore from earlier.

"Sorry," Emery whispered, stilling. "Are you okay?"

I wanted to laugh at the ridiculous question. I was way better than okay. *Orgasm number four, here I come.* "Don't stop. Just go slow."

Nipping at my neck, his hips rolled in that sensuous rhythm I enjoyed so much. He kissed his way up my jaw until he landed on my lips.

Then with his face just an inch from mine, he locked eyes with me while linking our hands above my head. His breath puffed across my cheek.

Sex was never the same with Emery. Every time was like the first time. Sometimes he was rough and dominant, others he was so tender it made my eyes sting with tears.

I remembered back to a time—not too long ago—when I thought a dozen times with him would be enough. I was so wrong.

We'd already surpassed that number and I wasn't anywhere near being done. In fact, the more I had him, the more the hunger grew.

He was like a drug.

And I just had to face it—I was so fucking addicted to Emery Matheson.

Chapter 15

Emery

I was completely obsessed with Estelle Winters.

Infatuated. Smitten. Pussy-whipped.

Didn't matter what you called it. I was so gone for her.

Yesterday my head had been totally out of the game, which meant we didn't make much progress with the cats. I was supposed to do a follow-up visit with Marty and Greg to see how they were doing, but decided to push it back another day or two. Instead, I found myself hanging around the apartment.

Seemed that when it came to spending time with Estelle, everything else was secondary.

When I wasn't with her, I couldn't stop thinking about her. And when I had her in my sights, trying to hide how badly I wanted her was torture.

In between shoots, we couldn't keep our hands

off each other. We'd had some pretty heated make-out sessions in her bedroom. In the coat closet. In the bathroom. Anywhere the cameras wouldn't see us.

And as soon as the day was over and the door shut behind the last crew member, clothes came off and we practically sprinted to the bedroom.

Keeping the secret to ourselves was fun, but behaving during filming was becoming more and more difficult. Especially when she looked at me the way she was right now.

Estelle batted her eyelashes over the rim of her sweet tea before wrapping her lips around the straw. It wasn't rational to be envious of a flimsy piece of plastic, but fuck.

Then again, nothing about my quickly developing feelings for her was normal.

Placing the cup on the coffee table, she licked her lips and uncrossed her legs, primly keeping her knees together. She didn't need to spread her thighs for me to know what was under her dress.

I'd memorized every square inch of her.

My cock thickened and I shifted uncomfortably in my seat. Now was not the time to get a boner. But from the devious smirk on Estelle's face, I could tell she knew exactly what she was doing to me.

"Estelle." I cleared my throat. "What improvements have you noticed in the past few days?"

We'd already gone over the interview questions, but she delivered the rehearsed answer as if it was the first time we were talking about it.

"I owe everything to the pussy tamer. This is only day six, and I'm already over halfway to my goal. Cindy and

Greg found homes earlier in the week. Marcia and Jan were adopted—together—this morning. I couldn't have done it without him." She widened those doe-like eyes, blinking innocently like a damsel in distress.

Such a pro.

Over the past week, I'd learned she was neither innocent nor helpless.

In fact, she was hell on wheels—literally.

Her driving skills were still absolute shit, even after the lesson I'd forced on her last night.

After dinner, I'd insisted on taking her out to show her some basics. We worked on the importance of checking your blind spot, turn signals, and giving the vehicle enough time to slow before coming to a stop. By the time we made it back to her apartment, I needed a stiff drink.

"Tell us a little bit about the family who adopted Marcia and Jan," I requested, proud of Estelle for handling the double adoption so well. The middle-aged couple had been perfect for the unique pair.

She smiled. "They're empty nesters. In the past two years, both of their kids moved away to college and they don't have any other pets. It was an ideal situation for taking on two cats instead of one. The local shelter helped us get matched up. I couldn't be happier with the results for my pussies," she laid it on extra thick with a wink.

"That was perfect." Steve clapped, ecstatic with her stellar performance. "Emery, you're up next."

I took Estelle's spot on the couch and looked into the dark lens. "Four pussies tamed, three to go."

"Come on, Emery." Steve sighed. "Make me *believe*

it."

Behind him, Estelle rolled her eyes so hard I thought she'd fall over. Then she stuck her tongue out and mimed a cat cleaning itself.

I laughed.

Steve turned around to see what was so funny but in an instant, she reverted to a blank facial expression, nonchalantly tucking a strand of hair behind her ear.

Shrugging, my clueless producer faced me again.

And something about that moment—that insignificant moment—made something shift inside of me. That feeling of true happiness that had been few and far between over the past several years whelmed in my chest.

Estelle was making me feel something I'd never experienced before. I didn't know if it was love, but it had to be pretty damn close.

Everything was better when she was around.

Steve's shitty moods? I let them roll off my back.

Peter still being a dick? It didn't bother me. He wasn't responding to any of my positive reinforcement methods, but I'd get him to come around eventually.

And even if it was a life-threatening event every single time, I enjoyed riding shotgun in Estelle's Jeep. Sometimes I found myself making up reasons to go to the store, just so I could hear her rap about big butts. A simple trip to the gas station gave me a bigger adrenaline rush than skydiving—which I'd done once, and would probably never do again.

And as I watched Estelle go back to making ridiculous faces, my heart sped up and my stomach swooped, the same way it did when I jumped out of that airplane when

I was eighteen.

After I nailed my line, Steve called a lunch break and Estelle headed down the hallway to the bathroom.

I followed.

Just before she could shut the door, I stopped it with my boot. I quickly glanced around to make sure no one was watching, then I pushed my way inside with her.

"What are you doing?" she whisper-yelled as I quietly shut the door.

Instead of answering, I picked her up and set her ass on the counter next to the sink. Reaching under her dress, I disabled her mic. Her eyes widened because she knew what that meant.

Then I slid my hand between her legs to confirm what I already knew—she wasn't wearing panties.

"Did you do this on purpose?"

"What?" she asked, blinking innocently.

"This dress. No panties." I buried two fingers in her slick heat and she gasped. "You like to tease me."

Grabbing my wallet with my other hand, I retrieved a condom and started unbuckling my belt.

Disbelief, fear, and arousal lit up her face when she realized I wasn't messing around. We were going to fuck right here, right now.

It was the first time we'd ever had sex with people still lingering around the apartment, and the risk of getting caught made my dick even harder.

I rolled the protection on, then replaced my fingers with my cock, slipping my tip into her tight heat. Just an inch.

"Has anyone seen Emery?" Joel's voice came from down the hallway.

Estelle and I both froze.

"I think he went out to the RV," Rhonda answered.

Out of instinct, habit, or whatever, I switched off the light. Estelle flipped it back on.

I grinned.

"Everyone is right outside," she hissed, but her protest sounded weak and half-hearted. "They could hear us."

Placing my palm over her mouth, I pushed forward and she whimpered behind my hand. "Guess you better be quiet then."

"This is ridiculous," Estelle complained as we got into her Jeep. "I've never been in an accident or anything. I don't drive under the influence. I'm not *that* bad." She threw her hands up. "I've never even had a ticket."

"How many times have you been pulled over?"

Her eyes turned to the darkening sky as she silently counted to herself. "Like, six or seven."

"And how many of those cops were dudes?"

"I know what you're thinking," she accused, those brown orbs narrowing. "Either I cried or flirted to get out of a ticket."

"Did you?"

"Well, yeah." She huffed, but she couldn't stop her lips from curling up at the corners.

Even though she pretended to be annoyed with my nagging, I knew she wasn't. She was so transparent. It was one of the things that made getting to know her so easy. Her every thought, all her feelings, her heart—they were all on her sleeve.

No apologies. No regrets. Just Estelle. Hard, but vulnerable. Wild, yet gentle. Crazy and kind.

She was wearing her leather jacket again. And those fuck-me boots. And the red lipstick. It was almost enough to make me say *to hell with the lesson* and drag her sexy ass back inside.

But my concern for her safety outweighed my desire to get her naked.

"Now, we need to do something about this." I pointed at the nonfunctional gages. "How long has it been like that?"

She shrugged. "Only a few months."

Resisting the urge to scold her, I grunted. "Estelle, you're playing with fire if you drive around in a broken vehicle for that long. What happens if you run out of gas?" Then I spoke my true concern. "I don't want to worry about you after I'm gone."

"You'd worry about me?" she asked softly.

My eyes met hers. "Every fucking day."

Biting her lip, she looked away. "I'll get it fixed then."

Like I said—so transparent. Even in rare instances when she tried to hide, I could see right through her. She liked the fact that I'd worry about her.

I liked it too. A lot more than I should.

What had started off as something fun was turning into something more—for both of us.

Chapter 16

Estelle

WHY DID EMERY have to be so fucking perfect? I mean really, the guy had no flaws.

I'd been actively searching. Waiting for him to slip up and say something rude or hurtful. Watching for the moment when he'd look at me with judgement or disdain because of my *many* flaws.

It never happened.

Waking up without him beside me was way more unpleasant than I liked to admit. As I ran my hand over the cool covers, I felt a stab of disappointment.

It wasn't like I expected him to stay—we'd already agreed it was best for him to go back to the RV before morning so no one would catch onto our tryst. He was doing it to protect me, and it wasn't like we were in a relationship or anything.

Still, it sucked.

Staring up at the ceiling, I reminded myself to live in the moment. To enjoy this fun while it lasted. For now, I wasn't alone.

It was a Sunday, so we had the day off—a much-needed reprieve from filming. And despite Halloween being just around the corner, the costume shop was closed. It was one condition my aunt had when I took over the business. She'd said taking a day off every week was good for the soul.

I puttered out to the kitchen to load up on caffeine. My only complaint about this arrangement with Emery was that we had most of our alone time at night—meaning I'd lost a lot of sleep.

I'd just poured my coffee when my phone pinged with a text.

Emery: Spend the day with me.

Not a question—a demand. God, he was so hot when he got all bossy. And a whole day? I tried not to squeal with excitement, but I wasn't very successful. My shriek was so loud, several of the cats bolted from the living room.

Play it cool, Estelle.

Me: Sure. That would be great.

Emery: Can I get a tour of your shop?

Giddiness made my fingers shake, and I was smiling like a loon.

166

Me: Yeah! I'll be ready in 30 minutes xoxoxo

I hit send before I could think better of it, then read over the message.

xoxoxo?! Not just one or two Xs and Os. Three of each.

So much for playing it cool.

Groaning at my awkwardness, I let my head fall back against the fridge with a thud.

My phone pinged again, and I immediately felt better because Emery had sent some goofy cat emojis along with a heart.

See? Perfect.

Emery gave my fingers a squeeze as we walked hand in hand on the sidewalks of the downtown district where my shop was located. The funny thing about this area was that parking lots basically didn't exist. Most of the spots were metered, which was one of the reasons I usually rode my bike.

But I didn't mind that we had to park a few blocks away. Sunny and seventy degrees, the weather was ideal for a short walk and perfect for the blue long-sleeved tee and skinny jeans I'd picked out.

Pulling Emery closer, I rested my temple against his upper arm as we passed a pawn shop. Butterflies skittered in my abdomen when he dropped a soft kiss to the top of my head.

Most of the businesses here had a hipster vibe with vintage clothing stores, coffee shops, and cafés. Musicians often set up on the street corners and played for anyone who would listen.

I tossed a dollar bill into the guitar case of a dreadlock-sporting man singing an Ed Sheeran song. Not to be outdone, Emery threw a five in after mine.

I poked his side. "Show-off."

He retaliated by hooking his arm around my shoulder, then he placed an open-mouthed kiss on my neck. I shivered and suddenly felt short of breath.

"I can't believe Turner's is still here." Emery nonchalantly pointed at the ice cream shop across the street, like he didn't just turn me into a quivering mess of lust.

"Believe it or not, I've never been there."

"They only serve four flavors, but it's the only ones you need."

"Rocky Road?" I asked hopefully.

His thumb grazed my collarbone. "I bet they could mix something up for you."

I nudged him away with my shoulder, linking our fingers once again. He needed to stop touching me like that if he didn't want me to jump his bones in the middle of the street.

"I keep forgetting you're from here. You know this town way better than I do."

"Like the back of my hand." He brought our clasped hands up to his lips and lightly brushed my knuckles. "My old studio apartment is that way, on the other side of the railroad tracks."

Glancing left as we crossed the street, I peered at the haggard structures in the distance. I spied graffiti, broken windows, and chain-link fences. "Not the best part of town, huh?"

"No," he replied simply.

We were silent for the next block, and I studied Emery out of the corner of my eye.

Whenever we were in public, I noticed his mannerisms were different. He kept his head down, his shoulders hunched. The red plaid button-up and dark-wash jeans he wore were a vast difference from the signature gray T-shirt he always had on for the show. And he didn't try to push his hair out of his face, letting it just hang over his eyes.

I knew why he did that. He was worried about being recognized, and I couldn't blame him. Every outing was a risk. A risk he took for me.

My shop came into view. Excited, my footsteps sped up and Emery laughed as I dragged him behind me.

"What do you do when it's not busy season?" he asked as we approached the brick-front building. The ancient wooden sign displayed 'Estelle's Costume Shop' in big yellow letters. I'd thought about having it replaced with something more modern, but it was one of the things about the place I couldn't bear to change when I remodeled.

"I sell party supplies and sew new costumes in my spare time," I replied. "And I do face painting."

Impressed, Emery raised his eyebrows. "You're an artist too? Talented, beautiful, and you love cats. Are you sure you're real?"

He playfully pinched my cheek.

I giggled. "It's face painting. Believe me, I'm not winning any awards. I do mostly kids' birthday parties or festivals. It's a good way to bring in extra money year-round and I love it." Turning my key, the heavy door opened and a jingle rang out. "I've changed a lot of things, but you'll probably recognize the clown mural." I pointed to the wall over the cash register. "It's creepy as shit, but I like the history behind it. Aunt Estelle's late husband painted it back in 1977."

"Still smells like lemons in here," he commented, doing that adorable sniffing thing.

"It's the wood cleaner," I informed him. "A lot of these old buildings have the original woodwork. Adds character, but takes a special kind of care to maintain it."

Turning in a circle, he took in the front part of the store. It used to be crammed full of seemingly endless racks of costumes, but now it was mostly filled with shelves of gag gifts, party favors, and decorations. Only a few headless mannequins displayed popular costumes for this year.

"It's a lot like I remember it." He walked behind the checkout counter to the adult-only section and picked up some penis-shaped suckers. "I believe these are new, though."

I nodded, eager for him to see the rest. "There's more. A lot more. Most of my Halloween inventory is on the second floor. My aunt used to have an apartment up there, but it was time to expand."

"Well, show me the way."

As he followed me up the stairs, pride swelled in my chest at the renovations I'd done a year ago.

The old floral wallpaper had been stripped away and replaced with a modern gray paint. Framed pictures of Hollywood icons lined the wall—Judy Garland as Dorothy, Elvis Presley in his white jumper, Elizabeth Taylor as Cleopatra.

When we reached the top step, I happily bounced on my feet as Emery admired the space. The soles of his boots quietly padded over the hardwood floors as he made his way to the other end of the large room.

"Holy shit." He slowly walked the rows, running his fingertips over all the different fabric hanging on the racks. "How many costumes are here?"

"About ten thousand. Most were already here when I took over ownership. My aunt was really proud of this place, and rightly so. She made a lot of the costumes herself. I've made about fifty in the last couple years and bought some new ones because they're popular with the college crowd." To make my point, I picked up a slutty nurse dress. "Gotta keep up with the times."

Emery laughed and took it from my hands. Then he held it up in front of me and licked his lips. "What would I have to do to get you to model this for me?"

Grinning wickedly, I got an idea. "Say it."

His head tilted to the side. "Say what?"

"*It.* Your line. I want you to say it to me. Make my fangirl dreams come true."

Grunting, he rolled his eyes to the ceiling, feigning annoyance.

"Come on, Emery," I goaded, letting the hanger dangle from my finger. "If you want me to put this on, those are my terms."

He advanced on me. When his face was just inches

away from mine, he begrudgingly gritted out, "I'll tame your pussy."

"Nope. Try again." Spinning away from him, I put a rack of clothing between us and made my voice deeper. "I need you to make me *believe* it." It was a poor imitation of the whiny producer, but Emery laughed anyway.

"Oh yeah? Maybe I should show you instead." His voice dropped. "Here, kitty kitty."

I squealed, partly with delight over the fact that he'd said not one, but *two* of his lines to me, but also because he was coming after me in earnest.

Stalking toward me with wide strides, he made a swipe for me, but I skirted to the side, knocking into the mummy statue by the wall.

Giggling, I ran into the used-to-be bedroom that was now the 'mask room', and hid in the small closet. Emery's heavy footfalls weren't far behind.

"Here, kitty kitty…" he said again, gruff and seductive as he walked by.

I peeked through the crack in the door to watch him approach the window.

Putting his hands in his pockets, he rocked back on his heels. "Really, Estelle? Hiding behind the curtain? I can see your feet."

He whipped the yellow and white chevron drapes to the side, and disappointment was evident in the slump of his shoulders when he didn't find me there. He'd been tricked. Those shoes were tacked to the floor—a permanent fixture in the décor just to freak people out.

I clamped a hand over my mouth to stifle my laughter, but a snort escaped.

Emery turned, a smile on his face as he scanned the

wooden door separating us. He had that predatory glint in his eye—the one that got my blood pumping.

When the door swung open, I threw myself at him. Laughing, he caught me around the waist as I linked my legs behind his back.

I didn't hesitate to deepen our connection, bringing my mouth to his. Pushing my tongue past his lips. Tasting him. Running my fingers over his scruffy jaw. Sucking on his bottom lip.

Panting, I rested my forehead on his. When I opened my eyes, I realized Emery had backed up against the wall, his body embedded in all the rubber and hair of the masks on display.

"We can't do this in here," he said, his gaze darting around. Wall to wall faces started back at us. "It's fucking creepy."

I laughed. "I have a better idea."

Chapter 17

Emery

"WELL, DO YOU like it?" Estelle struck a pose in the doorway of the dressing room.

It took me a second to realize I was just staring, slack-jawed. Hell, I was almost drooling.

"It's great," I croaked.

The slutty nurse costume was everything I'd hoped for and then some. On the hanger, it was just a piece of flimsy white fabric with red trim and a cute little heart over the left breast pocket.

On Estelle, it was pure seduction. It hugged the curve of her hips, accentuated her narrow waist, and pushed her breasts up, showcasing inches of cleavage.

She turned around.

I groaned out loud.

The short skirt barely made it past her rounded, supple ass cheeks. Before I knew what I was doing, I was on her. With my hands on her hips, I moved us both inside the tiny room and shut the door.

Three of the walls were plated with floor-to-ceiling mirrors, giving an endless view of my front pressed to her back.

Hugging her from behind, I met Estelle's hooded gaze in the reflection in front of us as my hands glided over the silky material on her belly.

Her hand came up to the back of my head, and I lowered my mouth to her neck, sucking at her sweet skin. There was a tremble in her fingers as they gripped my hair.

"Did you know I fantasized about fucking you in a dressing room?" I asked huskily, pushing her shoulders down until she was bent over in front of me.

"When?" she asked, breathless.

"After we went shopping that first day." Flipping the bottom of her outfit up, I groaned when I saw she wasn't wearing panties. "I jacked off thinking about you just like this."

"That's really hot." Bracing her hands on a small stool, she confessed, "I think about you all the time. I get so wet when I think about having your cock inside me."

Dirty girl. My erection throbbed behind my zipper.

Estelle impatiently wiggled her ass, and I undid my pants before rolling the condom on. Lining myself up at her entrance, I could feel how ready she was.

She wasn't kidding—always so wet for me.

I pushed forward, using her shoulders for leverage until I was fully seated. Then I moved my hands around to her front and pulled the stretchy fabric down, letting her tits spill out of the lowcut neckline. I thumbed both nipples and she whimpered.

My palms slid to her hips. Guiding her body back and forth, I slowly pumped her over my dick. The old wooden planks beneath my feet creaked rhythmically with my movements.

"Fuuuuck, baby," I moaned.

Turning my head to the side, I watched us in the mirrors. It was awesome, seeing the infinite reflection of our connected bodies at every possible angle. With each thrust, Estelle's tits swayed and her ass cheeks jiggled.

My eyes zeroed in on the tight ring of her ass. Stroking my hand down her backside, I gently circled it with my thumb.

With a grunt, she jerked forward and her questioning eyes flew to mine in the mirror.

"Shh." I gave her a reassuring nod as I continued to rub her there, conveying all the things I wanted to say with just one look.

That she could trust me. That she was safe with me.

Her stiff body relaxed, and she pushed back on me. I circled her puckered hole again.

I'd never been into anal play before, but her moan encouraged me to keep going. I didn't push inside—just massaged it, stimulating the nerve endings there.

With my other hand, I reached around her front and did the same to her clit while delivering deep strokes with my cock.

Watching her face in the mirror was one of the hottest moments of my life. Cheeks flushed with arousal. Eyes screwed shut. Mouth open.

"How do you do this to me?" Pressing her palm on the glass, she began pushing back harder. "How do you make me feel so good?"

I didn't think she expected me to answer her, but I did it anyway. "I just want to touch you in as many places as possible."

She responded with an unintelligible moan.

I kept pumping my hips, matching her stroke for stroke as I sped up the action of my fingers.

Estelle's body trembled and her fingernails scratched over the surface of the mirror. A sheen of sweat broke out on her forehead. Sounds tumbled out of her mouth as her pussy squeezed my dick in a vice-like grip.

I could tell she was so close but she was fighting it.

"Come on, baby. You're almost there." I drove my cock deeper.

"I can't," she whimpered, her legs shaking. "I can't. I can't. If I come, I'm gonna fall over."

"I've got my arm around you. I won't let you fall," I promised, tightening my hold around her stomach.

"Shit. Emery. Fuck," she squeaked, her voice getting higher with every word.

And then it happened. Her legs gave out as her inner muscles clamped around me with an impossibly powerful orgasm, and I held on tight, my own release right behind hers.

Her scream echoed off the walls, and a roar left me as my balls drew up tight, blinding pleasure slamming through my body. It was so intense that I almost fell over with her.

I braced an arm on the mirror in front of us while Estelle's pussy milked my cock.

With my dick still inside her, I folded my body over hers, wrapping my arms around her trembling form.

I kissed her hair, her shoulder, her neck. The side of her face was pressed against the cool glass, every ragged breath fogging up the mirror.

We stayed like that for a minute, basking in the moment. Finally, my softening erection slipped out and I turned Estelle around.

Her eyes were dazed. Her body languid in my arms. Both of us were still shaking and out of breath. I tenderly kissed her forehead before my mouth claimed hers, our lips lazy and uncoordinated.

"Thank you," Estelle said, pulling back.

"Baby, you never have to thank me for great sex," I responded, amused.

Tucking her breasts back into the outfit, she laughed. "I meant for wanting to see my shop. It means a lot to me."

"You're welcome. You have a lot to be proud of," I told her honestly. And now it was my turn to be excited because I had plans for us. "Get yourself together." I gave her a light swat on the butt. "I have someone I want you to meet."

IT WAS A bad day for Pops. Estelle and I had just arrived to find Dad cranky and agitated with the nurses.

"I don't want that pureed potato crap." He pushed the plate away for the tenth time, refusing to eat his dinner.

"Mr. Matheson, you need to have something in your stomach so you can take your medicine." Gretchen's tone was soothing, but he wasn't having it.

"You're trying to poison me!"

"It's medicine to make you feel better."

"I feel fine," he argued. "There's nothing wrong with me. I want to go home. I want my wife. Where's Mary? She won't let you poison me. Mary!"

"Dad. Dad, calm down." My plea only seemed to make it worse. He knocked his juice from the table and the orange liquid splattered all over the floor. Sending an apologetic look to the nurse, I said, "I'm sorry."

"It's not a problem," she replied patiently. "I'll go get a towel."

Today was the Windsor Lakes annual trick-or-treat event for the residents and family members, but all the new people could be confusing for some of the patients.

The decorations were minimal. All the round dining tables had the usual plain cream tablecloths, but each had a small festive centerpiece: a wicker basket with a variety of multicolored squash. Pumpkin pie was being served, and the heavenly aroma filled the air as the guests devoured their desserts.

Disheartened, I turned to Estelle.

I should've prepared her better, but I'd been so excited for her to meet my dad that I had glossed over his condition, simply telling her not to be surprised if he didn't know who I was.

"I'm sorry. Maybe today was a bad time to come with everything going on. Sometimes he doesn't want to eat his dinner, so that's normal," I explained. "And he gets confused in the lounge because there's a TV, and every now and then he'll think he's actually inside whatever show is on—"

"Emery." She put a hand on my forearm. "You don't have to apologize or explain."

"We should go," I told her, my shoulders sagging.

But Estelle wouldn't accept defeat. She gave my arm a reassuring squeeze before stepping forward. "Hi, Mr. Matheson. It's nice to meet you."

Dad's eyes landed on her, and I waited for more of his paranoid outbursts. Instead, the hard lines on his face went soft and he stilled.

"Call me Robert."

"Okay, Robert. I'm Estelle."

"My wife has hair just like yours. Do you know Mary?"

Shaking her head, Estelle smiled and leaned her hip against the table. "No. Will you tell me about her?"

"She's the most beautiful woman in the world—not that you're not pretty, but my wife…" Dad let out a whistle.

"Does she like animals?" Estelle sat down in the chair next to him, tentative, yet confident.

He let out a laugh, going from the mess he was a minute ago to a cheerful, boisterous man. "Does she ever. If I let her have twenty pets, she'd do it."

She smiled. "Your wife and I have that in common too. What about you? What's your favorite animal?"

"I'd have to say cats. We have a cat named Fuzzy. Spoiled rotten, that one."

They laughed together. Estelle didn't skip a beat, even though she knew my dad was talking about his late wife and a deceased pet.

As I watched them fall into an easy conversation, I felt my eyes sting, filling with happy tears. I hadn't seen this side of my dad in a long time—years even. He was never like this with my sister and me. The closest he ever got was when he recounted the stories from his childhood.

Seeing him come to life made me blindingly happy. I blinked, desperately trying not to cry like a baby in the middle of the cafeteria.

Dumping her huge-as-hell purse onto the tabletop, Estelle said, "Halloween is coming up soon. I couldn't help noticing you're not wearing a costume."

"Bah." Dad waved a dismissive hand. "It's been years since I dressed up. My kids love it, though. I take them trick-or-treating every year. We hit all the best houses—the ones with the king-size candy bars."

Estelle sifted through all the contents of her bag and started gathering small, circular compacts—red, blue, yellow, white. Face paints. I wasn't even surprised that she carried them around with her.

Dad laughed at something else she said, but I was too busy trying not to fall apart to hear what they were talking about.

"I'll be right back," I announced, my voice gruff, before moving quickly down the hall.

Stopping outside the restrooms, I pinched the bridge of my nose and took a deep breath. I counted to ten, every second helping me to get my reeling emotions in check.

I'd just gotten myself under control when a scratchy voice spoke next to me.

"Your girlfriend is really good with him."

I looked down to see Agatha, one of the housekeepers.

She smiled behind her rolling cart of cleaning supplies.

Possessiveness flared through me at the title of *girlfriend*. I hadn't referred to Estelle that way yet, but it felt strangely satisfying to hear someone else say it.

"Yeah, she is," I agreed.

Although, 'good with him' didn't quite describe the interaction I'd just witnessed. Estelle was amazing with him. I wanted to tell myself it was because she reminded him of Mom, but I knew that wasn't true. It was just her. Her openness made people feel at ease. There was no one else in the world like Estelle.

Fidgeting on her feet, Agatha stepped closer to me. "You know we're all a fan of the show around here."

I smiled. "Thank you. The project I'm working on now is a tough one, but it's been fun."

"Well, that's kind of what I wanted to talk to you about," she started, seeming nervous. "See, my cat died from kidney failure last year. I'd had her for twenty years and I loved her like she was my own child. The other day, Nikki mentioned you might be looking for homes for some cats and I feel like I'm ready now... I don't suppose you might have one for me?"

"Agatha." I placed a hand on her shoulder. "Did you think I'd say no?"

She shrugged, looking hopeful. "What requirements are there? I'm old and I don't make a ton of money, but I've got a lot of love to give."

There were shelters filled with animals that only wanted exactly what she was offering—a home. Hell, sometimes you couldn't even pay people to take them in. Listening to a lonely woman try to convince me she was worthy of a companion was one of the most touching moments I'd had in my career.

"A good home is the only requirement."

Face brightening, she lunged at me with a quick hug. She pulled away, appearing a bit embarrassed about her uncontrollable display of affection. Righting herself, she smoothed down her gray uniform.

"Mitzy was one of the most irritating cats I'd ever met," she reminisced fondly. "She used to tear up my toilet paper and stash it in places around the house. Sometimes I'd find big wads of the stuff in my underwear drawer."

"Irritating, you say?" I asked, already thinking of Carol.

She nodded emphatically. "Oh gosh, there were times when I wanted to strangle her—not for real, of course. But at the end of the day, she'd curl up in my lap and I just couldn't stay mad at her."

"I think I have the perfect cat for you," I told her, taking out a business card. I scribbled my number and Estelle's address on the back. I was about to put the 'pussy emergency' code, then thought better of it. The last thing I needed was a booty call from Agatha. "Call me tomorrow, and we'll set up a time for you to come meet Carol this week."

"Thank you so much!" she exclaimed before practically skipping down the hall with her cart.

As I made my way back to the cafeteria, a realization hit me—if Agatha adopted Carol, there would only be two cats left to go. And that meant my time in Remington was quickly dwindling. I couldn't imagine going back to my solitary existence, continuing my life without Estelle in it.

My unpleasant thoughts were interrupted by booming laughter combined with feminine giggles. When I turned the corner, my footsteps halted at the entertaining sight in front of me.

Estelle had painted Dad's face to look like a pirate, with a realistic-looking eye patch and a scar on his left cheek.

I barked out a laugh, gaining her attention. She whipped her head around and smiled.

Her face was painted too, only she was a rabbit. Pink nose, white cheeks with whiskers, and big bunny teeth were painted below her bottom lip.

"Did I ever tell you I have a thing for buckteeth?" I joked, pulling out a chair and sitting across from them. It was then that I noticed several other residents were lined up to have their faces done too.

"I request buckteeth," an elderly woman called from the end of the line, prompting laughter from several onlookers.

"I feel like the only thing I'm missing is a parrot on my shoulder," Dad said, smiling like a kid on Christmas.

"How about a skull bandana instead?" Estelle finished off dad's costume by wrapping the black material around his head. "All right, Robert. You're ready to set sail."

Sometime in the few minutes I'd been gone, Gretchen had brought out a fresh plate of food for Dad. She'd replaced the 'pureed potato crap' with the tapioca he liked.

Estelle got up to sit at another table and waved the next person over.

Taking her seat, I picked up the bowl and came face to face with a transformed man—and I wasn't just talking about the pirate ensemble. Dad's smile was easier, his eyes a little more focused. Just a few minutes with Estelle and he looked five years younger.

"Boy, she's really something," he said before accepting a bite of the pudding from me.

"You're not telling me anything I don't already know." I wiped his chin with a napkin. "The fact that she convinced you to put makeup on is a miracle."

"Makeup?" He sounded offended. "No, I'm a swashbuckling rogue."

I snickered. "Well, she got you to sit still long enough, so that's something."

"Son, when a beautiful woman raps Dr. Dre, you keep your ass in the seat until she's finished."

My own laughter hit me so hard, I almost dropped the bowl. It was a deep belly laugh, and tears sprang to my eyes for a completely different reason as I tried to picture Estelle quietly busting out lyrics about God knows what to my father.

She smiled at me over her shoulder, then went back to painting a clown face on a gray-haired woman.

Once I could fully form a sentence, I said, "Truest statement ever made."

"You better hold onto that one." Dad's eyes flitted to Estelle. "She's a keeper."

"I know," I agreed with him.

Problem was, keeping her had never been part of the plan. I'd meant it when I told Estelle I wasn't in a good place to be starting a relationship.

But I knew better than anyone that plans could change.

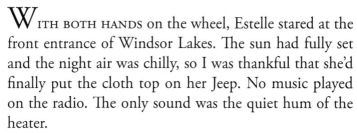

WITH BOTH HANDS on the wheel, Estelle stared at the front entrance of Windsor Lakes. The sun had fully set and the night air was chilly, so I was thankful that she'd finally put the cloth top on her Jeep. No music played on the radio. The only sound was the quiet hum of the heater.

I braced myself for Estelle's pity, but she surprised me.

"He's great, Emery." Her eyes swung my way. "You're so much like him."

That made me smile. "If you'd known my mom, you wouldn't be saying that. Even Dad would tell you I take after her."

Estelle shook her head. "I don't need to know her to be able to see the similarities between you and your dad. You have the same smile, and this part…" She rubbed a thumb over the cleft in my chin.

"This is the first time I've ever introduced a woman to him," I told her, feeling like the confession splayed me wide-open.

Her plump lips made an 'O' shape. "Seriously?"

I nodded. "Unless you count a homecoming date, yeah."

"Wow. That's kind of a big deal."

"Yes. It is." I held her stare, willing her to understand the depth of my feelings for her and for the first time,

I witnessed an uncharacteristic fear in Estelle's eyes. A sense of hesitancy I'd never seen before. It was like shutters fell over the openness I'd gotten so used to.

Her gaze darted back to the building. "Does he ever get to leave?"

Changing the subject. Ouch. I'd be lying if I said that didn't sting a little.

I grimaced, thinking about the few unsuccessful outings we'd had. "Not anymore. He becomes disoriented if his routine is scenery changes. It took him a long time to get used to Windsor Lakes and he's happy here, for the most part."

"I'm sorry, Emery."

"Hey," I said, softly gripping her chin as I turned her face my way. "What did I say about feeling sorry for me?"

"I can't help it. Seeing that"—she tipped her head toward the building—"is a lot different than hearing about it. It must be so hard for you. And him."

"The hardest part about living so far away is wondering if he'll still know me next time I come visit," I admitted quietly. As hard as it was to say out loud, this was something I needed to let Estelle see if I wanted her to know me. She'd been so honest, it was only fair I did the same. "What if today was the last time he'll ever look at me like I'm his son?"

Blowing out a breath, she shook her head. "He'll always know you." She leaned over the middle console and pressed her lips to mine. "He'll always know you," she whispered again before coming back for more.

This kiss was different than all the others. It was slow and sweet. Soothing. Much better than words of sympathy.

Warmth spread through my chest as she held both sides of my jaw, controlling the kiss. She was comforting me. Reassuring me. She was simply *giving*.

And I let her, all while pushing thoughts of eventually saying goodbye far from my mind.

Chapter 18

Emery

W HEN I WOKE up in Estelle's bed with her naked body snuggled against mine, I couldn't find the motivation to get up. Leaving her bed before the sun came up had gotten harder every time.

Last night, instead of sneaking back to the RV, I made the conscious decision to stay.

We didn't even have sex after we got back from Windsor Lakes. We channel surfed until stopping on a bad infomercial, but paid no attention to the TV. I had no idea it was possible to talk about literally nothing for hours, but that was what we did. With Bobby in my lap and Alice curled up with Estelle, we laughed about random things, our conversation veering from one insignificant topic to the next.

After taking a shower together, we collapsed onto the bed, both naked and exhausted. I'd managed a soft kiss to Estelle's forehead before my eyes closed.

And now I had this amazing woman in my arms, and I didn't want to let go.

I couldn't let go.

I never should've assumed I could do casual with Estelle. Somewhere along the line, she became mine.

Mine.

But given her reaction to my candor last night, it was safe to say she might not feel the same. Maybe she was just scared. Hell, I was scared too, but I wanted her in my life.

This wasn't temporary for me. Not anymore.

I wasn't sure how we were going to make it work, but we could discuss it later. Today, I just wanted to pretend we had all the time in the world.

As early morning light filtered through the curtains, I did something I'd never done before: I called in sick.

Lovesick counted as an illness, right? It had to be legit, because the way I felt was downright disturbing. Every time I thought about my numbered days with Estelle, my stomach felt like it was in knots.

I sent a text to Steve.

> **Me:** I'm not feeling well and I don't think I'll be able to film today.
>
> **Steve:** Are you serious? How bad is it?
>
> **Me:** Remember the food poisoning you got while we were working with the cat who wouldn't stop eating clothes?
>
> **Steve:** Good God, do I ever.

I could almost imagine his sour expression at the reminder of the time he and half the crew got lunch from a taco van in Arizona. They were out of commission for two days.

I wasn't asking for much—all I wanted was twenty-four uninterrupted hours with Estelle.

> **Steve:** I guess we'll have to do as much as we can without you today. We can get more interviews done.

Shit.

> **Me:** I think Estelle's sick too. She and I ordered food from the same takeout place last night.
>
> **Steve:** Damn it. We're going to be set back a whole day.
>
> **Me:** If I feel better this afternoon, I'll try to do a couple follow-up visits with the adoptees.

The suggestion wasn't a lie. Going to see Cindy at Nikki's would make Estelle's day, and I'd get to see my family. Win-win.

> **Steve:** Okay. I'll let everyone know.

Shifting, Estelle sighed. I wondered if my movements had woken her, but when I looked down, her eyes were still closed, those long lashes resting against her cheeks. Her breathing evened out before hitching again.

I set the phone back on the nightstand and held her

tighter.

She let out a quiet moan, her hand clenching, digging her fingernails into my chest. Her hips jerked slightly, causing her soft pussy to rub against my thigh. Another whimper followed a gasp.

A sex dream? Fuck yes.

My morning wood became a raging hard-on. What was happening inside that pretty little head of hers? Was it me between her legs? I sure as shit hoped so.

"Emruffft." She sighed. My name on her lips wasn't fully formed. Close enough, though. It told me what I needed to know—she was dreaming about me.

Estelle's thigh came up, crossing over the lower half of my body. Smooth skin caressed my balls.

"Fuck," I whispered, my erection trapped between her leg and my stomach.

Estelle let out a long humming noise before climbing on top of me. Wild hair covered my chest and she buried her face by my neck.

As her breathing evened out again, every inhale made her body rock back and forth, and my dick grazed her slick entrance.

Fuuuuck.

She wiggled her hips and the tip slipped inside her heat.

That woke her up.

Although she didn't lift her head, her body went rigid and her breaths came faster. I ran a hand down her back to let her know I was awake too. I was a little bit sad that our unexpected morning playtime had to end.

Only it didn't end.

Instead of moving off me, she tilted her hips up then

pushed down. She was so wet that I slid easily through her tight pussy until my dick was buried halfway inside.

The sensation was so intense, a string of whispered swear words left my mouth, but I had no idea what I was saying. I'd never been inside someone bare before, and it eclipsed every thought I had inside my brain.

I didn't even realize I had shut my eyes until Estelle whispered, "Emery, look at me."

I did as she said.

And seeing her hovering over me—hair mussed up from sleep, pupils dilated—made my heart thump.

Brushing the hair out of her face, I rubbed her cheek with my thumb and whispered, "Hey, beautiful. I see you."

Her mouth dropped open and she blinked. "You're still here."

My lips quirked up. "We're playing hooky today."

"Really?" Smiling, she shifted slightly, causing the most unbelievable friction on my cock.

"Estelle." I licked my lips and tried to form coherent words. "No condom."

Biting her lip, she appeared conflicted. "I've never had sex without one. It feels different. Like, really-fucking-good different."

"Yeah," I grunted as she swiveled her hips, pushing me deeper. "So fucking good."

"Your skin is so hot… so smooth." Her walls clenched around me.

I gasped. "Shit. I don't want to stop."

She stilled. "Neither do I. I have an IUD. And I'm clean. You?"

I nodded.

"And—" Estelle hesitated, glancing away.

Placing my finger under her chin, I tilted her face toward me. "And what?"

"And we're not with anyone else, right? We're monogamous." Her cheeks pinked. "For the time being, I mean."

Maybe it was a good time to have that talk. The one where I told her she was mine and I was hers, end of discussion.

"Estelle, I don't want anyone else," I stated, my tone certain.

"Okay." She gave me a naughty smile. Then she began to move, and any speech I could have prepared about all the ways we'd be good together flew out the window.

Letting out a long groan, my back bowed off the bed as my fingers dug into her hips.

I felt everything. Her heat, her slickness, her silky walls gliding over every inch of my dick. It was too much.

"Baby," I rasped. "Oh, shit. You're so fucking good."

She kissed my neck. "Tell me when you're gonna come, okay?"

Making a sound of agreement, I nodded.

It was the first time she'd ever been on top. I loved being the one in control, but this was awesome.

I let her ride me. Let her use my body. Her nipples grazed my chest as she ground herself on me, rubbing her clit on my pelvic bone.

I palmed fistfuls of her ass, completely lost in her.

So wet.

Hot.

Tight.

So fucking intimate.

I wanted this. Just her skin and mine. We were completely connected. From now on, I didn't want any barriers between us.

Sitting up, Estelle's arm went behind her and she lightly grabbed my balls. My hips jerked.

I pressed the heel of my palm to her clit. I needed her to get there. Now.

Estelle rocked faster until her body stiffened above me. Throwing her head back, she let out a strangled moan. Even as her orgasm subsided, she didn't slow her pace and I couldn't hold back any longer.

"Now," I grunted. "I'm gonna come."

I was about to roll us over so I could pull out and come on her stomach, but she lifted off me. Quickly scooting down my body, she sucked my cock into her mouth.

My hand went to her hair and my hips bucked, fucking the inside of her warm mouth. I came with a shout as I watched her swallow my cum down.

Shocked, I gaped at her. Panting. Speechless.

"That was so much fun." She sat up with a naughty grin, primly wiping at the corners of her mouth.

Holy fuck, she was dirty.

Calling in sick was one of the best decisions I'd made in a long time.

Chapter 19

Estelle

"This is Nikki's place," Emery said, pointing to the two-story suburban home at the end of the cul-de-sac.

Parking my jeep out front, I observed the immaculate lawn, the cute blue shutters, and a couple chairs on the wraparound porch. Four pumpkins sat outside the door, and I couldn't help noticing one had a cat face carved in it. I caught a flash of light-orange fur in the bay window.

"This house is adorable." I smiled. "Cindy's got it made."

"I'm sure she's having the time of her life," Emery agreed.

As we walked up the front steps, I couldn't help feeling overwhelmed.

This was the second time Emery was taking me to a family event. Not exactly something you do in a fuck-buddy arrangement.

And he wasn't shy about being affectionate, even when we were in public. He was constantly holding my hand and finding ways to touch me. It seemed like now that the cameras weren't around, he wasn't holding back at all.

Honestly, it scared the shit out of me.

Everything about us was starting to feel real. Too real.

I couldn't fall for a TV star. Out of all the stupid, crazy things I'd done in my life, that would be at the top of the list.

"You okay?" Emery asked before ringing the doorbell. "Nervous about seeing Cindy?"

I shook my head.

"What is it then? You're walking all stiff." His eyes scanned my body and he lowered his voice. "You didn't put on underwear for this, did you? Honestly, it's not worth the wedgie. No one would know if you were going commando."

Laughing, I shoved at his shoulder. "Be serious. Of course I'm not wearing panties."

He let out a sexy growl. "Of course not."

Stepping closer, his hand gripped my waist before his thumb slipped under my white sweater. The goosebumps on my skin had nothing to do with the chill in the air.

The moment was broken when the door swung open and Lizzie came flying out.

"Uncle E!" she squealed, launching herself at Emery. He caught her and gave her a big bear hug until she complained through giggles that she couldn't breathe.

What was it about seeing men with kids that was such a turn on? It was like a mainline straight to my libido.

Then again, everything Emery did was sexy. It was becoming a problem, just like my too-real feelings for him.

After getting inside, Cindy greeted me with a sniff and a purr before curling up on Lizzie's lap. Emery introduced me to Nikki's husband, Tom. Tall and lanky, with glasses and reddish hair, he had an endearing geeky vibe. It totally matched up with the fact that he was a sixth-grade science teacher.

Nikki hooked her arm with mine. "Estelle, would you like to help me in the kitchen?"

Uh-oh. I knew what that meant. Clearly, that was woman-code for 'I'd like to talk to you alone.'

"Sure," I agreed reluctantly.

She'd seemed super nice last week at my apartment, but that was before Emery and I were involved.

Nikki gave me the task of putting together the salad while she sliced a ham she'd gotten out of the oven.

I thought maybe she would immediately start grilling me about what my intentions were with her baby brother, but she didn't. We were working side by side when she spoke.

"I just wanted to take a second to thank you for Cindy."

"You're welcome." I scooped up the chopped tomatoes and dumped them into the bowl. "But it's me who should be thanking you."

"A cat with a cleft lip." Nikki laughed lightly, shaking her head. "What are the odds, huh? As you can imagine, Lizzie is self-conscious about her appearance. Having a friend who's just like her has done wonders for her self-esteem."

"You have no idea how happy I am to hear that. It's like they were meant for each other."

"Speaking of meant for each other," she started, "he likes you a lot."

"Who does?" I knew exactly who she was talking about.

"My brother."

"Oh. Yeah, he's really great," I said, proud of myself for not adding *in bed* at the end of that sentence. I didn't think his sister would appreciate the joke.

"I mean, he *really* likes you. As in, completely crazy about you."

As much as her statement made my heart flutter, I frowned. "I don't think it's like that. He was very upfront about not wanting a relationship. Besides, he's not here for very long."

"I'm telling you, I know my brother," she insisted as she wiped down the counter. "It's the way he looks at you. He used to look at Lizzie McGuire like that."

I laughed. "What?"

"That Disney show." Her smile mirrored my own as she threw the dish rag down and faced me. "He would totally kill me for telling you this, but I can't resist. When he was, like, nine years old, he was so obsessed with that show. I'm talking posters on the bedroom wall. Of course, he grew out of that phase by the time he was a teenager, but I made fun of him for years. It was a bit of a running joke between us when I named my daughter Elizabeth. He thought I'd done it just to torture him forever."

"That's pretty funny," I told her, going back to cutting up a cucumber.

We worked silently for a minute and I thought the conversation was over, but Nikki was relentless.

"Emery brought you to see our dad," she said, and I was reminded of the way Emery had looked at me when he said I was the first woman he'd ever introduced to his father.

Alarm bells went off in my head, shouting at me to deny, deny, deny.

I shook my head. "He was planning to go there anyway, and we were already hanging out, so…"

"Did he tell you about how Dad ended up at Windsor Lakes?"

I nodded. "He told me the basics."

"The nursing home he started out at… It wasn't a good place. Fortunately, he wasn't there for long. I remember the exact moment Emery and I realized we couldn't let our dad stay there anymore. There was an old woman in a wheel chair, trying to make it down the hall on her own. She seemed so lost. When a nurse walked by, the woman reached out to her and said, 'I want to go home.' The nurse just patted her hand and said, 'Oh, honey. You are home.'"

"What did the woman say then?"

"She just said, 'Oh' and looked down at her lap. I'd never seen someone look so devastated and defeated in all my life. It's one of the saddest things I've ever witnessed. As we were leaving that day, Emery told me he was getting Dad out of there. Three days later, he made a payment to Windsor Lakes."

"Using his college fund," I filled in.

"Yep." Her voice was clipped.

"Why do I get the feeling you weren't happy about

that?"

Letting out a sigh, she leaned back against the counter. "Because I wasn't. I know there wasn't any other way, though. If Emery hadn't done what he did, our dad would still be in that place, miserable. Maybe he wouldn't even be alive today. Emery saved his life."

"Your brother is an amazing person. And he is successful—like, epically successful. He's smart, he's got money, he's good-looking, and he freaking loves cats." I ticked the list off on my fingers. "Emery could have anyone he wanted."

"Then I would consider yourself pretty lucky." Smiling, she gave my shoulder a squeeze. "And just keep in mind—when Emery wants something, he goes after it."

If everything Nikki said was true, I was in deep shit.

Chapter 20

Emery

So there I was, totally kicking ass at strip poker with five cats as witnesses. You know, just a typical Monday night.

Winning was awesome, but the drawback? Being forced to sit across from a very naked Estelle while concentrating on my cards at the same time.

An extremely difficult task.

"Okay." Estelle sighed dramatically, and the action made her tits jiggle. Standing up, she hooked a finger into the one sock she had left. She tossed the white scrap of material to the pile of clothes on the kitchen floor, then sat back down in her chair. "I guess I really suck at this game."

"You won a few hands," I offered, pointing to my bare upper half.

Honestly, she wasn't terrible. I was down to my

boxers and socks. Tossing my three-of-a-kind down, I started gathering the cards.

While I was distracted by Estelle's nudity, Carol jumped up onto the table and swatted at my sweet tea. I tried the catch the cup before it tipped over, but failed. A good amount of the liquid spilled, soaking some of the cards and running onto Estelle's lap.

"Cold!" she shrieked, standing up. "Very, very cold. I'll go grab a towel."

As she took off down the hall, I watched her luscious ass bounce with every move.

I snagged a small rag from the counter and started cleaning the mess on the table. Satisfied with the mayhem she'd caused, Carol leapt to the floor and sauntered away. Didn't even stick around to watch the aftermath of her destruction.

Estelle came back with a towel for the floor and a towel around her body.

"Hey, no fair," I complained.

She gave me the stink-eye as she knelt down. "It's freezing in here."

She was right. Mike had insisted on having outdoor time, so she'd left the balcony door open for him to go in and out as he pleased. The night air seeping in was pretty fucking cold.

I flipped some of the cards over to dry them off, and I sputtered in disbelief when I saw Estelle's hand.

"You had a flush?" I asked incredulously.

"Oh, is that good?" Widening her eyes to the point of comical, she gazed up at me, trying to play it off like she hadn't just lost on purpose.

"Uh-uh. You're not fooling me. I know that look,

Estelle." Shaking my head, I laughed. "You're the only person I've ever met who'd intentionally lose at strip poker. That's cheating, you know."

"Only on a couple of the hands. I wanted to get to the naked part."

"You're a piece of work." I snickered. *My crazy girl.* "I demand a rematch."

"All right, one more hand, but not for clothes this time," she bargained as she finished cleaning up the tea. "My nips are so hard they could cut glass."

I barked out a laugh at her crass comment. "Upping the stakes. I like it. What are we playing for?"

"If you lose, you have to fuck me in the shower."

I slapped the deck down on the table and held up my hands in surrender. "I fold."

Looking amused, she sat back down in her seat. "*And* you have to ride my bike—"

"Tricycle," I corrected, earning a scowl.

"—all around the neighborhood. And after you experience its gloriousness, you'll have to admit that it's far superior to traditional bikes."

"That's two things," I told her.

"Okay, I take the first one off the table then."

"Let's not be hasty, now," I said, backpedaling. "You drive a hard bargain, but I think I can accept it."

She giggled. "What are your terms?"

I didn't hesitate with my answer. "If I win, you have to go on a date with me this weekend. I want to take you to the beach."

Even if I didn't win, I'd still insist on taking her there. It would be the perfect setting to bring up the topic of continuing our relationship beyond my time here.

A grin pulled at Estelle's lips. "That sounds like a daytrip, not a date."

"It is what it is."

"Do I get to drive?"

"That depends." I crossed my arms. "Are you gonna rap on the way?"

"You bet your ass."

"Eminem this time?"

"Sure." She shrugged.

"Then you've got yourself a deal." As I shuffled the somewhat damp cards, I noticed Estelle was studying me, nibbling her bottom lip. "What?"

"I was just wondering why you don't talk with an accent." She cocked her head to the side. "Nikki does. Your dad, too."

"My producers thought I'd be more relatable without it."

"I think it would be sexy."

"Darlin', you have the best sweet tea on this side of the Mississippi," I drawled, laying it on extra thick.

Estelle threw her head back and laughed.

Just then, my phone rang. It was a number I didn't recognize, but it was local. "Hello?"

"Uh, yes, Emery? This is Agatha."

"Hey." I smiled, trapping the phone between my shoulder and my ear so I could continue shuffling the deck. "I take it you're calling about a certain cat?"

Estelle stilled, her eyes questioning.

"I am, and I'm so excited," Agatha replied. "When can I come see her?"

"When are you available?"

"I have tomorrow morning off. I could come around

eight."

"That would be perfect," I told her. "We'll see you then."

I dropped the phone to the table.

"I meant to tell you earlier," I said to Estelle. "One of the employees at Windsor Lakes is interested in Carol."

"Oh, that's great." Her face turned skeptical. "Are you sure she wants Carol?"

I nodded. "She used to have an annoying cat. Apparently she misses having her toilet paper shredded."

Grinning, Estelle hiked a shoulder. "Whatever floats her boat."

I gave her a smile, but it was forced.

We'd had such a great day together, but Agatha's call reminded me that reality awaited us tomorrow. I should've been ecstatic about another adoption, but it meant I was one step closer to being done in Remington.

Earlier, Estelle had been the main source of entertainment at Nikki's while we ate dinner, telling stories about the cats and her costume shop. When she told us about the time in eighth grade when she dressed up as the rapper Flavor Flave and paraded around her classes with a blowup doll as her date—which landed her ass in detention for a week—we all thought it was hilarious. Tom laughed so hard Sprite came out of his nose.

I was in awe of how effortlessly Estelle fit into my life here. How easily she got along with my family. How quickly she'd managed to work her way into my heart.

But what if she turned me down at the beach? How could I possibly convince her that we could make it work when I was a thousand miles away and she hated flying on planes? Why couldn't we have met at a different time in my life, when I could settle down in this city full-time?

Pushing down the tightness in my chest, I dealt the cards.

My hand was shit. After exchanging three of the lowest numbers, it was still shit.

I glanced up at Estelle. Looking down at what she had, her lips twitched. It was her tell—she had something good.

I could've folded and asked for new cards.

I could've walked away, but giving up on a losing hand had never been my style.

Chapter 21

Emery

Pussy-whipped for sure.

That was the only explanation for why I was staring down at 'The Flying Purple People Eater' at six o'clock in the morning. Estelle didn't waste any time cashing in on that bet, and it was time to pay up.

She handed me a hot pink helmet. "Now, before you go on the ride of a lifetime, I need to tell you why this bike is awesome."

"Still a trike, Estelle."

She let out a cute growl. "First, it has three wheels, which means I don't have to balance. My core strength isn't up to par, and there's, like, zero chance of falling over on this thing."

"My core strength is fine," I announced cockily. She ignored me.

"Second, look at this seat." She patted the black

foam, which was at least a foot wide. Then she picked up a large, oddly shaped piece of cardboard. "I know this looks like a giant upside-down ball sac," she said, making me laugh, "but it's not. This is the actual size of my ass when I'm sitting down."

I laughed even harder, clutching my burning abs and questioning my claim about having great core strength. "You mean to tell me you sat down on that and traced your butt?"

"I needed it to be accurate for the demonstration." Placing the cutout over a standard-sized seat on a bike next to hers, she pointed at the massive size difference. "Can you see why sitting on something that's literally the width of a pop can would be uncomfortable for me?"

"I didn't hear you complaining last night," I quipped, snickering at my own crude joke.

She smacked me with the cardboard ass.

"And third, look at this basket." Sweeping her hand through the air, she made a big deal of the large metal crate between the two back wheels. "It's great for hauling all kinds of cargo."

Sighing, I straddled the seat. I didn't want to admit out loud that it was the most comfortable bike seat I'd ever sat on, but damn. "Is this memory foam?"

"It is." She grinned.

"How far do I have to go?"

"To the gas station."

Dismayed, I let out an obnoxious scoff. "That's almost a mile."

She ignored me again. "While you're there, can you pick up some more Rocky Road ice cream for me? I'm hungry." Following up with a sweet smile, she leaned down to give me a peck on the cheek. "You look adorable, by the way."

Shaking my head, I chuckled. "Unbelievable."

By the time I got back, filming was already underway. Taking a day off had set us back, which was exactly what I wanted, but it seemed Steve was hell-bent on making up for lost time.

He stopped me in the apartment hallway outside Estelle's door. "Yesterday I made some calls to the shelter."

My eyebrows shot up because he usually left that stuff to me. "You did?"

"We've got three potential families coming to see Mike today."

"Wow, uh…" Why couldn't he be this motivated all the time? "That's a lot of traffic coming through the apartment. And Mike hasn't been cleared for the UTI yet."

Waving a hand dismissively, he said, "Just send some crystals home with them."

"It's not that easy."

Obviously, he had no idea how much detail went into the adoptions. It wasn't like we just found anyone off the street and gave them a cat. I investigated the families first. There was a screening process and paperwork. I needed to make sure they were serious about providing a loving home and that they weren't just in it to get their fifteen minutes of fame.

"Make it that easy." He shrugged. "They're getting a free cat."

He was such a jackass. There was no point in arguing with him, so I walked away, knowing I'd do whatever I damn well pleased. To hell with what he wanted.

As soon as I got into the apartment, my eyes went straight to Estelle. She was by the kitchen sink, filling a new pitcher full of water. Probably about to make a new batch of sweet tea.

Grinning, I held up the pint of her ice cream before stashing it in the freezer. Then I went into the living room where Agatha was on the couch with Carol, Alice, and Bobby.

"I wish I could take them all." She beamed up at me.

"You'd have to fight Estelle for these two," I joked, pointing at Alice and Bobby.

It wasn't until I sat down that I realized I was getting weird looks from pretty much everyone in the apartment. Well, everyone except for Estelle, who was silently laughing her ass off in the kitchen.

"What?" I glanced around.

"Did you go for a ride this morning?" Agatha snickered.

"Yeah… Why?"

She pointed at my head. "I like your helmet. Pink's a good color on you."

Shit. I'd forgotten I was still wearing it. Shooting a half-hearted glare at Estelle, I undid the clasp under my chin and took it off. She came into the living room carrying an armful of small plastic shot glasses.

"A little early to be hitting the bottle, don't you think?" I teased.

Rolling her eyes, she started lining them up on the coffee table. "I'm giving Agatha a demonstration."

Now it was my turn for an eye roll. "Another demonstration?" I turned to Agatha. "Estelle's demonstrations tend to end with someone wearing a pink bike helmet, riding around town on a tricycle."

"It's a *bike*," Estelle hissed.

Amused, Agatha chuckled at our banter, but her laughter was cut short when Carol began swatting at the shot glasses, knocking them to the floor one by one.

"See?" Estelle shrugged. "I can't have candles or decorations." She pointed at the yellow flowers. "That vase? It's glued to the table. I just want you to understand what you're getting yourself into."

Agatha raised her eyebrows in challenge. "You think this is bad? Mitzy would only drink out of the toilet. It was her only source of hydration."

"That's pretty gross." Estelle's face screwed up. "But while we're on the subject of bathrooms, Carol will only sleep in a sink. You might have an issue if you want to brush your teeth or wash your hands."

"Mitzy used to climb the walls. Literally," Agatha countered. "I had claw marks all over the drywall."

As the two women got into a contest about whose cat was worse, I sat back and watched with a smile on my face.

Scoffing, Agatha leaned forward and scooped Carol into her lap. "Oh, and we can talk about bathrooms some more. Mitzy used to tear up my toilet paper and leave it all over the apartment."

Standing up, Estelle laughed. "Follow me."

Joel and I traipsed after the women and hovered outside the bathroom. Estelle held up the tissue container that housed her toilet paper.

"That's why I got this. Carol does the same thing. If you want her, I'll even let you have it. I wouldn't have a reason to keep it anymore." Her fingers curled around the yellow plastic, a flicker of sadness seeping through.

Agatha nodded. "I want her. And I'll love her. I promise I'll give her a good home."

Estelle's forlorn expression filled with happiness. "I know you will."

"I REALLY LIKE this one, Dad." One of the nine-year-old twin boys looked up at his parents from the floor as he dangled a bird toy in front of Mike.

This was the third family from the applicants Steve had chosen and they were my favorites so far.

I liked that they had children. Not every cat did well in a family with young kids, but Mike had a lot of energy. If he was going to be happy living indoors, he'd need constant stimulation.

"It says on your application you have a screened-in porch?" I asked. Because of Mike's specific needs, creating the illusion of being outside was important for his well-being.

"On the back of the house, yeah," Mr. Carter

answered. "We spend a lot of time out there."

"We also have a large bay window where he could sit and watch the neighborhood," Mrs. Carter added, scratching Mike behind the ear. "He can be our guard cat."

The boys laughed.

Estelle and I locked eyes, and an unspoken communication passed between us—the Carter family was perfect.

At this point, I was pretty sure most of the crew knew about Estelle and me; we hadn't exactly been covert about it today. The sexual tension was impossible to miss.

After Agatha left with Carol, I almost kissed Estelle in front of Joel during active filming. Showing her affection was just natural and automatic. I'd been a few inches from her face when I realized what I was doing, then I tried to play it off like she had a piece of fuzz in her hair.

But I didn't want to hide anymore. Part of me wanted the whole world to know she was mine, no matter what the consequences were.

And no way in hell was I spending one more night in that RV.

"We'll need to keep Mike for one more night," I told the Carters. "He needs to be tested for a possible UTI before he can come home with you. Once he gets medically cleared, he's all yours."

The parents grinned as their kids cheered. Mike showed his enthusiasm by chewing on one of the twin's shoelaces.

A loud hacking sound came from Steve. He sent a look that said, 'absolutely-fucking-not.' I sent one back that said, 'fuck you. I'm doing it my way.'

"You all right there, buddy?" I asked him, pretending to be concerned. "If you need something to drink, I recommend Estelle's homemade sweet tea."

Mike staying one more night wasn't hindering the process, and I refused to send him out the door without a clean bill of health.

Obviously pissed that I'd gone against his wishes, and that I was being a smartass, Steve stormed out of the room. Good riddance.

But I didn't like the look he sent me before he walked out the door. Because that one said, 'I'm going to get back at you for this.'

Chapter 22

Emery

FUCKING PETER. I'D spent the last couple of days searching for the right owner, but he didn't like anyone. The level of distain he had for people was surprising even to me, and I'd seen a lot of crazy shit during my career.

Three out of the four people who had come to meet him ended up leaving the apartment with a big 'hell no.' And the fourth was just too polite to say it.

I had no idea how I was going to find him a home.

He'd spent the past two nights isolated with the crystal box, but we'd gotten nothing from him. Either he was holding it, or he was peeing in the tub just to spite me.

Someone on the crew had been assigned to watching the twenty-four-hour playback from the camera in the cat room—a mind-numbing job—but so far, there'd been no footage of anyone peeing outside of the litter boxes.

Frustrated, I went to the tiny RV bathroom to bandage up my injury from the most recent encounter with Peter.

This morning I thought I was finally getting somewhere with him. He seemed to enjoy my petting until I reached his tail. Then he lost his shit. Apparently that was a no-touch zone, and he let me know it by sinking his claws into the back of my hand.

Mental illness was rare in cats, but it did exist. As much as I hated the idea, I was starting to think a long-term anti-anxiety medication was the only option for him.

The plus side to Peter's dick-ish behavior was getting more time with Estelle.

I should've been upset with our lack of progress, but I'd happily stay at a standstill if it meant I got to spend my days with her. My nights with her. Laughing, talking, fucking. Riding in that death trap she called a Jeep.

Didn't matter what we were doing—if I was with Estelle, I was happy.

My phone buzzed with a text and I pulled it from my pocket.

Estelle: I found the pisser!

Well, I'll be damned.

Since it was Halloween, Estelle was supposed to handle business at the costume shop, and I had planned on making a few well-check visits to the adoptees. But a new development called for some impromptu filming.

I sent a text to Joel.

Me: How fast can you get here?

Joel: Ten

He didn't ask what it was about and he didn't need to. That was Joel—always ready.

Three minutes later, I was freshly showered. I threw on some jeans and my gray T-shirt. Joel rolled into the parking lot shortly after and had the camera on his shoulder in record time.

Just as we made it to the front entrance of the apartment complex, Estelle stumbled out, holding a cat carrier and wearing the most hideous costume I'd ever seen. If she wanted to scare small children, I suspected she was going to succeed.

"What the fuck?" Joel breathed out in horror at the same time I said, "What the hell happened to your eyebrows?"

"Eyebrow stamps," she replied, waggling the brown caterpillar shapes. "I'm a crazy cat lady for Halloween and I figured someone who spends every waking moment with their cats doesn't have time to tweeze."

I laughed.

My eyes traveled down her body. She wasn't kidding about taking this holiday seriously.

The pink threadbare robe was tied at the waist, bunching around her hips. She had several small stuffed cats pinned to her outfit. She even wore a headband that had a kitten attached, making it look like the animal was clinging to her frizzed-up hair. Instead of shoes, she had on fuzzy cat house slippers. With the over-the-top eyebrows and the smeared red lipstick, she looked nothing short of deranged.

An angry screech came from the carrier, and I peered through the bars. Peter.

"How did you figure out it was him?" I asked, walking back toward the parking lot.

"He peed on the TV remote this morning. Right in front of me. And the worst part? When some of it got on my couch, it was tinted pink, not yellow. That's a bad sign, isn't it?"

Wincing, I gave a nod. "Blood in the urine. Not abnormal with a UTI, though it must be more than just a mild infection if it's changing the color that much."

"I already called the clinic and they're expecting me." The urgency in her tone and her pinched facial expression told me she felt guilty, probably for not figuring out Peter's problem sooner.

"Do you want me to bring him in since you have to work?"

She shook her head. "No. I want to be there for him."

"We'll come with you," I offered, taking the crate from her hands.

After we piled into her Jeep, she pulled a red foam clown nose from the middle console and handed it to me.

"It's just not right for y'all to not be wearing costumes on Halloween," she said, grabbing a bushy glue-on mustache. Reaching for Joel, she halted with her arm halfway stretched between them. "Well, I guess you're already covered in this department." She motioned to her upper lip, then pointed at us. "You guys switch."

And that was how I ended up sporting a '70s porno 'stache in a pink Jeep with a crazy cat lady, a howling feline, and a clown to document it all.

I tossed a glance over my shoulder. "Hold onto your tits, Joel."

Chapter 23

Estelle

"Ms. Winters, while this is a serious procedure, Peter shouldn't have any long-term complications if it's successful." The middle-aged woman delivered the news with a reassuring smile.

We'd been at the clinic for over an hour while Peter was sedated for an exam, X-rays, and other tests. The diagnosis: He had the worst case of bladder stones the doctor had ever seen in a cat so young. Our only option was to have them surgically removed.

"How did this happen?" I asked, distraught.

Emery put his hand on my knee in a comforting gesture, probably because he could tell I was one step away from losing it. My chin trembled, and I blinked rapidly to keep the tears at bay.

"It could be genetics combined with the fact that his urethra is quite narrow, which is usually the case with male cats. When an infection persists for a long period of time, crystal formations can build up in the bladder, and that's how stones are made."

My face flushed, but unlike the first day of filming, I didn't have to wonder where the sudden heat was coming from—it was good old-fashioned shame. The truth was, I had no idea how long the infection had been going on. Possibly most of his life.

Swallowing around the lump in my throat, I asked, "What if the stones come back?"

"There's another procedure called perineal urethostomy where we reconstruct the opening of the urethra to make it wider."

I felt the blood drain from my face. "Like, you *reconstruct* his penis? That sounds painful."

"It isn't pleasant," she confirmed. "Let's hope it doesn't come to that. He's young and otherwise healthy. With medication, dietary changes, and monitoring, I think he should bounce back from this fairly quickly."

"Can I see him before I leave?"

The doctor nodded. "Of course. He's still pretty out of it from the anesthesia, though. We'll be performing the surgery as soon as possible, so try to make it a quick visit."

"Emery, can you wait outside for me? Joel too?" I was grateful to have him with me, but I needed a moment alone with Peter.

"Yeah," he said, reaching for me, like he wanted to touch my face. But he thought better of it after a quick glance at the camera and dropped his hand. "We'll be right outside."

The vet tech Emery used to work with led me to

the pre-op room. The walls were stacked with floor-to-ceiling kennels, and several of them were occupied. My nose wrinkled at the strong sterile smell of disinfectant.

"We'll take good care of him," Christine said, stopping outside Peter's cage. "We do the best we can for all our patients, but anyone who's a friend of Emery's gets top priority."

"Thank you. I really appreciate that."

After she left, the tears I'd been trying so hard to hold back finally fell, making hot tracks down my cheeks while I mentally beat myself up over the whole ordeal.

How long had Peter been in pain? He'd been suffering and I didn't even know it. I should've seen it. Looking back, I realized there were signs—the biggest one of all being his irritable personality. Hell, I'd be grumpy too if I had a bladder full of stones.

If only I'd paid more attention. If only I'd fed him the right food. The list of all the ways I could've been a better pet owner went on and on in my mind.

Sticking my fingers through the metal bars, I traced the soft orange stripes on his head as the guilt ate away at me.

"I'm so sorry, Peter. I let you down." I swallowed down a sob and wiped my eyes. "I promise to do better. We'll get you fixed up, and Emery is going to find you the best home ever."

I ripped a paper towel off a nearby roll and blew my nose. Knowing I needed to keep my visit short, I willed away my emotional breakdown while I fanned my face.

Tossing one last look at Peter, I took a deep breath and went out to the lobby. With a shaky hand, I signed the consent form, then shelled out the hefty payment to the receptionist.

I walked out of the double doors in a daze, eyes red-rimmed from crying and still looking like a lunatic in my costume. I pulled my robe tighter, trying to ward off the late-morning chill of the air.

Emery immediately drew me in for a hug, dropping the platonic act we'd both been trying to pull off. I relished in the feel of his strong arms engulfing me, warm and comforting.

This wasn't a simple hug between friends with a pat on the back. This was an embrace—the kind where it was obvious that two people had known each other intimately.

Burying his face in my hair, Emery just held on to me, one hand gripping my waist while the other went to my ass.

Yeah, definitely not platonic.

I was vaguely aware of Joel's presence, but when I glanced over Emery's bicep, he was sitting on a bench with his camera down while pretending to look the other way. I knew I liked that guy.

"My poor baby." I sniffled. "Peter had an infection for months? No wonder he was pissed. No pun intended. I'm the worst cat owner ever."

Cupping my jaw, Emery forced my eyes up to his. "Don't be so hard on yourself. UTIs and behavioral issues are extremely common in cats, and the two don't necessarily go hand in hand. These things happen all the time."

"I just wanna go home," I murmured, burying my face in his chest. "But I can't. Today is the busiest day of the year at the shop."

"I'll go with you," he offered.

Surprised, my gaze bounced up to his face again. "You will?"

"Yeah. Well, I don't know anything about costumes, and I might just be in the way… But if you want me there, I'm there."

I grinned wide. "I want you there."

Just then, a white news van drove by at a snail's pace before hitting their brakes.

"Shit," Emery breathed out, stepping back. "I'm surprised it took them this long to track me down."

"Maybe because you chopped off your man bun," I wondered out loud. "Or because no one gives a damn about Meemaw's Rodeo and Cattle Show."

Clearly bothered by being found, he raked a hand through his hair. "I wonder if someone inside the clinic tipped them off. Christine wouldn't do that… but anyone else would."

"Is it paparazzi?"

"No, just some local press. But paparazzi won't be far behind once they give away my location." Emery didn't take his eyes off the van. The sliding doors opened and two female reporters emerged with a camera man close behind. "You and Joel go wait in the Jeep. I'll handle it."

"Mr. Matheson! How does it feel to be back in your hometown? Are you here for personal or professional reasons?" The questions started immediately. Those people were hungry for a story.

Emery strode confidently across the grass, meeting them halfway, and I climbed into the Jeep. I watched in fascination at how cool and calm he seemed when he answered.

"Filming for season three is underway," he said vaguely. "Unfortunately, I can't tell you anything about the case we're working on because I'm under a confidential agreement. Be sure to tune in on January third to see the most dramatic season yet."

"We noticed you got a new haircut," they persisted. "And the mustache is interesting. Are you starting a new trend?"

His hand went to the hair above his lips that he'd obviously forgotten about. I snorted and Joel let out an amused chuckle.

"Who's the woman with you? Do you have a new relationship to report?"

"You'll have to excuse me," he said politely with a parting wave. "I've got pussies to tame."

One of the women blatantly stared at his ass as he walked away, and I had the sudden urge to go over there and punch her in the face.

That would be one hell of a headline: Catfight of the Century! Reporter Gets Mauled by Crazed Pussy Tamer Fangirl.

Deciding it wasn't worth it, I stayed put.

A second later, Emery got into the passenger seat and sighed. "They're going to follow us, I guarantee it." He nodded his head toward the crew hurrying back to the van.

One of the women got her stiletto stuck in the grass and almost fell. I smiled, because I'm kind of a bitch like that.

"I can lose them," I said confidently.

"I'm sure." Emery braced himself by grabbing the door handle. "But I'd like to live to see another day."

"I take it I'm supposed to hold onto my tits again?" Joel piped up from the backseat.

Cranking up the radio, I laughed. "Definitely."

Chapter 24

Emery

"A DRAG QUEEN? Really, Estelle?"

"Hush. You look pretty."

We were in her small office at the back of the shop. Just like her apartment, splashes of yellow decorated the tiny space in the form of wispy curtains over the window, a picture frame above the desk showcasing the two Estelles side by side, and a canary paperweight holding down a stack of wrinkled papers.

I could hear the commotion of customers outside of the door—footsteps, voices chattering about what to wear, and kids yelling. It was a warzone out there, and I was about to walk out in the craziest costume ever.

Estelle had been right about losing the reporters. Those high-speed police chases I'd seen on TV had nothing on her. If there was one good thing that came from her reckless driving, it was her ability to make people want to avoid her on the road as much as possible.

And if there was one good thing about being dressed up like a hooker celebrating every holiday all rolled into one, it was watching Estelle's face while she made me 'pretty.'

While she was concentrating on getting my look just right, I had a front row seat to every expression she wasn't even aware of.

When she applied the foundation, her tongue poked out between the right side of her lips. When she put on my blush, her nose scrunched up. When she did my eyes, a wrinkle appeared between her caterpillar eyebrows.

So fucking cute.

A blond strand came loose from her kitty headband, but she didn't bother to move it out of the way. "Don't tell me you've never wanted to wear makeup."

"I do wear makeup for the promotional shoots," I pointed out.

She shook her head slightly, being very careful to keep her hand steady as she applied a bright blue eyeshadow above my fake lashes. "Doesn't count, because then it looks like you're not wearing any."

I tucked the rogue piece of hair behind her ear. "I thought that was the point of makeup."

Twisting her lips to the side, she gave me a look. "No."

"Nikki used to put me in all her dresses when I was too little to have an opinion about it. How about that?"

"Didn't happen unless I see pictures as proof," she quipped. "There." Sitting back to admire her work, she picked up a small mirror and some bright pink lipstick. She handed them out to me. "I'll let you finish."

I held up the mirror.

"Holy shit," I barked at my reflection, turning my face to view all angles. The wig she'd put on me was the same pink as the lipstick. "I don't even recognize myself."

"That's the point. No one will know it's you."

"I can't believe I'm doing this," I grumbled before clumsily coating my mouth with the obnoxious hue. "I'm drawing the line at panty hose and heels, though."

Frowning at the long, silky, cream-colored dress she'd put me in, she nodded. "No one will be looking at your boots."

I huffed out a laugh. "That's for sure."

Estelle pulled a small blue binder from the top drawer of the wooden desk and opened it to the front laminated page.

"I think you'll be the most useful helping people find things. For example, if they're looking for an adult animal costume"—she flipped the page—"they'll find them in this section on the second floor. And the kids' costumes are here," she said, pointing to a yellow square.

The color-coded sheet was a map of the entire store. In alphabetical order.

"Wow, this is crazy organized," I praised. "Makes it easy for me."

"I have it on good authority you're familiar with the location of the dressing rooms." Estelle snickered and threw me a wink.

My cock twitched at the reminder. At least my dress would hide my boner.

"Hats and gloves are here—"

"Estelle." I took the binder from her hands and stood up. "No worries. I've got it. You go do your thing."

"Thank you." Beaming, she raised up on her tiptoes and pressed her lips to mine, making a noise when she realized some of the pink transferred to her mouth. Rubbing her lips together, she glanced at the mirror. "Perfect."

"One more," I demanded, bending to give her a soft kiss. I wanted to mark her all over. Instead, I made a shooing motion with my hand.

Estelle opened the door, and the mayhem was unreal. I caught sight of the checkout line that wrapped halfway around the front room.

Adjusting my chiffon collar, I took a deep breath.

It was time to go out there and be the best drag queen ever.

"How does it feel to be down to these two?" I gestured to Alice on Estelle's lap and Bobby on mine.

"Strange," she replied, ignoring whatever was on TV. "But I'm happy for everyone who found homes. I'm worried about Peter, though."

"Try not to be. Think of it as a good thing. This explains a lot about his behavior, and I bet he'll be happier now."

It was 10 p.m. and we were both exhausted. The craziness at the shop had finally died down around six because of parties and trick or treating.

But the entire building looked like a bomb had gone

off in there. We'd picked up as much as we could, trying to put all the costumes back in the right places, but it was a lost cause.

Around eight, Estelle suggested we go back to her place and drink. I whole-heartedly agreed.

"I like you like this," I said, grinning at her post-shower bedtime look. She'd chosen to wear one of my T-shirts with pink cat pajama pants. Estelle always looked beautiful, but her natural state was my favorite. Softer. More vulnerable.

"Like what?" Scoffing, she self-consciously touched the still-wet ponytail on top of her head. "You mean the hot mess I've got going on right now?"

"You look good with no makeup."

She grinned wickedly. "That's funny, because I was about to tell you how much I loved that mascara on you today."

Amused, I grunted. "The things I do for you."

"I'm so grateful for your help today." Estelle's face got serious. "With Peter and the shop."

I responded with a kiss and playfully tweaked her chin.

"Out of all the cats, what makes Alice and Bobby so special?" I asked, trying to keep her mind off Peter. "Why do you want to keep them?"

Smiling, Estelle ran a hand down Alice's back. "Bobby and I bonded during all the bottle feeding. He'd always stick around to snuggle afterward. He used to fall asleep in my hoodie pocket."

"And Alice? I assumed it was because you had her first."

Estelle shook her head. "I can see why you'd think

that, but no. Alice gives backrubs."

"What?"

"Here, watch." Removing Alice from her lap, Estelle got down on the floor, lying flat on her stomach. She made some kissy noises at Alice. The cat jumped down, climbed onto Estelle's back, then started kneading the muscles with her paws. Letting out a sigh, Estelle gave me a cheeky grin.

"You've been holding out on me," I grumped, slightly offended. "Where are my backrubs?"

She laughed.

Just then, something on the TV caught my attention.

"*… tamer might have a new love interest,*" the woman said as a picture of Estelle and I appeared on the screen. "*We have this steamy shot of the pair sharing a romantic moment and some Halloween shenanigans outside of an animal hospital in Emery Matheson's hometown. An inside source says the woman is Estelle Winters, a cat hoarder he met on the set of season three of The Pussy Tamer.*"

Without taking her eyes off the screen, Estelle took the seat next to me on the couch again.

"*A cat hoarder?*" the guy next to her chimed in. "*That sounds pretty crazy.*"

"*It sure does. Has Emery Matheson fallen for the crazy cat lady? Perhaps the pussy tamer has finally met the untamable. Stay tuned to find out.*"

Shit.

The rumors had spread fast. That wasn't even a local channel. It was one of those entertainment networks that had the audacity to call themselves the news.

"Fucking gossip television." Grabbing the remote from the coffee table, I hit the off button and turned toward Estelle.

"We made national news, huh?" She was still looking at the dark screen.

"I'm really sorry. I never wanted this for you." I made a sound of frustration. "It's all my fault."

She shrugged, like it wasn't a big deal. "Well, I guess we don't have to sneak around anymore."

"You're not mad?"

Her eyes flitted my way, worried but not angry. "All they did was insinuate that we're dating. That's not embarrassing—people date. I'd be pissed if they said something that wasn't true, but it's not like we can deny it. And that's nothing compared to the dildo debacle. I can't wait to see what they have to say about that," she said sarcastically.

"This is just the tip of the iceberg," I explained, remorse evident in my tone. "They'll find out things about you. They'll interview old friends and neighbors. They'll be outside your apartment every damn day."

Looking down at her pajama pants, she picked at a loose string. "Well, when you're done here, they won't have a reason to stick around, especially when they realize how boring I am."

My heart actually hurt at how casually she talked about our time together ending.

"Estelle," I started, wanting to tell her how I truly felt—that I was in love with her.

That I had fallen in love with the potty-mouthed, no-panty-wearing, trike-riding, crazy cat lady. Maybe I'd even fallen in love with her a little during that first interview when she talked about bottle feeding her kittens.

But the words got stuck in my throat.

I'd never said I love you to a woman before, and I wanted it to be perfect and special. The beach trip was where my confession needed to happen.

So I just tipped her face toward mine and said, "You're a lot of things, Estelle. But boring isn't one of them."

Chapter 25

Estelle

"I HAVE A problem," I practically shouted at Janice as soon as my ass hit the seat in my office.

I'd called her over to the shop for an emergency session because I couldn't keep quiet about Emery any longer. The post-Halloween disaster upstairs needed tending to, but it would have to wait.

Janice nodded in agreement. "That's quite a crowd you've got out there. I had to bulldoze my way through the reporters just to get to the door."

I waved a dismissive hand because paparazzi were the least of my problems. "I don't really care about them, but since we're on the topic of the news, you probably already know what I'm about to say."

She gave me a small smile. "Well, out with it then."

"I know you don't dabble in the area of sex therapy," I started, anxiously bouncing my leg. "But Emery and

I have been *involved*. To be frank, we've been going at it like rabbits. And now I'm emotionally attached, even though I tried really hard not to let that happen."

"Ah. I see your dilemma. What are you going to do?"

I frowned. "There isn't really anything to do. Next week, he'll be gone."

"What's stopping you from continuing the relationship?"

"It was never supposed to turn into a relationship. We both agreed on that in the beginning."

"But things have changed for you," she said with understanding.

"Yeah." I sighed. "Remember how I promised myself I'd never date someone again if they didn't like me for who I am?"

Her lips thinned. "That's an issue with Emery?"

"No, that's the thing. He really gets me. He's fucking perfect."

"What about Emery's feelings? Do you think things have changed for him too?"

Nodding, I bit my lip. "Maybe. He hasn't come right out and said it, but I think so."

"I'm confused about what the problem is then. Talk it out."

"You say that like it's so easy." I leaned forward, spearing her with a look. "This is Emery Matheson we're talking about."

"And you're Estelle Winters and I'm Janice Hudson. I'm glad we all know who we are," she deadpanned, making me laugh.

Over the past couple of weeks, Janice and I had talked about a lot of things. Every time one of the cats found a new home, she helped me work through my feelings. I'd come to rely on her far too much. Was it sad that my therapist had become my closest friend?

"What am I supposed to do when he's away?" I asked, my voice heavy with sadness and uncertainty. "I'll be all alone."

Leaning forward to match my body language, Janice rested her elbows on her knees. "I know we've talked about this, but I'm going to suggest it again. Form new friendships. Be social. You're way too young to be spending all your time working and hanging out with your cats."

I let out a huff. "I know."

"You should talk to Emery. Confronting the issue head-on is the only way it'll get solved."

She was right. But the thought of bringing up the commitment talk made me feel all hot and twitchy. Hell, maybe Emery would cave first. That was probably the safest bet.

We still had several days together. Hopefully it was enough time for us to figure things out.

Chapter 26

Emery

Since Estelle had damage control to do at the shop, I'd offered to pick Peter up from the hospital. Knowing how cantankerous he could be, I told Christine I didn't mind retrieving him from his cage.

"He's actually been quite docile since coming out of surgery," she said as she led me to the back of the clinic.

"Docile? Really?" I asked and she nodded.

"Kinda sweet too."

Imagine my surprise when I was greeted by a pleasant cat. Not just pleasant, but downright friendly. He rubbed his head against the metal bars and meowed.

Shocked, I glanced around, making sure I didn't have the wrong animal. I opened the cage and ran my hand down his back. Once. Twice. Three times, ending at his tail. Still a happy cat.

"We'll see how you feel about me after this." I picked

him up, being careful of his surgical site.

He purred. Actually purred.

"What, no witty comeback? No 'fuck you, Emery?'"

He answered with a pathetic meow.

"Yeah. I guess almost getting your dick chopped off can change a guy. Tough luck, buddy."

The reconstructive penis surgery the doctor had mentioned as a last resort was cringe-worthy for any male, no matter the species. But given the vast improvement in Peter, I was pretty sure it wouldn't come to that. His new owner would just need to be diligent about keeping him on the right diet.

I gently tied the plastic cone around Peter's neck, then placed him in his carrier.

After getting his go-home instructions, medications, and a new prescription food, I left with a brand-new cat. I brought him back to Estelle's, using the key she gave me to get in.

He got odd looks from Alice and Bobby because of the cone, but after several minutes of sniffing, they finally accepted him as family.

I looked at the time on my phone. Almost 10 a.m. I needed to get moving because I had an appointment with my lawyer. I hadn't mentioned it to Estelle since the day of the 'dildo debacle', but I had plans to follow through on getting her contract checked out.

I just hoped I'd have good news for her.

"Y̲O̲U̲ ̲C̲A̲N̲'̲T̲ ̲A̲I̲R̲ it." I dropped the contract onto the dining table in Steve's hotel room, unable to keep the smug grin off my face.

"Excuse me?" he sneered.

"The dildo footage," I clarified, victoriously pointing at the papers. "Page five. Estelle is a business owner and you can't air anything that could be seen as defamation of character that might impact her financially."

Satisfaction flowed through me when he sputtered, "You took it to a lawyer?"

"You bet your ass I did. If you put that on the show, she would have every right to sue us. You wouldn't want that, would you?"

"Whose side are you on here?"

"The right one. We're here to make people's lives better, not drag them through the mud."

He let out a humorless laugh. "We're here to make good television. To get good ratings. To get people to sit their asses on the couch and watch the fucking show. That is the only purpose."

I shook my head at his callous claim, but he wasn't done yet.

"Oh, you thought it was about making a difference?" he went on. "The sooner you get your head out of the clouds, the better." Taking one more look at the contract, he tossed it down on the table. "Fine. I won't air the footage. Happy now?"

Not exactly, but Estelle would be—that was the most important thing. "Yes."

"Good. Now, if you wouldn't mind, could you get one last interview with Estelle today?" He looked at his Rolex. "I've got a flight to catch at five."

"Last interview?" I asked, confused. "What flight?"

"Rhonda didn't tell you?"

"Tell me what?"

"Today is the last day of filming here. Our next shoot starts on Tuesday. This one's gonna be a doozy. A divorced couple is going through a nasty custody battle over their three cats."

He couldn't be serious.

"Peter just got out of the hospital today." Now it was my turn to sputter. "He needs time to heal and we haven't found him a home yet."

"So?"

"So we haven't finished the job."

Seeming bored, he waved a hand. "We'll do a wrap-up segment where we say Peter found a home and all is well."

Anger bubbled up. "You mean we lie."

He sighed. "Nothing of significance has been filmed in days. We've just been sitting around, waiting for him to find a home. We can't fix them all, okay? We tried. But now we have a new shoot. Deadlines and all that."

"No."

"No? No what?"

"No, I'm not leaving until we're done. I can't let Estelle down."

Steve set his coffee mug down a little harder than necessary and liquid splashed onto the table. "You stay behind, and you're breeching the contract. You're really going to throw this all away for some fling? Come on, Emery. Be smart about this."

"It's not like that."

How could I explain that Estelle wasn't just some

fling? That it wasn't just about fucking a hot client? That she'd come to mean so much to me in such a short amount of time?

Most people wouldn't understand. And Steve, of all people, certainly wouldn't be able to grasp such a concept of falling in love so quickly. My dad used to talk about love at first sight all the time, but as I got older, I thought he was just romanticizing the whirlwind romance he'd had with my mom.

Love that easy couldn't exist.

But it did for me.

I had no idea how Estelle felt. Sometimes she looked at me like I hung the moon, but it was safe to say after I failed and got her evicted, she might not think so highly of me anymore.

Oblivious to how close I was to knocking his lights out, Steve continued, "Listen, I don't care who you bang, as long as it doesn't interfere with the show. In four days, we begin filming the next episode. Which means I need you back in Chicago in two. Everyone else is packing up tomorrow. You had your fun and now it's time to move on."

"Fuck you," I spat the words, slamming my hand on the table. "Why do you have to be such an asshole all the time?"

"Aha!" Grinning, he leaned back in his chair. "There's the attitude you need to have. Why do you always have to be so fucking polite? That good ole boy act you've got going on? It's great for the show. But behind the scenes, you need to have a little more grit."

Grit? Being a spineless prick was what he called grit?

I didn't have anything left to say, so I walked out of

the room before I did something I'd regret.

For a long time, constantly butting heads with Steve had been tiresome and annoying. But I always wanted to believe that deep down, there was a good person under the suits and the rude remarks. That maybe he was just jaded by the business or life in general.

But I was wrong. He was just a selfish, narcissistic asshole.

There were a lot of things I could look past, but leaving Estelle high and dry wasn't one of them.

Maybe I should've had my lawyer look into my contract too. Because right then, I wanted to say to hell with it and quit.

Legally, I was locked in with the network until next summer, and the execs had already mentioned renewing it for another three years. I had always assumed I'd stay on with the show, but maybe that wasn't the best idea.

For the first time in a long time, I didn't have a plan. And I felt completely lost.

I climbed into the van, but I didn't start it up.

Resting my head in my hands, I thought about the conundrum I'd gotten myself into. It was partly my fault we hadn't found homes for all the cats. I'd purposely delayed the process for my own selfish reasons.

And now Estelle might get kicked out of her apartment.

I couldn't let that happen. I'd made her a promise and I intended to keep it.

There was only one solution. Only one way to make things right.

I was going to have to adopt Peter. Not that I was complaining. Sure, we'd had our conflicts, but he seemed pretty loveable now that he felt better.

A text from Estelle let me know she was still at the shop, and this wasn't a conversation I wanted to have on the phone or in public. So, I decided to kill some time at Windsor Lakes.

When I got there, the receptionist told me my dad was resting in his room and I was surprised to find him awake and alert.

Looking up from the encyclopedia—Edition K—he smiled. I smiled back. One of my favorite quirks about my dad was his unusual reading habits. If you asked me, encyclopedias and the dictionary weren't entertainment, but Dad used to tell me he always learned something new, and that was exciting to him.

"Hi," he said, his face lighting up with clear recognition in his eyes.

Good day.

"Hey, Pops." I pulled the chair closer to the bed.

The ballcap he almost always wore was on the bedside table. His salt and pepper hair had been trimmed recently, reminding me of how well he was taken care of.

Closing the book, he set it down next to his hat. "I'm feeling like myself today. They started me on a new medication and I've been told it's working well."

I let out a relieved sigh. "That's great."

"How are things going with your girlfriend?" He didn't waste any time getting right to the good stuff.

"Ah…" I let out an uncomfortable laugh. "I don't know if she'll be my girlfriend for much longer."

The look of tragedy on my dad's face might've been comical if I wasn't so damn upset. "Well, why the hell not?"

"I'm not sure it was ever going to work out," I told him, trying to hide my sadness but failing. "She's not really into traveling and my job doesn't allow me to stay in one place for long. This will probably be my last visit for a while. My time here is getting cut short."

His frown deepened. "You work too hard."

"It's necessary," I replied cryptically.

He speared me with his 'dad look'—the one I remembered from when I was a kid.

"You think I don't know what you've sacrificed for me? I don't always know what's going on, but I know you." He pointed to his chest. "In here. I know you, Emery. All those years you should've been in college. You were working so I could be here."

I wasn't about to apologize. "Best decision I ever made."

"It's not your responsibility to take care of me."

"No, it's not," I agreed. "It's an honor. You did a great job raising me, and I'm returning the favor."

"When you were a kid, no one could stop you from doing anything you wanted to do. Once your mind was made up, that was it," he said, smiling. "Always admired that about you. But it made me worry, too."

"Why?" My eyebrows furrowed.

"Don't let your determination be your downfall. Don't let it cloud your judgement and blind you from the end goal. Sometimes we get so caught up in *doing*, that we forget why we're doing it in the first place."

"And what's the end goal?" I asked, feeling desperate for the wisdom he once possessed all the time.

Shrugging his shoulders like it was the easiest answer in the world, he said, "Happiness."

"It's not that simple."

"Sometimes it is." A small smile played on his lips before a frown took over. "Some days it feels so hopeless for me—knowing I'm losing my mind, but there's nothing I can do about it. But you know what the best part of all this is? I get the opportunity to see what my kids are really made of. And you?" His eyes got misty. "You're my greatest something."

"Thanks, Dad," I whispered, overwhelmed by emotion. I needed to change the subject before I lost it. "How about you tell me a story."

He smiled. "Which one?"

"Anything."

Glancing down at his hands, he said, "You were six pounds and eleven ounces. Tiny little thing. I could hold your entire body with these hands."

Following his line of sight, I looked at the width of his spread-out fingers, the wrinkles and age spots on his weathered skin, the place where he once cradled my body.

Suddenly, I felt like crying and laughing all at once. I couldn't remember the last time he was able to tell me something specific about my life. About our life.

"But this was where you wanted to be," he continued, holding his palms up. "Right here, in my hands. Boy, you gave your mother hell when I had to leave the hospital. Nikki was home sick with strep throat, so your mom had to brave it alone. Said you screamed bloody murder for the whole eight hours I was gone. I wish you could've seen how offended she was when you quieted down as soon as you were in my arms."

Then I really did cry. Just let the tears fall down my

face because there was no stopping it.

We both chuckled as I wiped the wetness off my cheeks.

"My boy." He lovingly patted my hand.

"It's so good to see you, Pops."

"You too, Son."

If I'd ever doubted my decision to pay out the ass for his topnotch care, any uncertainty I might've had vanished. I truly believed the reason he was still alive was because of Windsor Lakes.

And that meant one thing.

As much as I wanted to, I couldn't quit the show. Not now and maybe not even next summer. If I did, the medical bills would drain my college fund again in just a few short years.

I'd come full-circle to where I was two years ago—forced to choose between my dad's health and my dream. There was no contest between the two.

Only this time, there was more at stake—my happiness.

Chapter 27

Emery

Knocking on Estelle's door for what might be the last time was agony. I'd wanted to use my key, but I didn't think it was a good idea with Joel standing right behind me.

When Estelle opened the door, her eyes widened with surprise when she saw the camera, then she immediately looked concerned when she noticed the slump of my shoulders and the hair on my head that was surely a disaster from repeatedly raking my hands through it.

"Is everything okay?" she asked, biting her lip.

"Yeah," I answered, then looked over my shoulder at Joel. "Can we have a few minutes?"

"Sure." He casually leaned against the wall and placed the camera on the floor.

As soon as the door shut, Estelle started fixing my hair and asked, "What's going on? You look so serious."

Her scent overwhelmed me. The fingers gently sweeping through my strands gave me comfort I didn't deserve. I stepped back.

"We have to leave. The show, I mean. There's another project to be filmed back in Chicago," I told her, then answered the question I could see was on the tip of her tongue. "Tomorrow. We pack up tomorrow."

Her pretty mouth fell open in shock, disappointment written all over her features. "Tomorrow?"

Distressed, I paced the room. "I'm so sorry, Estelle. I didn't expect this. Steve just dropped it on me today. I think he's pissed at me because I didn't do things his way. Oh, and by the way, he won't be showing the dildo debacle—I made sure of it."

The unhappiness on her face was replaced with hero-worship. "Really? Thank you so much, Emery." Then the sadness took over again. "But what about Peter?"

"He'll be taken care of. I want to adopt him, if you'll let me."

The hero-worship was back. "Emery…"

"Don't look at me like that." I stopped pacing. "I don't deserve it."

"Of course you do." Estelle plastered the fakest smile ever onto her face and a shadow fell over the openness I loved so much. "Hey, we both knew this time was coming. It's just a little sooner than we thought."

"Estelle."

She started scrubbing her already-clean countertops with a yellow dish cloth. "And all the cats have homes now, thanks to you. I bet you and Peter will get along just fine."

"Estelle."

Bending down to scratch the orange tabby's head, she continued to ignore me. "Isn't that right, Peter? You're a new man now. You'll be very happy—"

"Estelle," I said again, more forcefully this time.

She finally stood and faced me. I almost wished she hadn't because the devastation in her eyes made my chest ache.

"We need to talk about this."

"Okay," she conceded, but we were interrupted by Joel knocking on the door. He had a flight to catch in a few hours, so he was pressed for time.

"We're supposed to get one more interview, but you don't have to do it," I told Estelle. "I'm not going to make you sit there and lie, pretending like this is okay, because it's not."

She straightened her shoulders. "No, I want to do it. I have things I want to say, and I won't lie."

Good.

Truth be told, I hoped she'd give them hell. This was a shitty deal, and I wasn't about to censor anything that came out of her mouth.

I opened the door for Joel, and Estelle headed straight for the couch.

She hadn't bothered with the normal preparations she usually made before being filmed. No lipstick. Hair in a messy bun. She was wearing my gray T-shirt, the excess material baggy on her petite frame.

This was a woman who had zero fucks left.

After Joel gave the thumbs-up, I thought she'd open with a rant full of profanity. Instead, she surprised me.

"Emery Matheson is more than just a guy who says pussy a lot on TV." Estelle's eyes flitted past the camera to me as she spoke. "He isn't a miracle worker—he's just really damn good at his job. He succeeds because he sets his mind to it. He's a great person and an even better friend. I couldn't have done this without him." Finally allowing a chink in her armor to appear, her voice shook as she finished. "We were lucky to have him in our lives, and we'll miss him after he's gone."

As awesome as her words of praise were, it sounded way too much like a final farewell speech.

Lowering the camera, Joel stepped forward and extended his hand to Estelle. "It was a pleasure working with you, ma'am. Emery, I'll see you back in Chicago."

After he left, it was just Estelle, me, and the deafening silence that would be filled with the inevitable goodbye.

Chapter 28

Estelle

"WE WERE SUPPOSED to have more time," I whispered, standing at the sink, my hands gripping the counter.

I'd been prepared to give Emery up—that was what I'd told myself repeatedly. Sometimes I had to remind myself of it several times a day.

But not yet. It wasn't enough time.

As I stood there, the reality of Emery's job hit me full force.

It had been so easy to pretend we could have a future together. But the truth was, Emery was never supposed to belong to me.

The heat of his body warmed my back as he stepped behind me.

"I know." Emery placed his hands on my shoulders and turned me around. "Plans changed." His pleading eyes burned into mine. "We can change our plan, too. It doesn't have to end here."

A desperate suggestion. Words that sounded good when said out loud, but actually doing it? Living it? That was a different story.

"And how would that work?"

He rubbed the back of his neck. "I could come here in between shoots."

"How often?"

"Once a month or so. Maybe more, depending on my schedule. I'll be back in a few weeks for Thanksgiving. And then again at Christmas."

"And how many years would that go on for? How long would I have to wait for you?" It was starting—the chin trembling. And I really didn't want Emery to see me cry.

"Until next summer, at least." Frustrated, he growled and tugged at his hair. "I'm thinking I might not renew my contract with the show. I don't know. I don't know anything right now, except that I don't want to lose you."

"We have to be practical." I pivoted toward the fridge because it was too hard to look at his beautiful face while trying to be rational. "You live in Chicago. I live here. You travel all over the country for your job. My shop is here. Besides, you're the pussy tamer. You're this big star—"

"Stop," he interrupted, his voice sharp. "You know that's not me. That's not who I am."

I hung my head. He was right.

"This is crazy," I muttered.

"People make long-distance relationships work all the time."

"Yeah, when they have a solid foundation to go on."

I turned back toward him. "We've known each other for what? Two weeks?"

"Twelve days."

Throwing my hands out, I made an exasperated noise. "See? Crazy."

"I love you," he blurted out, and I sucked in a breath so fast I thought I might choke on it. "I love your potty mouth and the way you don't give a fuck if anyone approves or not. I love that you bottle fed kittens. I love that you lose at strip poker on purpose. I even love the way you drive." He took a deep breath. "You've shown me *everything* about you, Estelle. *I see you*. And I love all of it."

The trembling in my chin spread throughout my entire body until I was hugging myself to try to hide it. "You just said the word love a lot of times."

"I meant every single one."

A tear tried to escape, but I swiped at it before it could fall.

It was so tragic. I had finally found something I thought I'd never have—someone who loved me for me. And I loved him too, even if saying it out loud was too scary at the moment.

Emery and I were right for each other—a perfect match—but our lifestyles simply didn't mesh.

"I'm so sad," I said honestly. "And disappointed. And scared."

Closing the few feet between us, Emery took my face in his hands and pressed a kiss to my forehead. "Me too."

I wrapped my arms around him, slipping my hands beneath his T-shirt and clinging to the strong muscles of his back. His scent simultaneously comforted me and tormented me. I was so addicted to his smell. Burying my face at the place where his shoulder met his neck, I ran my nose along his skin, breathing him in.

He threaded his fingers through my hair. "We still have tonight."

Another desperate suggestion.

But this was one I was absolutely on board with.

If I only had one more night with Emery, I was going to make it count.

Chapter 29

Emery

SHE TURNED OFF the lights.

She never did that—not once in all the times we'd been together.

When darkness cloaked the room, I didn't ask her why because I already knew. Our connection was too deep, and seeing it reflected in my eyes would be too much for her. Too emotional. Too painful.

Fine. If she didn't want to see it, I'd just make sure she felt it instead.

I took my time with her.

Slow.

Gentle.

Sweet.

Every time she tried to take control, I snatched it back.

Letting out a tortured moan, she clawed at my ass,

the dig of her fingernails begging me to go faster. I didn't.

I grabbed her hands and pinned them above her head before continuing the painfully slow rhythm of my hips.

"Emery, Emery, Emery," she chanted my name like a prayer.

A quick glance at the clock on the nightstand told me we'd been going at it like this for forty-five minutes. Sweat slicked our bodies. We were both panting and shaking with the need for release.

But I didn't want it to end yet. I was drawing it out on purpose, wanting to savor every second with her.

Outside in the parking lot, someone started up their car and the headlights hit the window, throwing light into the room. In the dim glow, I saw wetness on Estelle's eyelashes, but I wasn't sure if it was sweat or tears.

"I love you." I kissed her nose. "I love you." Her forehead. "I love you."

A tear slipped down her temple. Fuck.

She'd been right to turn the lights off. Because the eye contact was too much, and seeing her fall apart wrecked me.

Gazing down at her unfocused eyes, I kissed her lips so softly I almost didn't feel it.

She bit me.

I definitely felt that. It wasn't hard enough to draw blood, but the slight pain sent a jolt straight to my cock.

I let out a growl and kissed her harder, finally giving in as I pounded hard.

Deep.

Fast.

"Come inside me," she gasped. "Please. I want to feel it."

That was a line we hadn't crossed yet. Although we hadn't bothered with condoms since our literal slipup the other day, I always pulled out.

I had never come inside of a woman bare before. I'd never been in love with anyone.

Estelle was the owner of so many of my firsts. And I wanted her to have every other first I had left to give.

I circled her clit, determined to get her off before I did. She was so close that it didn't take much. Her snug walls gripped my dick as she let out a moan.

My balls tightened and I buried myself as deep inside her as I could, my cum shooting in hot spurts. I fought the urge to close my eyes because I wanted to watch the ecstasy on Estelle's face as I filled her up.

"I can feel it," she breathed out. "So good."

Groaning, I rested my forehead against hers as I tried to slow my racing heart.

I stayed inside Estelle for a minute while I kissed her and wiped her tears away with my thumbs.

After I pulled out, I rolled onto my back and wrapped my arms around my girl. Enjoying the feel of her in my arms. Soaking up the time we had left. Wishing tomorrow would never come.

We'd been lying there for so long, I thought she'd fallen asleep.

"I love you, too," Estelle whispered into the darkness, her fingers curling into my chest.

God, I needed to hear that. Needed it like I needed air. But hearing it only amplified the emotions I already felt. Could she feel my heart thundering under her palm?

"We can make it work," I told her confidently.

She didn't say anything for a long time. "I don't want

to lie to you."

"So don't."

"If I say I think we can make it work, I'd be lying."

Ouch. "Think about it?"

I felt her nod. "Falling in love with each other was never part of the plan."

"I know."

"I blame you entirely."

"That's fine."

"All I wanted was to get help finding homes for the cats. You've ruined everything," she said petulantly, but I felt her lips tilt up against my skin.

"I could say I was sorry, but I don't want to lie to you either."

She lifted her head. "Why do you have to be so good? Why couldn't you have been a douche like I originally thought?"

I didn't think she expected me to answer those questions, so instead I asked one of my own. "Is it because you don't trust me? Because I'd never mess around on you. I'm not like that."

"No." Estelle propped herself up on her elbows. "That's not it at all. I do trust you, Emery."

"Well, what is it then?"

"I'm just so tired of being alone," she quietly spoke one of her fears.

The weight of her confession hung in the air like a heavy cloud. Because even if we continued our relationship, she'd be alone most of the time. I wouldn't be able to give her the physical presence she wanted.

Still, the thought of letting her go so she could be with someone else made me feel sick.

"Will you think about it? We can decide at Thanksgiving. See what it's like to live apart for a few weeks. Please," I begged, not even trying to hide the desperation.

I needed her to give us a chance.

I remembered what my dad said to me at our visit earlier—that I was his greatest something.

Well, Estelle was mine. She was it for me and I needed her to know it.

"You're my greatest something," I told her, my voice thick with emotion.

"What?"

As I idly toyed with her fingers, I told her about my dad and how that was his thing. How he always wanted to know the best parts of my life. How I wanted to say that to my kids someday on their first day of kindergarten, their last day of high school, and all their most important moments.

"So it doesn't matter how far apart we are," I said, squeezing her hand. "Wherever I am, you'll still be my greatest something."

"Emery," she whispered shakily. I suspected she was crying again and that wasn't what I wanted.

"Shh, baby. It's gonna be okay."

"We can try it," she said, placing her head on my shoulder. "Just for these next few weeks. Let's see how it goes. It'll be like we're on pause."

"No, not on pause. Never on pause, okay?"

"It's just…" Estelle absentmindedly drew circles on my pecs. "Give me some space for a few days to think."

"You mean, you don't want me to call or anything?" I asked, and I felt her nod. My heart clenched beneath her hand, but I had to respect her wishes. "Okay. If that's what you want."

"Right now, there's something else I want." Her tone was a little playful as her fingers slowly drifted down my stomach.

Now that was something I could give her.

Chapter 30

Emery

The next morning, the dread I felt was like a punch to the gut.

The RV was being returned today. It wasn't like I needed it—I'd been staying at Estelle's for days. After all the rumors, there was no reason to hide our relationship.

I'd arranged for a mechanic to come pick up Estelle's Jeep too. They assured me it would be brought back by the end of the day, and I insisted on taking care of the bill, much to Estelle's dismay.

The parking lot looked so empty in the early morning sunlight as I hopped into the van. I'd be returning it to the rental place soon, then renting my own car for the trip back. With Peter still recovering, traveling by plane was out of the question. The stress of the car ride was already going to be pushing it, but luckily, I still had some of the catnip drops left to help him stay relaxed.

I made my rounds to all of the adoptees. Made sure everyone was adjusting—felines and family members—and offered advice to anyone having issues.

I already knew Cindy was doing great, so I didn't have to make a trip to Nikki's house. When I sent her a text to let her know we were pulling out of town early, she went big-sister mode on me, asking a bunch of questions about Estelle and what was happening with us. And I did something out of character for me—I didn't answer her.

When I got to Marty Miller's house, I found him clean-shaven. Greg had chewed away most of his beard, so he was bare-faced for the first time in twenty years and couldn't have been happier about it.

Out of all the cats, Marcia and Jan had the easiest time getting acclimated to their new environment. Probably because as long as they were together, they were happy.

Carol was shredding toilet paper at her new home, and Agatha was thrilled. She'd had to resort to brushing her teeth in the kitchen because Carol had made the bathroom sink her new sleeping spot, but it didn't bother her in the slightest.

Mike seemed restless with the screened porch already. I gave his owner a harness and leash so they could take him for walks. The kids thought it was so cool because they could walk their cat like a dog.

Overall, it seemed like everyone was doing great.

Everyone except for me.

On the drive back to Estelle's I let the fake smile I'd been keeping on my face slip away.

Chapter 31

Estelle

I NEVER THOUGHT I'd be one of those people—the blubbering mess who couldn't handle saying goodbye.

But here I was, standing outside my apartment complex with tears running down my face.

My mascara was shot to shit. Wiping at my cheeks, I cursed myself for not getting the waterproof kind. I knew what I'd be getting from Target next time. I had a feeling there would be a lot of tears shed in the near future.

Watching Emery drive up in the blue rental car that would take him back to Chicago was surreal. It all seemed so final.

The crew had left. Emery, Janice, Joel… they'd all move on to the next exciting project, while I remained here.

Emery pulled up to the curb in front of me and

parked, but didn't turn off the car. There was no need for him to go back into my apartment because he'd already packed up. He had a long drive ahead of him. I'd already given Peter half a dose of the sedative along with his other meds, so he was sleeping soundly in the carrier.

As soon as Emery made his way around the vehicle, his arms engulfed me. It only made me cry more.

"I'm sorry," I choked out with a sob. "I don't want to make this harder than it already is."

Shaking his head, he gave me a half-smile. "I think I'd be more upset if you weren't crying. At least I know you'll miss me."

I pressed the side of my face against his chest and listened to his heartbeat. I wanted to remember it forever.

"I'll always be thankful for everything you've done," I said softly. "I mean it, Emery. You changed my life, and I don't just mean with the cats."

"Baby, stop," he rasped, tightening his hold on me. "That sounds way too much like a goodbye, and this isn't the end. Three weeks," he reminded me. "Just think about what I said."

"I will," I promised.

I already regretted my request for us to limit contact for a while, but the time apart would give me the opportunity to experience what missing Emery would be like.

I wasn't looking forward to it.

"I love you, Estelle." Emery pressed a kiss to my forehead.

"I love you, too. Now get outta here." I sniffled and tried to muster up a smile. "I can't think straight with all your sexy in my face."

Hooking his arm around my waist, he drew me in for one last hug. "God, I'm gonna miss your crazy ass."

Emery put the box full of Peter's things in the trunk, then placed the carrier on the passenger seat. After shutting the door, he grabbed me by the waist and kissed me, deep and slow. It reminded me of our first kiss, how hungry and desperate he was that night.

"Call me when you're ready," he whispered against my lips.

I nodded.

And just like that, he was gone.

Chapter 32

Estelle

I TRIED TO take Janice's advice about being social, but all it did was make me miss Emery more. Every man bun reminded me of him. Every gray T-shirt I caught a glimpse of had me craning my neck to see if it was him.

It never was.

I'd been moping around the shop all morning, so when Julia insisted that we go to lunch together, my spirits lifted a little. Maybe a little girl time was just what I needed.

However, I didn't realize she was trying to set me up on a date. She played it off like it was just a 'casual get-together with friends', but there was way more interest than that from the guy across the table. His hazel eyes—which were undressing me right this very moment—did absolutely nothing for me.

"So, Ester," he started, shooting me a grin. "I hear

you're going to be on TV. Should I be asking for your autograph?"

"It's Estelle," I corrected him. I wasn't even offended that he didn't know my name because I didn't have a clue about his either. Jerry? Terry? It didn't even matter.

"Brett," Julia hissed. "Don't be rude."

Brett? Oh, hell, I wasn't even close.

Nervously glancing around the downtown café, I adjusted the big sunglasses on my face.

It was a little ridiculous for me to wear them inside, but the paparazzi had been following me around. Apparently, I wasn't old news yet. It seemed like every time I left the apartment, they'd pop up, asking all kinds of questions about my relationship with Emery.

I wondered how he was doing. Were they harassing him too?

It'd been two days since he left. Forty-eight agonizing hours since we'd talked.

Just then, a bright flash went off from the other side of the restaurant and the photographer called out, "Estelle Winters, is that you?" He almost tripped over a chair in his rush to get closer as he rattled off questions. "Are you on a date? Have you moved on from Emery Matheson?"

Damn. I guess my half-assed attempt at going incognito failed.

Emery wasn't kidding about these guys. They were ruthless. But while the paps were a little annoying, it gave me the perfect excuse to leave.

Slinging my purse over my shoulder, I stood up. "I'm sorry to cut things short, y'all, but it looks like I've been spotted."

Julia's face turned sympathetic. "Are you okay?"

I tried to give her a smile. "Yeah. I just need to go home."

I didn't go home.

When I got out onto the road, I just kept driving without any specific destination in mind, taking several random turns to lose the reporters.

As I held my hands securely positioned at ten and two on the steering wheel, I remembered how patient Emery had been with me during those damn driving lessons. Although I'd acted annoyed at the time, I would've given just about anything to have him sitting next to me now.

I glanced at the speedometer—which worked now, thanks to Emery—and made sure I stayed at the speed limit.

Okay, maybe I broke the speed limit a little, but I didn't have much of a choice with paparazzi on my tail.

When I got close to my apartment, I went straight instead of turning into my parking lot.

Then I drove by the costume shop. I took a right, heading into the rougher part of town. The graffiti and broken windows got closer as I neared the area where Emery used to live in that crappy studio. Slowing, I looked at the buildings, wondering which one had basically been his prison. He'd never stated it that way, but I knew he felt trapped during that time in his life.

I kept driving.

The radio quietly played "Uptown Funk", but I didn't even feel like singing along. That was how bad the heartache was—not even Bruno Mars could cheer me up.

Much to my surprise, I found myself parked outside

of Windsor Lakes Retirement Home. For a good five minutes, I watched the fountain while debating whether I should stay or go.

I decided to go in. Just like the first time I had come here, the floors were gleaming. People were smiling. There was so much life within these walls.

Approaching the front desk, I nervously twisted my hands. "I'm looking for Robert Matheson."

"And you are?" The receptionist smiled up at me.

"Estelle Winters. I've visited him before."

"Oh, you did the face painting last weekend!" she exclaimed, then whispered, "You're Emery's girlfriend, right?"

Refusing to confirm or deny my relationship status, I said, "The face painting was a lot of fun."

"I was hoping you'd stop back in. The director thinks making it a regular thing would be great for our residents. Of course we would pay you. We have a budget for entertainment and social activities."

"I would do it for free," I said honestly. Handing her my business card, I told her to call me anytime and she let me know Robert was hanging out in the lounge.

I found him sitting on the couch and I hesitated before taking a seat at the other end. Muttering to himself, he seemed agitated. I hadn't brought my face painting supplies like last time, so I didn't have any distractions to offer him.

"Hi," I spoke softly, gaining his attention.

Robert gave me a small smile, but I couldn't tell if he recognized me.

"I don't know why I'm here," I blurted out awkwardly.

"Neither do I." Chuckling, he shrugged, and I

laughed at his ability to joke about his condition.

"It's really nice out today." Oh my God. Was I seriously talking about the weather? I was the worst at small talk.

Squinting at me, Robert asked, "You gonna go on pretending everything's fine behind those sad eyes, or are you gonna tell me what's wrong?"

Alzheimer's or not, he was still sharp as a tack. I sighed.

I wasn't sure what to say. I didn't know if I was supposed to avoid talking about his family members. I had a lot to learn when it came to his disease.

But that didn't stop me from confessing the best and worst thing that had happened to me in a long time.

"I'm in love with your son."

Reaching over, he patted my hand. "I know, dear. I know."

"Yeah? How do you know that?" I asked curiously.

"Mary told me."

Pausing, I took a good three seconds to process what he'd said. "Your wife?"

He made a sound of confirmation. "Dreamed about her last night. She tells me all sorts of things." When he glanced my way, he had a sly smile on his face. "Not even death can keep us apart."

I gaped at him, speechless. Robert and his wife were separated in the most final way possible, and he wasn't letting that get in his way.

And I was letting a thousand miles scare me away from being with Emery?

To hell with our three-week trial. If I really wanted this thing to work, I needed to make it happen. I needed to show Emery that I was willing to do whatever it took to be committed.

Even if it meant facing one of my biggest fears.

A DING SOUNDED through the airplane cabin, followed by the pleasant voice of the flight attendant explaining something about how the seat cushion can be used as a floatation device in the event of an emergency.

Closing my eyes, I swallowed hard as I tuned her out. If the plane crashed, I was pretty sure I wouldn't be alive to use the damn thing.

Nearby, someone sneezed twice and another person coughed. The little fan above my seat was pointed directly at me, causing my hair to repeatedly tickle my nose. My hands white-knuckled my purse. All the while, I tried to convince myself this was a good idea.

I could get through this flight. For Emery. Besides, it was too late to get off now because we were moving. Takeoff and landing were always the worst parts.

I braved a peek out the window next to me and immediately shut my eyes again. The plane was speeding down the runway and I felt the wheels leave the ground. My ears popped, my heart pounded.

After a minute, it leveled out and I let go of the death-grip I had on my purse.

Okay, that wasn't terrible.

Then a foul smell invaded my nose, and my entire

face wrinkled with disgust.

Motherfucker.

Someone definitely farted. Holding my breath, I glanced around at my fellow passengers with narrowed eyes. Who did it?

Could've been the bald dude in front of me. Or the lady to my right. There was a baby across the aisle. Maybe she crapped in her diaper. Actually, I would've been totally okay with that. I'd prefer baby poop over old man gas any day.

My lungs were starting to burn from lack of oxygen. I wanted to give the stench time to dissipate, but I couldn't hold my breath any longer.

Gasping loudly, I drew in much-needed air, earning a few strange looks. The offensive odor still lingered, but not quite as bad as before.

Deciding to distract myself with some reading, I took out my Kindle and began chapter five of a beautifully written historical romance.

Sensing the elderly woman next to me, I cut her a glance. She quickly looked away, pretending like she hadn't just been reading my book.

A devious smile pulled at my lips when I got an idea.

Tapping the screen a few times, I scrolled through my library and picked one of the most risqué books I owned. I pulled up *Trailer Park Virgin* by Alexa Riley and didn't bother with the beginning, skipping straight to the raunchy stuff.

I made sure to angle the screen a bit, just so Nosy Nancy could get an eyeful.

About ten seconds later, I heard a scandalized gasp. I had to bite the inside of my cheek to keep from laughing.

Twenty seconds later, another shocked huff.

She didn't stop reading, though. I swiped the screen, turning to one of the best parts.

Buckle up, lady. I've got an entire collection of these and two hours to kill.

Maybe flying on planes wasn't so bad after all.

Chapter 33

Emery

FATIGUE WEIGHED DOWN on me as I plopped onto my couch. I remembered a time not too long ago when I sat in this very spot, looking forward to meeting the mentally unstable cat hoarder.

I had no idea I was going to meet the love of my life.

As I rubbed my tired eyes, I almost laughed at how ridiculous it was.

Since I'd gotten home, I hadn't even left my condo. All I'd done was wallow, surviving on pizza and beer.

I missed Estelle.

I missed her bed. Her smell. Her smile. Her soft body against mine.

The fourteen-hour drive from South Carolina to Chicago had worn me out, and I'd slept like shit the past two nights. Tossing and turning. Repeatedly reaching for the other side of the bed, only to find cold, empty sheets.

Even during sleep my body knew Estelle wasn't nearby, and I was experiencing some serious withdrawals.

I needed caffeine. Lots of it. If I was going to be coherent for the new shoot tomorrow, I'd need to snap out of the funk I was in.

I headed to the kitchen to get some coffee.

Peter let out a meow as he jumped onto the kitchen island, the cone around his neck bobbing up and down as he gently headbutted my mug.

"How do you like your new place? Fancy Keurig, flat screen TV, million-dollar view." I gestured to the living room. "That couch is real leather. Bet your claws could do some serious damage there."

He let out a yawn and paced the granite countertop, looking around like he was searching for something. Or someone.

"You miss her too, huh?"

Meowing again, he jumped down and took off down the hall.

My phone rang, and excitement shot through me as I pulled it from my pocket, thinking it was Estelle. This whole no-contact rule was bullshit.

When I saw 'unknown caller' flash across the screen, disappointment made my heart plummet and I wanted to throw it against the wall.

"Hello?" I ground out.

"You can tame my pussy anytime," a female voice cooed.

Completely losing my cool, I barked, "Don't you have something better to do with your time?"

Several seconds of silence.

"Ah—sorry. I—it was just a joke," the girl stammered.

"My friend bet me twenty bucks that I wouldn't call you, and I really wanted that money…"

"How did you get this number?"

"Someone just posted it on Twitter. You know how it goes." She let out a nervous laugh. She was right—I shouldn't have been surprised by it. Still, it pissed me off.

"Well, I hate to break it to you, but there's only one pussy I'm interested in and it's not yours."

"So it's true then? You're really off the market?" She sighed. "I figured if your own producer was saying it, then it had to be real."

My whole body locked up. "What's my producer saying?"

"Uhh, just that you and the woman you worked with are dating or something. He's on TV talking about it right now."

"What channel?" I seethed.

"NTT. It's an exclusive interview—"

I ended the call and promptly turned my phone off as I marched over to the couch.

Picking up the TV remote, I turned it on. Steve filled the screen, a sleazy smile on his face as he blabbed my personal business to the gossip reporter at his side.

"*—impossible to miss the sparks flying on the set. The romance between Mr. Matheson and Ms. Winters added a special element to the show. You'll definitely want to tune in for the next season.*"

The brunette turned toward the camera, grinning like the cat that ate the canary. "*Well, there you have it folks. Sounds like perpetual bachelor Emery Matheson isn't single anymore. The tamer has been tamed.*"

I turned it off.

If Steve had been in the room, I would've clocked him for sure. He was the leak. He was the one who'd tipped off the press. He'd thrown me under the bus, all for the sake of his fucking ratings.

My concern immediately turned to Estelle. The reporters would definitely be hounding her now, if they weren't already.

I turned my phone back on and had to hit ignore three times on unknown numbers.

Then I called Estelle, to hell with her rules. I needed to make sure she was okay.

It went straight to voicemail. Not a good sign. She never turned off her phone, so there was a good possibility that her number got leaked too. I hated thinking about her dealing with the harassment all by herself.

As soon as I hung up more calls came through, all numbers I didn't recognize.

I growled.

This was just a part of the business I was in, and I should've been grateful for the popularity. After all, that was what kept the show going. Ultimately, it was the fans who signed my paycheck.

But was this really the life I wanted? Changing my number every few weeks, going where I was told to go, saying what I was told to say?

I couldn't even cut my damn hair without someone's permission.

And Steve had made me into a puppet. A front man. An image.

Success meant nothing if I didn't have integrity, and he'd pulled that right out from under me when he made me leave a job unfinished.

He'd known from the second he spotted me that I was desperate, and he'd been using it to his advantage for far too long.

Then he went and aired details about my private life for his own personal gain.

That was the last straw for me.

Suddenly, the answer became clear. I couldn't keep working for him, regardless of the consequences.

I sat down on the couch to think, and Peter climbed onto my lap. He purred while I mentally added up the cost per month at Windsor Lakes. With what I had saved, I figured my dad was set for about three years. Not much time, but enough for me to make a new plan.

Certified vet techs made decent money. I could sell my Range Rover and get something economical. I could move in with Nikki until I found an affordable place of my own.

Who was I kidding? I didn't want to live with my sister. Or alone. I wanted to be with Estelle 24/7.

And I needed to get to her. Fast.

But first, I had to call Steve. Normally I would text, but I wanted to hear his voice when I delivered the news.

Dialing his number, I made my way to my bedroom.

He picked up after two rings. "You back in town?"

"I am," I confirmed, while quickly stuffing a small duffle bag with clothes. "But not for long."

"What do you mean?"

"I'm done."

"Done?"

"I'm leaving the show. You're an asshole, Steve. I've decided I don't like you much, no matter how funny it is to watch you piss your pants over your horoscope results."

Silence.

I zipped up the bag and headed to the master bathroom. "And before you start making threats about breeching contract, I'd like for you to think about how the execs will react to your recent unethical decisions."

"What the fuck are you talking about?"

Putting the phone on speaker, I set it down and searched the top drawer for my electric beard trimmer.

"Giving cats out like candy without having them medically cleared first. I'm sure animal endangerment rumors would be very damaging to the show." I smiled to myself as the sound of buzzing filled the room. Without hesitation, I ran the clippers over my head, cutting the hair down to about a quarter of an inch. "I'm sure we can negotiate when it comes to terminating my contract early."

"Animal endangerment?" Something crashed on the other end of the phone. Oh, yeah. He was pissed. "Are you fucking with me right now?"

"Nope. How's that for grit?"

After ranting about me being an ungrateful twat, and then some uncharacteristic begging, Steve finally accepted the fact that I was done with the show.

He wouldn't have any trouble finding someone to fill my shoes. There were hundreds of highly qualified dudes out there who'd love to be in my position.

It felt so fucking good to hang up that phone. And to be able to see without hair in my fucking face.

Grinning, I smoothed a hand over the short hair on my scalp.

After quickly cleaning up the bathroom and taking a

shower, I made sure Peter was set with his medications, food, and water.

Charles just about had a stroke when I handed him the pet-sitting instructions, but I balanced the tedious task with a fifty-dollar bill and the promise that I wouldn't be living in the condo much longer.

As I drove to the airport, I waited to feel sadness, fear, or grief over my lost career. But instead, I felt invigorated. Sure, I was uncertain about what the future held, but I knew I wanted Estelle at my side while I figured it out.

FOUR AND A half hours later, I was punching Estelle's front door code in and sprinting up to her apartment. There'd been a shady-looking SUV parked out front, but with my oversized hoodie and the new haircut, the camera-wielding men didn't even give me a second glance.

Excitement coursed through me as I made it to Estelle's door. I knocked and waited.

No answer.

I knocked again.

Pulling my phone from my pocket, I turned it on and cringed at the forty-eight voicemails and ninety-six random texts waiting for me. I quickly dialed Estelle's number.

"Hello?" Her voice was music to my ears.

I grinned. "I have a pussy emergency."

Chapter 34

Estelle

"**W**HAT?" CONFUSION WAS evident in my tone as I glanced around Emery's penthouse, the afternoon sun beaming through the wide windows. I bent down to pet Peter, who seemed very happy to see me.

"I'm hitting you up for a booty call," Emery replied, and I could picture the cocky smile he surely had on his face.

"Well, considering I'm already at your place, I'd say we could make that happen," I quipped, grinning from ear to ear.

"You're *where*?"

"I'm in Chicago, standing in your kitchen. You need an interior decorator, like yesterday." Meowing, Peter rubbed up against my leg. "And I think your cat agrees with me."

Emery laughed. "Ah. Shit, Estelle. Does that mean

you got on a plane for me?"

"You're damn right, I did. Someone farted, too. I'm traumatized," I deadpanned. "It wasn't so bad, though. I tormented an old woman with smutty erotica, so that part was fun."

"You troublemaker. So, what made you change your mind?"

I went for the truth. "I realized I'd rather be alone and know you're somewhere missing me than not be with you at all."

"Baby," he breathed out, then chuckled. "Well, here's the problem—I'm at your place too."

"What?" I gasped. "Why?"

"Well, for one, I never got to take you on our beach date."

"You came all the way back to take me to the beach?"

"No," he said reluctantly. "I wish that was the case. The real reason is because I needed to make sure you're okay."

I was confused. "Why wouldn't I be okay?"

"I take it you haven't watched TV much today?"

"No," I replied warily. "What happened?"

"Steve outed us during an official interview this morning. Then your phone was off and I got worried… But now I realize it's just because you were traveling."

"We're so ridiculous." I laughed, flopping down onto his couch. Emery's scent lingered on the leather. Pressing my nose into the back cushion, I took a big whiff and sighed happily.

"Stay at my place," Emery said, sounding out of breath. I heard a car door shut. "If I can get the next flight, I should be there in about four hours."

"Oh, that's no problem. Take your time. Charles and I are supposed to grab a bite to eat at the café down the street anyway."

"Wait, how did you get past Charles? And how the hell did you get him to agree to hang out with you? I can't even get him to smile at me."

"I told him I was your cat nanny, and he didn't even question it. Also, I might've charmed him with some face painting."

"So that's what it takes, huh? Guess I've been going about it all wrong."

"What can I say? I'm a tough gal to turn down."

He laughed. "Don't I know it."

Chapter 35

Estelle

I'D JUST DOZED off when I heard the penthouse door open. I shot up from the couch and ran toward the sound because I missed Emery so much. But as soon as I saw him, my feet skidded to a stop so fast I almost fell over.

"What happened to your hair?" I gasped.

Emery sheepishly shrugged while rubbing his hand over the buzz cut. "Got tired of it being in my way all the time."

With the new hair, sweatpants, and hoodie I barely recognized him. I couldn't believe how different he looked.

"Oh, Steve is going to be so pissed at you."

Emery smirked. "He's already pissed at me. Because I quit."

"You did what?" I practically shouted.

"I quit."

"But-—but you can't."

"It's already done," he replied, closing the gap between us. He wrapped his arms around my waist and buried his nose in my hair. "Mmm. I missed you."

I melted into him while trying to keep my thoughts straight. It was so easy to get lost in the feeling of being in his arms again. Running my nose along his neck, I placed a soft kiss on his collarbone.

"Are you doing this for me?" I managed, nipping at his skin. "Because that's not what I want. We can be together, no matter what."

"This wasn't just about you." He shook his head. "There were a lot of factors that went into this decision."

A sexy sound rumbled in his chest when I licked his throat. I needed to stop if we were going to finish this conversation.

I pulled back to look at his face. "What about your dad?"

"Fortunately, I've got enough in my savings account to keep him covered for a few years," he said optimistically, but I didn't miss the hint of melancholy in his voice.

"Your savings account, meaning your college fund?"

He sighed. "Yeah. And I might be facing some fines for breaking the contract early, but I'll deal with that when I come to it."

"What about vet school?" I frowned.

"I don't know. It'll have to wait. Guess I'm back at square one, but things are different this time."

"How so?"

"I've got a vet tech certification, so I can still work with animals. And now I have you."

My lips tilted up. "I could always hire you on at the

costume shop."

Emery let out an amused grunt. "I think my drag queen days are behind me, but I appreciate the offer." Then his face got serious. "Will you still love me even though I'm poor and bald?"

"You're not bald." I snickered as I felt the short bristles with my fingertips. "Although, I have to admit I'm gonna miss holding on to it when your face is between my legs. Maybe you should think about growing a beard."

Raising his eyebrows, he grinned. "You'd like that?"

I nodded, rubbing a hand over his jaw. "That would feel good between my legs too."

Growling, Emery's hands gripped my hips and he backed me up until my ass bumped into the kitchen island. "You know, this place looks a lot better with you in it."

"I bet it'd look even better if we were naked."

He pretended to think about it before picking me up caveman style, tossing me over his shoulder. He smacked my ass, and I giggled as he dumped me onto the couch.

"How long are you here for?" he asked. That predatory look was in his eyes as he gazed down at me.

"Julia agreed to watch Alice and Bobby for three days," I replied, licking my lips while boldly eyeing Emery's body. His loose pants did nothing to hide the bulge beneath the fabric.

Hooking his thumbs in his waistband, he pulled down and his thick cock bobbed out. My clit throbbed.

"I've never had sex in this condo before," Emery said huskily. "So that means I've got about 1500 square feet of uncharted living space and three days to fuck you on every surface possible. We better make good use of the time."

Epilogue

Two Years Later

Emery

"Uncle E! Look, I'm Rudolf."

Glancing down at Lizzie, I smiled at her red nose, painted cheeks, and headband antlers. "The cutest reindeer I've ever seen."

She skipped away to rejoin Estelle at her face painting station.

We were having our first annual Black Friday Fundraiser at our animal shelter, One Home at a Time.

It was chaos. People of all ages explored the rooms and halls filled with cages—cats on the right side of the lobby, dogs on the left. All of them were ready for adoption.

Turns out, quitting The Pussy Tamer had not only been the right move for my personal life, but it also opened a lot of doors I never even knew existed.

When a rival TV network heard about my early

departure from NTT, they'd pounced on the chance to recruit me for a brand-new show.

And I promptly turned them down… Until they told me they wanted to film a documentary—a real documentary—about the rehabilitation of abused and neglected animals.

There were no cheesy lines. No unethical practices. And best of all, no traveling around the country.

The producers had allowed me to have a say in where the permanent shelter location was, and of course, I chose Remington.

They provided the start-up money and paid me to run the rehabilitation center in exchange for filming one week out of every month. I was in charge of everything: hiring employees, finding volunteers, working with the rescue animals, and finding them suitable homes.

And in the process, I found my real passion—fixing the unfixable.

The ratings spoke for themselves. People were genuinely interested in the journey of damaged dogs and cats, watching them go from utterly unadoptable to happy and loved.

Fortunately, I never had to make good on my threats to Steve about animal endangerment. Rhonda took care of that for me. She was pretty upset about my decision to leave, though she understood. She'd seen firsthand what a dick Steve had been and made a misconduct complaint to the network. He resigned before they had a chance to fire him.

I had no idea where he was now. Possibly shearing llamas in Peru. Maybe those tests weren't so far off after all.

The best part was, NTT was very willing to negotiate on the terms of my contract so they could avoid bad publicity or a lawsuit. I would always be grateful to them for the opportunities they'd given me. They were my leg up in the world.

And without The Pussy Tamer, I never would've met Estelle.

They did end up finding a replacement for me. At first, it was a little weird being on the other side of the screen, but the new guy did a great job. Estelle and I were sure to tune in every Wednesday night to watch it, surrounded by Alice, Bobby, and Peter.

After I moved back, Estelle refused to let me get a place of my own. But her landlord still wouldn't allow us to have three cats, so we found a new apartment together.

Then the following summer we took a leap, getting engaged and buying a house all in the same week. We'd found a cute one-story home just two blocks from Nikki's house. The first night we moved in, Estelle lost at strip poker on purpose and we made love until the sun came up.

I was pulled from my thoughts by a firm clap on the back.

"I think it's safe to say we should do this again next year," Dr. Knight muttered out of the corner of his mouth. "We've raised over ten thousand dollars this afternoon."

"Holy shit," I whispered, relief filling me. It wasn't that we were in trouble financially, because the network covered what donations couldn't. But I was also in charge of the budget, so I knew how costly it was to keep this place going. "Thanks for the update."

Dr. Knight was our full-time veterinarian until I got my degree. I'd just gotten accepted into the vet med program at the university, but I had several years to go before I could practice medicine. Someday in the future, I would be the vet here, but until then I was happy in the present.

Estelle stood up from her chair, sending the last kid away with a butterfly on her cheek.

I watched my wife, outright leering at her ass as she swayed out of the room.

We'd gotten married the year before on Halloween and it was the costume party of all costume parties. Estelle had looked gorgeous walking down the aisle toward me in the Marie Antoinette dress made by her great aunt— the same eccentric aunt who shot Silly String at us as we left the church.

Since Dad hadn't been able to make it to the wedding, we brought the wedding to him. In between the ceremony and the reception, we went by Windsor Lakes for a visit. As soon as he'd smiled at us, I knew he was having a good day, which made my day even better. We hung around for over an hour, laughing, taking pictures, and making memories he couldn't recall today.

His speech was slipping more and more. Basic activities such as swallowing or walking were difficult for him. His mind was forgetting how to take care of his body. But at least I was nearby to help him through it, even if it had been three months since he'd recognized me.

Before Estelle turned the corner down the hall, she tossed me a wink over her shoulder.

I followed, stopping a few times to thank people for

coming and directing them to the front desk for adoption applications.

Then I headed for the back room, where we kept the animals who weren't ready for homes yet.

My absolute favorite cases were the feral kittens—the ones who'd been born in the woods, under porches, behind dumpsters. They didn't know how to be domesticated house pets because human contact was a completely foreign concept. They often came in emaciated, flea-ridden, and aggressive as hell.

But with patience and love, eventually they came around.

"You're going to enjoy this someday, I promise," I heard Estelle say softly.

I shut the door, and I saw her cradling one of the wild ones. She was gently petting his gray head while holding the scruff on the back of his neck, just like his mother would. He let out a tiny hiss, but Estelle just smiled at him.

Coming up behind her, I wrapped my arms around the swell of her round stomach and kissed her neck. "You better not be cleaning litter boxes. It's not good for the babies."

She turned her face toward me, a smirk on her red lips. "Are you kidding? Being off poop-scoop duty is literally the best thing about being pregnant."

I knew she wasn't even joking—she'd had a rough six months. Her morning sickness had been all-day sickness that lasted until she made it to eighteen weeks. Then the fatigue hit. She'd had to hire extra employees at the costume shop this season, and I knew it bothered her to hand over the reins.

"How are you holding up?"

"Exhausted," she said, putting the kitten back in the kennel with his litter mates. "And my feet feel like they got hit by sledgehammers."

I winced. "Sorry, babe."

She shrugged. "Guess that's what happens when you're carrying twins."

I couldn't keep the smile off my face. Twins. A boy and a girl.

"Of course you'd knock me up with a litter," she went on with a playful tone. She loved to give me a hard time about it, even though she'd been elated at the news. Two birds, one stone, she'd said.

We both gasped when I felt a strong kick against my palm. I rubbed my hand there, hoping to feel it again. Our babies didn't disappoint. A foot, or maybe an elbow, pushed back.

"No." Estelle sighed. "*That's* the best part about being pregnant."

"You know what the best part is for me?" I nuzzled the side of her neck, inhaling the jasmine and honey scent I loved so much.

She scoffed. "The fact that I'm a horny, sex-crazed maniac?"

"You say that like it's any different from how you've always been," I retorted. She elbowed me, and I chuckled. Tightening my arms around her, I cupped the underside of her stomach. "You see… Right now, I'm holding my three greatest somethings."

"Emery." Turning in my arms, she tipped her head back to look at me with watery eyes. "My mascara isn't waterproof. You can't say shit like that to me when I'm hormonal."

"There's no limit to the things I'd do for you," I said, starting the game we played at least once a week. "I'd ride a tricycle for you."

That got her to laugh. "You did do that. And it's a *bike*."

"I'd dress in drag for you."

"You did that too."

"I'd go broke for you."

"That almost happened. I'd get on a hundred planes for you," she said, playing along.

It was a never-ending game of which one of us loved the other more. We always tried to one-up each other. I usually won, bringing Estelle to uncontrollable laughter or tears or both.

"I'd go to the store to get Rocky Road ice cream for you at 3 a.m." That actually did happen. The middle of the night was the only time my wife's morning sickness had left her alone.

"I would pull all-nighters, helping you bottle feed these guys." She tipped her head toward the wild ones.

"I know you would," I responded. "But I gotta draw the line somewhere. You need your rest."

Estelle's smile faded as she ran her finger over the indent in my bottom lip, her tone no longer joking. "If we ever get separated—by death or otherwise—I'd dream of you every night just so we could be together."

It was a punch straight to my heart, in the best way.

Now I was the one with watery eyes. The 'otherwise' she talked about was the disease that had consumed my dad. I'd been open with her about my fears when it came to Alzheimer's. There was a chance it would come for me. It was genetic, after all.

But knowing she'd be there for me, that she'd stick by me through it… It made it seem less scary.

Blinking away the sudden stinging in my eyes, I touched my forehead to hers and smiled. "Okay, baby. You won this round."

The End

Acknowledgements

To my husband and kids—I feel like a broken record every time I write this exact same thing in my acknowledgements, but I mean it when I say I couldn't do this without you. You're my greatest inspiration and my biggest supporters through this process. I love you!

Amie and Miranda—You two are listed together because you're a package deal (and I couldn't be happier about that). I've suffered through plane farts for you, and I'd do it again. We've only met once, but somewhere along the way, you've become my best friends. Thanks for embracing my crazy.

To my betas—Liz, Tina, Amber, Amie, and Miranda. You guys rock! Thanks for being the first to read Untamable.

Amber—As far as personal assistants go, it doesn't get better than you. I honestly don't know what I would do without your help!

Tina—Thanks for being such an awesome table assistant. My second book signing was so much fun because of you. Let's do it again someday!

My Significant Otters—I'm glad I found people who love otters and romance as much as I do. Not to be confused with 'otter romance', which would be an interesting book, right? Thanks for being part of my reader group and making this job so fun for me!

And to the readers, bloggers, PR teams, editors, graphic designers, and authors who have supported me along the way... Thank you so much for being my village and my tribe. Whether I'm a new-to-you author or you've been with me from the beginning, I appreciate more than you know. I couldn't do this without all of you!

About The Author

JAMIE SCHLOSSER grew up on a farm in Illinois, surrounded by cornfields. Although she no longer lives in the country, her dream is to return to rural living someday. As a stay-at-home mom, she spends most of her days running back and forth between her two wonderful kids and her laptop. She loves her family, iced coffee, and happily-ever-afters. You can find out more about Jamie and her books by visiting these links:

Facebook: https://www.facebook.com/authorjamieschlosser
Amazon: http://amzn.to/2mzCQkQ
Twitter: @SchlosserJamie
Bookbub: https://www.bookbub.com/authors/jamie-schlosser
Newsletter: http://eepurl.com/cANmI9

Also, do you like being the first to get sneak peeks on upcoming books? Do you like exclusive giveaways? Most importantly, do you like otters?

If you answered yes to any of these questions, you should consider joining Jamie Schlosser's Significant Otters!

https://www.facebook.com/groups/1738944743038479

Made in the USA
Lexington, KY
30 June 2018